TITUS RETURNS

He knew that the bishop was going to want to talk about his plans for the future and rejoining the church. He had always admired Bishop Ebersol, and the last thing he wanted to see on the man's face was the disappointment when Titus told him that his faith had slipped in the last five years.

He would go to the bishop's house and talk to the man face-to-face. Whatever conversation they had would hopefully remain between the two of them and no one else need ever be the wiser, until he decided what he wanted to do. Aside from the disappointment on the bishop's face he could only imagine the heartbreak and devastation on his mother's if he decided not to come back into the church.

Just give it some time, the voice inside him whispered.

It had only been five days since he had come back, and it hadn't been easy. But he knew that he was expected to rejoin the church or at least make a pledge to. Maybe that would appease his family. But more than anything, he needed to decide if he was going to stay in Wells Landing. Could he find his place back into the Amish community? He wasn't sure. One thing was certain though: he had to give it a try. . . .

Books by Amy Lillard

The Wells Landing Series
CAROLINE'S SECRET
COURTING EMILY
LORIE'S HEART
JUST PLAIN SADIE
TITUS RETURNS

E-Novellas

The Quilting Circle
MORE THAN FRIENDSHIP
MORE THAN A PROMISE

Published by Kensington Publishing Corporation

TITUS
RETURNS

AMY
LILLARD

ZEBRA BOOKS
KENSINGTON PUBLISHING CORP.
http://www.kensingtonbooks.com

ZEBRA BOOKS are published by

Kensington Publishing Corp.
119 West 40th Street
New York, NY 10018

All Kensington titles, imprints, and distributed lines are available at special quantity discounts for bulk purchases for sales promotion, premiums, fund-raising, educational, or institutional use.

Special book excerpts or customized printings can also be created to fit specific needs. For details, write or phone the office of the Kensington Sales Manager: Attn.: Sales Department. Kensington Publishing Corp., 119 West 40th Street, New York, NY 10018. Phone: 1-800-221-2647.

Zebra and the Z logo Reg. U.S. Pat. & TM Off.

First Printing: January 2017
ISBN-13: 978-1-4201-3975-4
ISBN-10: 1-4201-3975-4

eISBN-13: 978-1-4201-3976-1
eISBN-10: 1-4201-3976-2

10 9 8 7 6 5 4 3 2 1

Printed in the United States of America

Chapter One

Titus Lambert pulled the strap of his backpack a little higher onto his shoulder and stepped to the side of the road as the car whizzed past. A stream of laughter and music trailed behind and mixed with the exhaust fumes to leave a bitter taste in his mouth. He had never quite gotten used to the speedy movements of cars. Even during the short time he actually drove himself, he was always a little unnerved when he stopped to think about how fast he was really going. So he never stopped. At twenty that was easy. But five years had passed and things were different. Much, much different.

And yet some things were the same. He hitched his bag a little higher once more and studied the sign looming ahead: WELLS LANDING. It was just as he remembered. Pristine white that had barely started chipping around the edges. Flowing green letters that made it seem like a fancier place than it really was.

He stopped and stared at the sign, his heart pounding in his chest. His mouth went dry as ash. What was he doing here?

He had no business being here. But where else could he go?

Wells Landing had been his home all of his life. Until the night everything had changed forever. Now he had no idea where home was. He had no idea if he'd ever feel at home anywhere. It certainly wasn't the concrete cell that had been his shelter during the last five years.

He rubbed a hand across the back of his neck, the stitching in his shirt irritating his skin. These were the clothes that he had worn into the prison. The clothes that his mother had made for him. Nowadays the sleeves were a little tight and a little short, but the uncomfortable feeling that stole over him had more to do with memories than the fact that five years had passed since he had worn them.

He had heard the other guys talking about getting out and their families bringing them new things to wear, driving up to get them, and all the celebration that would be had that night.

But there was no celebration for Titus. He hadn't told his parents that he was coming home. He didn't know if he could call it home. He didn't know if he could actually go through with it.

Another car whizzed past, then he caught the low chug of a tractor.

The sound grew closer, the speed becoming slower until it practically stopped right beside him.

Titus kept walking.

"Titus? Titus Lambert? Is that you?"

He should have known that he wouldn't make it back into town without someone noticing. Wells Landing just wasn't big enough for that kind of secrecy. Wells Landing wasn't big enough for *any* kind of secrecy.

Unable to ignore the man who had called him by name, Titus turned to see who was driving the tractor.

Jonah Miller.

Emotions rushed him: anger, sadness, and an over-whelming need to hug this person he had known most of his life. He shoved them all into the box he kept buried deep inside and gave his onetime friend a brief nod. "Jonah."

Jonah swung down from the tractor, leaving it idling as he hit the ground. "It's good to see you." He stuck out his hand to shake.

Titus looked at it, unable to move. How long had it been since he had touched another person? One year? Two? Fistfights aside, it had been nearly four years since he had clasped another man's hand in friendship.

It hadn't taken long for word to get around the yard that he was Amish. The other inmates had considered it great sport to tease him and see if they could get the pacifist to respond. It took even less time for Titus to learn that if he wanted to have any peace at all he had to fight and fight harder and meaner than anyone else. He wasn't proud of the measures he had been forced to take, but he had done what any and every man does on the inside: whatever it took to survive.

He clasped Jonah's hand, then met his tawny-brown gaze. Jonah's eyes were the exact color of good maple syrup. How long had it been since he'd had a short stack with syrup and butter? A long time.

That was another thing he wasn't used to—making eye contact. He'd done whatever it took to stay off the radar of the harder prisoners. But he looked into Jonah's eyes, trying his best to begin his life on the outside. His eyes burned and his hand trembled. This was going to be harder than he thought.

"It's good to be here." His voice sounded rusty and unused as he uttered his lie. Was it good to be there? Or was this the only place he could be? Wells Landing was his home. At least it had been once . . . a long time ago.

"Are you on your way home?" Jonah jerked one thumb over his shoulder toward his waiting tractor. "I can give you a ride."

It was on the tip of Titus's tongue to tell him no, but the trip down memory lane was exhausting. He had seen just about all of Wells Landing he wanted to see for the time being, and he had barely made it past the welcome sign.

"Yes." He nodded. "I'd like that." He climbed up into the cab of the tractor next to Jonah and tried not to think about how many times they had ridden this way in their youth.

They were still young, he knew, but the innocence of that time was gone. And he could never get that back.

Jonah didn't say much as they chugged down Main.

Titus did his best not to stare at everything as they passed. Fitch's Furniture Store, Kauffman Family Restaurant, Lapp Bakery. He had spent so many hours hanging out in the park that divided Main Street that a part of him wanted to tell Jonah to stop and let him out. He could swing for a couple of hours, maybe use the time to get his head right. Then what? He would still have to go home. Still have to face his parents. Still have to learn to live again.

"You okay?" Jonah asked.

"Yeah," Titus lied. "How's Lorie these days?" Anything to change the subject. He wasn't okay. He was drowning in memories.

Jonah made a face that was somewhere between a frown and a grimace. "Uh, a lot has happened since you've been gone."

Of course it had. He'd been in prison for nearly five years, a stiff sentence for second-degree manslaughter.

But apparently the judge had been feeling particularly peevish that day about Amish who thought they could run amok in his district without consequences. Of course it didn't help that the state's plaintiff was an attorney himself. Titus hadn't known it would prove to be important at the time, but it was. Oh, how it was.

"You want to fill me in?" Titus asked.

Finally, they were through town and on the other side, where most of the Amish farms were located.

Jonah took so long to answer for a moment Titus thought he wasn't going to. Then he took a deep breath and started. "Let's see, we've had a few new folks moving in. Caroline Hostetler came with her daughter Emma. She went to work with Esther Lapp in the bakery, then she met Andrew Fitch. He's Abe Fitch's nephew. He moved down from Missouri. They ended up getting married—Caroline and Andrew—which you don't know either one of them but you'll meet them now that you're . . . home." He seemed reluctant to say that last word.

Titus couldn't blame him. The stench of change clung to him. He knew it. But it was more than change. Things would never be the same again and those around him didn't know how to handle it. Until he figured it out, he would just exist. And pray that one day he would understand.

"Then it was about that time that Esther Lapp married Abe Fitch."

That wasn't what Titus expected Jonah to say. "You don't say."

For as long as he could remember the man was absentminded euphemistically speaking and downright scatterbrained if a person really wanted to state the truth. But most people hated to say that about Abe. He was as kindhearted as they came, generous and caring, even if he was a little bit unkempt at times and would lose the thread of the conversation as easily as a fish slips off the hook.

"That is quite a bit," Titus said.

Jonah gave a small nod. "That's not the half of it. Luke Lambright ran off to drive *Englisch* race cars."

Titus nodded. "I'm not surprised."

"*Jah*, well, Emily wasn't very happy about it."

"Emily Ebersol?"

"Of course," Jonah said. "Except she's Emily Riehl now. Elam Riehl stepped in and started to court her. Now they're married and have a baby girl. Then there's his father."

"James?" It was so much easier talking about the many residents of Wells Landing and how they had been doing rather than dwelling on all the aspects of his own life.

He missed these people. He knew in his heart that he would never be a complete member of the community again. The Amish preached about forgiveness and understanding and that he could understand. But he wasn't the same person he had been when he'd left. How could he come back and pretend that nothing had happened? That was the saddest part of all.

"*Jah*, James was hurt. He got kicked in the head by a milk cow. He's not the same anymore. But he's doing all right. He and Joy had a new baby. They named her Lavender." He made a face telling Titus exactly what he thought about the name, then he shrugged it off. "He has a thing about purple."

"Thing?" Titus asked.

"You'll just have to talk to him. You'll understand then. Let's see, Sadie Kauffman is getting married this fall to a Mennonite guy named Ezra Hein. Clara Rose married Obie Brennaman."

"I knew that would happen," Titus said, nodding. "I think we all did except for Obadiah and Clara Rose." He chuckled.

"Then there's Lorie." An undeniable sadness crept into his tone. "Her dad died."

"I'm sorry to hear that." And Titus was. He liked Henry Kauffman. He was a good man, always happy. Titus would never forget him buzzing around the restaurant, big smile on his face as he made sure everyone had enough coffee and pie. His death was a shame.

"Lorie started going to Tulsa visiting with a grandmother she never knew she had."

"An *Englisch* grandmother?"

Jonah nodded and turned down the farm road that led to Titus's house.

His heart pounded a little heavier in his chest.

Almost home.

And then not. How could this ever be home again?

"It seems that Henry Kauffman was really Henry Mathis. And he wasn't Amish at all. It's kinda complicated, but when he died Lorie saw that he had a tattoo."

Titus whistled under his breath. Tattoos were strongly forbidden among the Amish. That was one of the many things he struggled with in prison. Everybody wanted to mark themselves to show what group they belonged to. Titus just wanted to keep to himself and do his time. He just wanted to get out with as few changes as possible. He did everything he could to come out of prison unmarked physically, but his marks were invisible, bolder, deeper.

"Anyway she met this sod named Zach something or another. I forget. . . ." He trailed off, and Titus had a feeling he knew exactly what this Zach's last name was, but he wouldn't press the issue.

"I'm sorry to hear that, too," Titus murmured.

"*Jah*, well, it's God's will."

Was it? Titus had lost faith in God's will. What proof was there that God wanted these things to happen? Why would God want some of these things that happened to happen? What good was it all?

He pushed those thoughts aside. He was going to see his parents again for the first time in four years, the first time since the trial. He hadn't seen his brothers and sisters since even before then. He'd had a few visitors that first year in jail, the year he served before the trial. But when he was shipped off to prison, he hadn't wanted them to come by. He didn't want anyone to see him in there. Now he was going to get to see them in just a few minutes. The thought sent his heart soaring even as it sank like a rock in his chest.

"Baby steps," the chaplain had said when he visited with Titus before his release. "Just take baby steps." And that's what he intended to do. What was that quote? "Do you know how to eat an elephant? One bite at a time." And that was what he was planning, to take one bite at a time until he figured out if he should swallow or spit it all out. Until then, he would enjoy what little remained of the life he had before.

"It's all right," Jonah said. "I'm doing okay."

Titus could spot a lie when he heard one. He'd been lying to so many people for so long that it had become easy. And he could tell that Jonah was lying now. As long as Jonah was trying to fool the outside and not himself, he'd be okay. Titus had fooled himself for years, and he knew that road led to destruction.

"It sounds like it's been a busy few years."

Jonah slowed the tractor as they neared the mailbox marked with the Lambert name. It hadn't changed. Their name was still spelled out in those gold and black letters. Half of the *T* was missing as it had been when he left. The mailbox seemed to have a couple more dents in it. But it seemed as if not much had changed at all, and he wasn't sure if that was a good thing or a bad thing.

Jonah turned the tractor, and they chugged down the drive. Once again Titus's heart was stabbed with the sameness of it all. Nothing had changed here. The barn still sat close to the road, the first building they came to when they turned down the driveway. It was still painted a bright red with a white fence wrapping around it. The white fence gave way to barbed wire and a sprawling pasture. On the opposite side of the drive the house sat, all pristine white with green shutters and a gray roof, just the same as it had always been. Only the flowers outside were different. How he knew that he didn't understand. But when he left there'd been flowers, mounds and mounds of beautiful blooms, spilling red, purple, and white all around the house. Now the flowers seemed a little tamer. They were more contained and looked thin as they stood straight and tall and reached for the sun. The flowers themselves were white with a couple of pinks mixed in, and it was definitely not what he had been used to seeing in the years before. Maybe that was what he needed, that one difference to bring him into the here and now.

Jonah pulled to one side of the house, then turned to Titus without cutting the engine. "Do you want me to go in with you?"

Titus stopped for a moment, mulling over every facet of the problem. He would love to have Jonah's familiar and steady support at his side as he entered the house he hadn't set foot in for five years. Yet this was something that he had to do alone. He needed to face the past and survive. And he needed to do it on his own two feet.

"Nah. You go on home." Titus climbed down from the tractor, grabbed his backpack, and slung it over one shoulder. He was standing on the opposite side of the tractor from the house, and yet he could see faces peeking out of the window to see who had come visiting.

"I had better get in there before everyone comes out on the porch." If that happened, then Jonah might not ever get to leave. That was one thing about his family: they were welcoming and loving and enjoyed having company of all sorts. If they knew Jonah was there, they would definitely invite him in, convince him he needed some pie and to drink some coffee, play a couple of games of Uno and twenty other things until they finally let him go. Titus wasn't sure they would treat him the same way. He was an outsider now, an outcast, a rebel, an outlaw, a convicted felon.

He couldn't handle them embracing Jonah with all the love that they always showed him before yet shunning him now.

He shook the thought away. Shunned or not, things would never be the same.

"Thanks for the ride," he told Jonah.

His friend nodded. "I'm glad you're home."

Jonah backed up the tractor and turned it around. He started for home, throwing a small wave over his shoulder as he putted along. Titus stood there, backpack slung across one shoulder, and watched him leave.

The front door opened and his youngest sister, Rachel, came to the door. She looked at him, turned her head one way and then the other. She had been only seven years old the last time she'd seen him. Plenty old enough to remember who he was.

"Titus." She breathed his name as if she never thought she'd speak it again. "*Mamm! Dat!* It's Titus! Titus is home."

He stood stock-still as inside the house movement erupted.

He heard his father's voice though he couldn't discern the words. Then Rachel responded. "I'm not kidding; he's right there." She pointed at him.

This was it. This was really happening. He was home.

His mother came out onto the porch, no doubt wanting to see what Rachel was so adamant about. She looked at her daughter and then looked at him. The moment froze. So many years had passed, but she looked the same as she had when he left. Maybe a few more lines around her face, a couple more wrinkles on her forehead, and a little more gray hidden under her prayer *kapp*. But somehow she looked just as she always had. Her blue eyes were kind and loving.

"Titus?" She said the word as if he would disappear if she said it too loudly.

"Hi, *Mamm.*"

"Abner, get out here! Titus is home!"

After that, chaos reigned. In an instant Titus was surrounded by the members of his family. His *mamm*; his *dat*; Rachel; his brothers Gabe Allen, Michael, and Paul; along with his oldest sister, June. As the oldest in the family, Titus had been the one who was supposed to set an example for them all. But after all the trouble he'd gotten into he was no role model, that was for sure.

But for now at least he was home. How long he'd be able to stay was anybody's guess.

Titus allowed himself to be pulled into the house. He did his best to seem as enthusiastic as his family. It wasn't that he *wasn't* happy to be home. It wasn't that he didn't love his family, but he knew that things had changed. And he knew that he wouldn't be able to stay. Not long anyway.

Before he knew what had happened he was sitting at

the kitchen table with everyone clustered around. His *mamm* was filling him a plate of leftovers as everyone tried to talk to him at once. He was the only one eating, so he was allowed to sit with them, but next time, he knew it would be different.

"How did you get home?" his *mamm* asked. "Why didn't you call us? We could have gotten a driver and come get you." She sat the heaping plate in front of him, and Titus resisted the urge to snatch up his fork and eat every bite as quickly as he could. That was how it had been on the inside. A person had to eat with single-mindedness or lose his meal to the next guy. The next bigger guy. Or the closest guy, whoever was meaner.

"I—" He stopped, unwilling to tell his mother that he hitchhiked home. That he hadn't wanted anyone to see him walk out of that prison. He was leaving it behind him and wanted them to as well. Or at the very least he was trying. "I caught a ride."

She reached out a hand to touch his face, but stopped short, just inches away from her target. She dropped her hand back to her side, then went around to the refrigerator and took out a large pitcher of lemonade. She poured him a glass, then hovered around him as if she wasn't sure what she should do next.

Well, that makes two of us.

"I joined the Turtles," Michael said. Titus could barely comprehend that his brother was old enough to run around much less that he had already settled on a youth group.

"*Dat* wouldn't let me join the Dragons like you did," Gabe Allen said. "I'm a Turtle too."

"The Turtles are a good group." He was sad that his parents wouldn't let his brothers join the youth group that Titus himself had been a part of, but he could understand their mindset. Titus had ended up in enough trouble for all of them. Not that it was the Dragons' fault or that being in a different youth group would have changed anything.

Titus took up his fork and steadied his hand as he tried to eat at an acceptable pace. A pulled pork sandwich with barbecue sauce and potato salad on the side. And as always there was applesauce, peanut butter spread, and biscuits most likely left over from breakfast. He took a bite and chewed as slowly as he dared. He didn't have to fight any longer. Didn't have to eat food that he wasn't familiar with. He was eating his mother's cooking, at home, at the table where he had eaten so many meals in the past.

The potato salad was as cool and tangy as he remembered it to be. Tears rose into his eyes. He blinked them away, swallowed the lump in his throat, and took another bite. He'd have plenty of time to think about what it meant to be home. But he would have to wait before taking out his emotions and examining them.

"If I had known you were coming I would have made something more special. Chicken and dumplings or fried chicken."

"Sit down, Jenny. Let the poor boy eat," his father groused.

His mother hesitated, then moved to the opposite side of the table.

"I've only got one more year of school," Paul boasted. "Then *Dat* said I could take over at the market."

Once upon a time that had been Titus's job and his dream: to take over at the market and run the family business. They sold anything and everything at the market. Canned goods, yarn items, produce, quilted pot holders. Name it and they had it. Once upon a time, Titus had thought that he would expand their operation. He'd had dreams of opening an actual store in town. He had even gone so far as to search for a place on Main Street. He'd found one too, but he had noticed on the way through town that someone had claimed that space. It appeared to be a specialty sports store selling jerseys and such for all the Oklahoma sports teams. It didn't add as much to the charm of the town as his store would have, but that opportunity was long past.

What were you thinking? That the place would still be empty, waiting for you to come home? Life went on; even while he felt suspended in time, everything in Wells Landing had continued without him.

"That's good, Paul." He was proud of his little brother. Truly he was. But with Paul in Titus's old spot where did that leave Titus?

"June's in love," Rachel sang.

He had expected protests from his oldest sister, but instead she turned a bright shade of pink.

"Who's the lucky guy?" When he had gone in, June had been seventeen and just getting into the swing of her runaround time. Back then she had been crazy about Noah Treger's little brother, Samuel. But the blush on her cheeks was not from a five-year-old relationship. No, this was something new.

"No one," she muttered.

"Timmy Glick," Rachel squealed.

"Rachel," *Dat* warned.

She covered her mouth and her eyes twinkled over her fingers.

"Jonah's cousin?"

June nodded.

Why didn't Jonah say anything about that?

Or maybe Jonah had recognized the fact that Titus

might not be in Wells Landing long enough for it to matter.

Titus wanted to ask what had happened between June and Samuel, but that was a story for another day.

He couldn't believe he was actually sitting there, in his *mamm*'s kitchen, listening to his family talk about everyday things as they struggled to catch him up on what he'd missed since he had gone to jail. The whole experience was almost more than he could bear. He was so thankful to be at home, so very glad to be free. Free! He was free. Though he had no idea what to do next.

He wanted to do everything at once and yet couldn't find the energy to get out of the chair. Titus pushed his plate to the side, and his mother was on her feet in a second. "Do you want some more? There's plenty."

He looked down at his empty plate. He had used the last of his biscuit to wipe up anything left. It was a habit from his childhood, but it served him well on the inside. Sometimes he didn't know where the next meal was coming from.

"No, thanks." He wasn't sure where he'd put all that he had just eaten. He was hungry and yet not. His stomach was tied in knots, his neck tight with tensions as he looked around at the faces of his family. The faces he missed so much in the last five years. The moment was so surreal he almost pinched himself to see if he was awake. Free. He was free.

His mother and father had come to the prison twice before he couldn't bear it any longer. He told them to go home and not to come back. He didn't want them to see him behind bars. His mother had protested, but he had held fast and strong. He would see her when he could. Now she sat across from him, her smile trembling, tears looking like they might fall at any minute. Still, she managed to blink them back and continued to smile. How long would it be before they got used to him being home and didn't stare at him like they were now? He was used to having his every move watched. But this was a little unnerving. He pushed back from the table and in a second his family was on their feet as well. He shook his head. "I just thought I'd go out for a little walk. Check out the farm."

Gabe Allen took a step forward, his chest puffed out importantly. "I'll take you if you want me to."

Titus shook his head. "That's not necessary. I know my way around."

Gabe Allen lost a little bit of his starch, but he picked it back up quickly. "I would like to spend some time with you."

And I'd just like to spend some time alone. He had spent the last five years knees and elbows to a bunch of angry, violent men. And as much as he loved his family and wanted to spend time with them, right now he needed the solitude he couldn't find on the inside. Still, he couldn't bring himself to tell Gabe Allen he wanted to be alone. "Come on then."

He could feel their eyes on him as he turned and made his way back to the door. He grabbed his hat off the peg, the motion so familiar that it almost made him cry. He hadn't been allowed his hat on the inside. Titus hadn't understood what about an Amish felt hat was so dangerous, but he knew the men on the inside were clever. They could make weapons from almost anything.

It hadn't taken long for him to realize that God might be everywhere, but He didn't listen through prison walls.

The sun was just starting to set as he and Gabe Allen made their way into the yard. Like everything else in Wells Landing, change on the farm came slowly. There were a few things different—a repair job in the fence, a new horse, a new dog. But as much as everything seemed the same, he was different. He rubbed a hand across the back of his neck again, that stitching a constant irritant. His clothes felt too tight, or maybe his body too big. He felt obvious, conspicuous, and so out of place he didn't know if he'd ever feel like a part of his own home again.

"It's so good to have you here," Gabe Allen said. "Was that Jonah who brought you home?"

Titus gave a small nod in response. Jail had been so full of shouting and banging that he didn't want to disturb the quiet that surrounded him. He could hear the birds chirping, the wind blowing through the trees, sounds of the animals all around, the hum of faraway engines, and the white buzz of silence.

He hadn't even been out for a whole day, and the change was almost more than he could handle.

Give it time.

He had no idea how much time it would take until he felt like he belonged here once again.

Chapter Two

"Did you hear?"

Mandy Burkholder looked up from the ham she was dicing to the other women all bustling around. Today was canning day and they were putting up soup for the winter. Days like today were Mandy's favorites. She loved getting out and being with her close friends, working together toward a common goal. Or maybe it was just that she wanted out of the house so bad some days she could taste it.

"Did I hear what?" Mandy used the back of one hand to push a loose strand of hair out of her face. She'd been in a hurry that morning and hadn't used a big enough dollop of baby lotion to smooth down all the wayward pieces. And now the wind was starting to pull a few of the hairs free.

Clara Rose Brennaman reached for another bag of carrots and started peeling them one by one. "Titus Lambert's back."

And just like that Mandy's world turned on its side. "Titus?" His name hadn't been on her lips for five years, not since the judge had sentenced him and he had gone off to McAlester to the prison.

"I'll wait on you, Titus," she said.

"Don't." The one word was clipped and cold. Even though she knew he didn't mean it. And she would wait on him forever, to the ends of the earth. Somehow they would manage to get through this together and somehow their love would survive. "I'll write you every day." She ran her fingers down those familiar features, across his smooth cheek. She wished she was as bold as those Englisch girls she'd seen in town. She would love nothing more than to intertwine her fingers in the silky strands of his blond hair and to pull his mouth to hers. They had kissed a couple of times before, little stolen moments on the way home from singings and on the porch when they thought no one was looking. But she had never been so bold as to initiate a kiss herself. A kiss she so badly needed to tell him that he was always hers and she was always his and that somehow, someway God would get them through this terrible time they now faced. She couldn't lose him. She couldn't lose Titus. He was her one and only. Her everything.

"Mandy? Are you okay?"

She roused herself from her thoughts, realizing only then that she had stopped chopping and was staring off into space. "Oh, *jah*, I'm—I'm all right. I'm fine." She gave a quick smile and started chopping once again as if to prove her words true. "Of course I'm fine. Why would I not be okay?"

Titus was back. Titus was back and after all her vows to wait for him, she had married another.

Five years was a long time. Much longer than she had ever dreamed as she watched her friends one by one fall in love and get married. The one man she wanted to marry was in prison for killing another. Never mind it was an accident. He was in jail, and she was alone. What else could she have done but marry Levi Burkholder? She couldn't wait on Titus forever. She wanted to have children. They weren't getting any younger.

And though she supposed by *Englisch* standards the
Amish have children much younger, it was hard to
watch her friends one by one bring beautiful babies
into the world while she felt as if she was still waiting
and waiting and waiting for Titus.

"You look pale," Clara Rose said.

Mandy could feel Clara Rose's sharp gray eyes fixed
to her. Mandy schooled her face into a carefully formed
mask. At least she hoped it was. She thought it was.

"You're not"—Clara Rose looked from side to side,
then leaned a bit closer—"pregnant, are you?"

The one word sent a knife straight through her
heart. It'd been three years, three years since she and
Levi had gotten married. Three long years of wishing
and praying for a baby and three long years of disappointment.

"No," Mandy said. "I'm not pregnant."

She wanted to go to the doctor to see if maybe there
was something wrong with one or another of them, but
Levi would hear nothing of it. His family was a little
more conservative than most in the area, even more
conservative than the rest of the community. She supposed it stemmed from their former bishop. William
Stoltzfoos had been a very traditional man. That district, on the far side of Wells Landing, was the smallest
in the area, not even having two hundred members. So
when Bishop Stoltzfoos died, instead of holding the
traditional lot, they had simply asked Bishop Treger to
serve as their bishop while they kept their own minister,
preacher, and deacon. The arrangement was supposed
to have been for a short time, but now it had turned
into years. It seemed to work well for them, being so
much more conservative than the rest of Wells Landing; they tended not to do much to shake things up.
Not that "shaking things up" would include going to

the doctor to find out why a person couldn't have a baby when it was the one desire of their heart. Was it so much to ask?

For Levi, it was. He felt that they would be blessed with the baby when the time was right, not before, not after, and certainly not with a doctor's help.

Mandy pulled herself from those thoughts and focused on the matter at hand, the ham. She made her slices, keeping her head down, her prayer *kapp* strings tied in the back. Normally, she let them hang free. At least when Levi wasn't around. They became something of a trial when working outside, and she found it easier to tie them to the back to keep them out of her way.

The *clink clink clink* of the carrot peeler in Clara Rose's hands complemented the dull *thunk thunk* of her knife hitting the chopping board. Down the line of their worktable she could hear other noises, the same comforting noises of every canning day they had ever had—the chatter of the children playing under the big apple tree, the clink of jars as everyone got ready to actually can the soup, the sizzle of the vegetables they sautéed on the open burner, and all the little noises of the world around.

Titus was home. She'd never thought this day would come. Or maybe she hadn't wanted to believe it. Maybe that was how she talked herself out of loving Titus forever and convincing herself that she could marry Levi and be happy.

She straightened her shoulders at the thought, then rolled them once to keep Clara Rose from suspecting anything out of the ordinary. She was happy. It wasn't that Levi couldn't make her happy. Just circumstances. She and Titus were over. They were finished. She was married to another. Amish married for life. It wasn't like she could run away with Titus and leave Levi behind, pray that she and Titus would have a baby and they would fulfill all of their dreams. That they would live happily ever after like those *Englisch* fairy tales. No, this was real life, real problems, real issues.

"You know what I heard?" Julie Fitch sidled up beside them using the guise of grabbing a bag of potatoes from under the table as reason enough for coming to their end of the workstation. "I heard Titus Lambert is back."

"He is," Sarah Yoder, Mandy's cousin, said. "Jonah told me last night. He picked him up outside of town and brought him to the farm. He said he looked sad."

The thought of Titus being sad sent pains through her heart. She didn't want him sad. She never wanted him sad. But as much as she had wanted to wait for him, she couldn't. It wasn't anyone's fault. It was just the way it was. Life had to go on. He had been suspended inside a prison, while she was out here trying to make life work. She couldn't do it without him, so she had married another.

"I wonder why no one had a party for him," Clara Rose pondered.

"Would you want a party if you were Eli?" Sarah asked.

The chatter of the girls grew silent. Mandy kept her head down and kept chopping, doing her best to pretend that none of the conversation around her affected her any more than on the surface.

Eli.

Eli was Levi's cousin and the only other survivor of the car crash that Titus had been responsible for. Yet even as Titus came away from the crash with a broken arm and a broken leg, an *Englisch* boy by the name of Blaine Carson lost his life. So had Alvin King. Eli had lost the use of his legs forever. The saddest part of all was that the boys had once upon a time been best friends. Now two were dead, one was crippled, and the other one had to go to jail for it all.

"No, I suppose not." It wasn't that they didn't forgive Titus for what he had done. His irresponsible actions that night might have led to the death of two people and basically the loss of a normal life for the third, but forgiveness didn't come automatically, regardless of what people believed on the outside. The Amish didn't have some sort of button they pushed that made them forgive anything that happened in their lives. This took time and energy, effort and prayer. But the first step was confessing that forgiveness. Everyone involved had said they had forgiven Titus long ago. But some hurts had to be dealt with and not celebrated. Having a party to welcome Titus back into the community would be completely disrespectful to Eli, everything he had done in his life and had not been able to do since the accident.

Mandy visited with Eli a lot, seeing as how he was her husband's first cousin. And Eli always seemed to be in good spirits. Unlike Johnny Flaud, Eli had the use of his upper body, even though it had been months since Johnny had fallen and years since the car crash that rendered Eli paralyzed. Only God knew if Johnny would have as much healing as Eli. Only time would tell. Still, Eli's life had been forever altered that night, and Titus was responsible, at least according to the *Englisch* courts.

"Do you think he'll stay?" Julie asked. She looked from one girl to the next and Mandy felt as if her gaze burned as it fell on her.

"I wouldn't know."

Julie straightened. "Of course not." She gave a nervous laugh and tossed her strings back over her shoulders. "I'm sure you stopped writing him long before the wedding."

The girls around all nodded, and Mandy did the same.

"Are you about ready down there?" Mandy's mother, Becky Yoder, sneaked a couple of cubes of ham from the chopping block as she looked from one girl to the next. "How much more do you have?"

Mandy thumped the side of the last package of ham with her knife. "I just have to cut this."

Sarah held up her bowl, a large stainless-steel container filled with onions. "Onions are done."

Clara Rose made a few more cuts, then nodded. "Carrots are too."

Mamm looked back at Mandy. "You had better get a move on." She snatched a couple more pieces of ham, then smiled. "You've fallen behind."

The words stayed with Mandy for the rest of the afternoon. Normally, she loved making soup with her family and it was a special time of bonding and memories. She loved seeing all the jars lined up and the big container filled with soup, enough to feed the five families who had gathered there. But today she couldn't find that joy. Today all she could think about was Titus.

Titus was home. He had come back to Wells Landing just as he had promised and yet she had broken her promise to him. Despite all of his pleas and then demands that she not wait for him to get out of prison, she had promised that she would wait forever. "Forever and a day," she told him more times than she could remember. And yet forever and a day turned out to be two years. Well, a year. She had waited a year. Then Levi Burkholder had come to her and told her how beautiful she was and how much he hated that she was wasting her life over someone who might not ever come back.

He told her how prison would change a person until they wouldn't be the same person they were when they left. Titus was a good man, he'd told her, but he was gone. Titus would spend five years someplace that they could not comprehend. And when he returned—if he returned—he wouldn't be the same as he had when he left. That was something she needed to keep in mind. Then Levi had explained that if she thought she might not be able to live with the man Titus would become while in prison, she should give serious thought to dating. More specifically she should give serious thought to dating him.

She had mulled it over for a week and prayed about it. She started to talk to her family, but chickened out. In the end, she prayed about it enough that the thought of not waiting for Titus didn't send that pain shooting through her stomach any longer. She thought about it long enough and hard enough that it didn't seem so out of place to marry another. Who knew when Titus would be home? How could she wait for someone if she really didn't know he was coming back at all? Despite Titus's claims that he would, she knew what Levi said was correct. Titus wouldn't be the same person when he came home as he was when he left. Five years was a long time of growing and experience. It would be better served to grow and experience with someone who was living the same life as she. So by the time Titus returned, she had married another. What was she supposed to do?

Abbie King smoothed a hand across the kerchief tied over her hair and patted the black-and-white cow on the neck. Of the twenty-five dairy cows they still had left, Edith was her favorite.

"It'll be okay, girl," she said.

Edith swished her tail to clear the flies off her back. Then she dipped her head for another drink of water.

"It'll be okay." But she was talking more to herself than to the heifer. Titus Lambert had gotten out of prison and had returned to Wells Landing.

Every day for the last five years she had known this day was coming, and she had dreaded it. It hadn't been easy to go on after her brother's death. He was her twin, her constant companion, the only two children that her mother and father had managed to bring into this world. She and Alvin had done everything together.

Well, almost everything. They hadn't gone to that *Englisch* party together. She had stayed at home while Alvin had gone with Titus and Eli and that *Englisch* boy named Blaine. She'd met Blaine once or twice and she knew his type. He was arrogant and self-assured. His family had money, enough to get him everything he wanted. Why he wanted three Amish boys as friends was anybody's guess. Maybe it lent him some sort of status symbol or made him the leader of their little group. Abbie had begged Alvin to stay home that night. She had known there was going to be trouble. But Alvin had scoffed and left, shaking away her protests. He had gone without her.

And then the things that she had shouted at him as he walked out the door.

She shook her head, then unhooked the milking machine from under Edith. She toted the full jug to the center aisle of the milking barn, only to unhook the apparatus, then re-hook it to the front, empty vat. She attached it to the next cow in line, Lena. Then she returned to pour Edith's milk into the "sputnik."

She missed her brother every time she came out to milk alone. There was a lot of work. It could be handled by one person, but it was more fun with someone to help, someone to talk to. She'd always made Alvin clean the cows' udders. It was silly of her, she knew, but she felt like he had a better touch. He said she just didn't want to get down so low and mess with the cows, but Alvin seemed to soothe the old girls. They seemed to do what he wanted when he wanted it done, instead of fighting her every step of the way as they had done for the last five years.

Yet what was she supposed to do? Alvin was gone, and she had to keep going. She was Amish. She couldn't just lie down and give up. Though that seemed more and more like what her parents had done.

She had gone to the library in town and read a couple of books about it, looked at some things on the Internet with the help of the librarian, and she knew that her parents suffered from depression. She was no expert, but she could see the signs. Neither one of them jumped out of bed and raced to greet the day as they had once upon a time. Their voices lacked the passion and caring that they once held. They went through the motions of everyday life as if somehow it had all been watered down to half of what it had been before. She knew they missed Alvin. She missed him more than both of them put together. But somebody had to keep this farm running. Somebody had to make sure that there was food on the table and money in the bank for the times when they needed it. But every day it grew a little harder to come out here by herself and milk the cows.

They only had twenty-five now, having lost the others to various problems in the last five years. She needed to do something about it. Buy a couple more heifers, let the bull have his way in the pasture, *something* in order to keep their stock up. But that was something she'd never learned about in her years growing up. And these days, her father didn't seem to want to talk about it. In fact, she had a hard time getting any man in Wells Landing to talk to her about cow breeding. She supposed that it was hard for them to talk with her about it. Though it wasn't because she was a woman, but her physical looks stood in her way. Everybody believed that the Amish didn't care about things like that, but they did. Everyone tended to assume that she was soft and loving and caring and couldn't hold a grudge and wouldn't hurt a fly and all those other sayings that she had heard over the years. What they didn't know was that behind her soft blue eyes and pale brown hair, she grew a little more bitter each day. Her insides felt like a shriveled-up persimmon. She prayed about it every day, prayed for understanding, prayed for help, prayed for change. But she got nothing. There was no change. Her parents were the same, day in and day out, listless, just a fraction of what they had been before. And she was at her limit as to what she could do to make the farm work. The buildings needed paint, and the barn needed a roof.

Just after Alvin died it was easy to find help, but now it seemed that other tragedies had taken time, money, and effort away from her farm and spread that needed assistance throughout the community. It was something that she had known would happen eventually and had prepared herself for. And it wasn't what caused her these feelings of darkness and spite. No, it wasn't that at all. It was Titus Lambert, free and coming back to Wells Landing as if nothing happened. As if his life could just go back to the way it was before. Before Alvin died. Before he killed Alvin.

Manslaughter, the attorneys had called it. Basically it was a case of negligence. She had learned all the boys had been out, that all had been drinking at a party, and somehow they had decided that Titus was driving Blaine Carson's car home. It wasn't like Titus didn't have a driver's license. He had gone on his *rumspringa* and gotten one. More and more Amish youth were getting a driver's license for the runaround time with some even buying cars. Even the ones who didn't have a vehicle to drive liked to have their license, a sign of their rebellion with the picture on it, tangible proof that they could push the envelope as far as they could in those few years between sixteen and joining the church. No, the big problem for her was that Alvin was gone.

It had been so hard, so very, very hard those first few months to accept that Alvin was no longer with them. The bishop had talked with them about God's will and understanding, about love, forgiveness, and all those other lofty things that bishops liked to talk about. But how could he consider a drunken car wreck part of God's will? God had nothing to do with that. Nothing at all. How could God have something to do with that?

Now Titus had returned. She hadn't been back in Wells Landing long herself, but after her numerous trips to Missouri under the guise of "getting herself together," Abbie realized that there was nothing wrong with her. But there was an awful lot wrong with the situation. Even more wrong with her parents.

She had come back for her cousin's wedding only to discover the effects of their quickly declining moods. She couldn't help but wonder why no one in the church had noticed that they needed help. And she felt even worse for abandoning them when they all should have been together. She should've never listened to everyone's urgings to go to Missouri to rest and relax and get herself back healthy before she returned. She thought she was doing good by all of them.

But all she had done was send her parents into a quicker downward spiral.

It'd taken a solid month of cleaning and organizing, scrubbing and more, to just get the milking barn in order. How her father's milk had passed inspection only the good Lord knew. She supposed he had managed to keep things going okay, but she had a feeling that he poured more milk down the milk-room drain than he had into the truck in the last few years.

And her mother was no better. *Mamm*'s clothes hung on her. Abbie knew that she had to have lost fifty pounds in the past few years. Her *mamm* had always been complaining about being a little heavy, and what was it the *Englisch* said? Be careful what you wish for. You just might get it. Her mother had wanted to lose weight, but surely not like this.

These days Abbie worked sunup to sundown, until she could do no more. Her father helped as much as he could and her mother did the same. But every effort they made seemed to zap their energy as if it were leaking from their body by the gallon. And that pushed the brunt of the work onto Abbie's shoulders.

Abbie unhooked the milking machine and moved it down. She poured the milk, then started another milking farther down the line of cows. One day, she vowed, one day everything would be back right again. Everything would be running smoothly, perfectly. Well, as perfect for a dairy farm as it possibly could be. Everything would be like it had been before. Or as close as it could be without Alvin there. Her parents would smile again, real smiles that reached their eyes and made them twinkle. Her parents would laugh again, not just that choking, coughing sound that they made to make her think they were happy. No one at the King household was happy and that was the saddest part of all. One person could be blamed for that lack of happiness and he had just returned home as if nothing was out of the ordinary. As if he hadn't ruined more than three lives in that car wreck.

How could he come back here and pretend like none of these things had happened?

She worked her way down the line of cows, nearly exhausted by the time she reached the end. And she still had to do all of the finishing-up chores—spread the feed, and unhook the cows, let them back into the holding pen, scrape the manure into the pit, pour the milk into the holding tank, clean and sterilize all of the milk machines, then let the cows back out into the pasture once more. Even with only twenty-five heifers, with only one person, milking took almost three hours. It was seven o'clock when she finished and she was almost asleep on her feet as she entered the house.

"Abbie? Is that you?"

"*Jah*, it's me." She wiggled her bare toes against the cool stone floor of their house entry. She always left her Crocs in the barn. They had too many unmentionables on them to wear them anywhere else. Just like the dress she had worn to milk. Even an hour in the barn left a person smelling like . . . well, barn. Hay, manure, and just stinky cows. She hated it.

"Come on in. Your supper's ready."

Abbie plucked at the front of her dress, preparing to tell her mother that she needed to shower before she came into the house itself. They had a bathroom complete with the shower off the downstairs foyer. It was perfect for dairy farmers who could come in, shower, and change before continuing into the house to join the rest of the family.

"What?" she called. Certainly she hadn't heard her mother right.

"Supper's ready."

Unable to resist having a peek, Abbie made her way into the kitchen. Her mother stood by the stove, though no pots bubbled there.

"Supper's ready?" Her eyes darted around the room, finally landing on the table. There sat a box of wheat crackers, a summer sausage, some olives, and a stack of cheese. There was also a tub of peanut butter spread and the loaf of bread that Abbie had baked the day before. Supper. If a person could call it that. It looked more like what they ate after church. Which was good. But didn't account for a hard day's work.

"You shouldn't have, *Mamm.* Thank you."

Her mother smiled but as usual it went no farther than her lips. "I thought you could use a break tonight."

It was times like this that Abbie knew her parents would be okay, eventually. They would come out of this dark mood that had engulfed them both. They would find their way to the other side and they would learn to live again without Alvin. Whether she would be as fortunate still remained to be seen.

"Where's *Dat?*"

Mamm shook her head. "He said he had a headache and that he was going to lie down."

Abbie pressed her lips together. Her father may have a headache, but it wasn't from natural causes. And that was something so beyond her grasp she didn't know what to do. She had seen the bottles in the trash, she had heard his unsteady footsteps at night. She knew her father was drinking alcohol. Whether her mother knew it or not Abbie couldn't ask. If *Mamm* knew, then what good would it be telling her again? And if she didn't know, telling her would only break her heart even more. This was something she should keep to herself. Until she could figure out what to do about it anyway.

She wasn't quite ready to go to the bishop yet. She needed a little more time to get to the bottom of the whys of the drinking. Like why had it started now? Was it because people around them were more comfortable talking about Alvin now that it had been five years since his death? They might be ready for those discussions, but she knew her *mamm* and *dat* weren't.

"I hate that he feels bad," she said. "Just let me shower, and I'll be right in."

Her mother smiled and this time Abbie could see that old sparkle. "Take your time," she said. "There's no hurry with this meal."

"I'll just be a minute." She turned to leave. But her mother's words stopped her in her tracks.

"Did you hear? Titus Lambert has returned to Wells Landing."

Chapter Three

Titus parked the carriage to the one side of the familiar white house, but couldn't bring himself to get out. He had been back in town for three days and this visit was two days overdue. He should've come sooner. He shouldn't have put it off. But the thought of looking Eli in the face, asking his forgiveness, and being denied it was almost more than he could stand. Not that he thought Eli would be angry. He knew better than that. That wasn't Eli's way. Then again, looking Eli in the face and having him say that it was okay, that it was all an accident, and that he shouldn't give it a second thought was even more than Titus could bear. He had given it a second, a third, and a fourth thought every day since the accident. Why was he the only one spared?

It wasn't that he hadn't heard from Eli since the accident. Of all the people involved, including his parents, Eli was the only one who had remained in contact with him all these years. While he was on the inside, Titus had received letter after letter from Eli. He talked about his physical therapy, the surgeries, and everything else he was going through. He talked some about what was going on in the community, but mostly his letters were about past times when the three of them had been together and all the things they had done. Each one had a conversational tone as if nothing had ever happened out of the ordinary. Like the person he was writing to wasn't in prison. Titus had responded to a few of them, but after a while the heartbreak of writing each word on paper and sending it to him became too much. He figured Eli understood because letters kept coming whether he received a response from Titus or not. Deep down Titus had been thankful for those little missives, the small bridge between prison and Wells Landing.

"Are you coming in? Or are you going to sit out there in your buggy all day?"

Titus swung around to see Eli sitting on the porch in his wheelchair.

Shock flared through him like a hard, white light, nearly taking his breath away. It wasn't that he hadn't seen Eli in his wheelchair before. He'd been in a wheelchair during the trial when he had testified how the events of that night were an accident. But to see him in a wheelchair now, at his home, broke Titus's heart all over again. The dumb choices people make . . .

"Come to think of it, why are you driving a horse during the week?"

On rubbery legs, Titus swung himself down from the buggy. "I don't want to drive anything with a motor." He shook his head, unable to finish with more. It was then that he noticed the ramp that led to the Glick's porch. Five years ago that ramp hadn't been necessary.

Eli watched him as he drew closer. Titus dropped his gaze to the ground as he approached. He felt unworthy, embarrassed to meet his gaze.

"It's about time you got here," Eli said. "I heard you've been back in town for three days."

Titus stopped, one foot on the ramp, the other on the ground. Finally, he raised his eyes to look at his friend. "I didn't know if you would want to see me."

Eli scoffed. "Why wouldn't I want to see you?"

Titus shrugged. He let his gaze wander over his friend, taking in every detail of his appearance. He looked about the same as he had all the other times. His dark hair on the unruly side, his green eyes as clear as glass with that telltale sparkle that told of his mischievous nature. For the most part he looked just the same as he had before. He dressed the same. Green shirt, black suspenders, black broadfall pants. But while his upper body seemed as trim and muscular as it had back in their runaround days, his legs were thin and frail beneath the dark fabric. Legs that had once worked but now couldn't.

Titus was overcome with remorse for everything that had happened. Stupid choices. Stupid choices that changed lives. He shook his head and started to turn away. "I can't do this."

"Can't do what?"

"I can't stay here. I'm sorry, Eli."

"You know, I never figured you for a coward."

Titus turned to his friend. "A coward?"

Eli raised his chin in a backward nod. "*Jah*, a coward. You spent all that time in jail, and you're still a coward. I just never thought it would be that way."

"I'm not a coward," Titus said. He propped his hands on his hips. Suddenly the urge to leave fled, leaving behind the need to defend himself.

"What else can I call it?" Eli shrugged. "You come all the way out here and then leave without even talking to me? That's a coward."

Titus shifted in his spot and tried not to snort like a bull. He and Eli Glick had been friends for so long, and now Eli thought Titus was a coward? Suddenly Titus had a few choice words to say to his friend. He wanted to tell Eli everything that he had suffered while he was in prison, the sleepless nights from always having to watch his back, the men who . . .

He shook his head. "Why are you trying to argue with me?"

That familiar grin spread across Eli's face. It was lopsided and bespoke his ornery nature. Titus had missed it. "Because if you're arguing, then you're not leaving."

The tension left Titus like the tide going out to sea. He nearly slumped with relief. "I'm sorry, Eli." His voice cracked.

"There's nothing to be sorry for, Titus. It was an accident. And that's all there is to it."

One foot in front of the other. Baby steps.

Titus made his way up the ramp to his friend's side. He hated that he towered over him. It was only because Eli was in a wheelchair. Otherwise he stood taller than Titus. Tall and slim and strong and capable and . . .

"I'm sorry, Eli."

Eli glared at him. "Say that again and I'll run over your feet. It may not look like I weigh much these days, but it will hurt. That I can promise you."

Titus stopped, a second passed, then laughter bubbled up inside him. He couldn't stop himself, and Eli joined in.

"Now come on in the house, and let's have a snack."

"Where's your *mamm*?"

Eli shrugged. "She's over at her book club meeting." He rolled his eyes. "If Bishop Ebersol ever finds out what they've been reading . . ." He grinned. "Of course, it's good for a bit of persuasion every now and again."

Titus chuckled. "Persuasion? Or blackmail?"

Eli shrugged. "It's all in how you look at it."

They laughed and together they made their way to the kitchen. A plastic container of seasoned pretzels and a jug of cool meadow tea waited on the table. It had been a long time since Titus had had meadow tea. Its minty taste brought back so many memories. Lazy afternoons at Millers' Pond, singings with Mandy, volleyball games with their youth group. The list went on and on and all of them included Alvin King, Eli, Abbie, and Mandy. All the people he knew and loved though so many of them wanted nothing to do with him now.

That's not true, that voice inside him whispered. Everyone had welcomed him back with open arms. Everybody but Abbie. Not that he had been to see her. But he knew that she wanted nothing to do with him. And he couldn't blame her. Of all the people he'd been around since he returned to Wells Landing, he felt that at least her feelings were genuine and sincere. Even if he didn't like them, even if they broke his heart all over again, they were her feelings and they were real.

They took their fare to the long table that sat in the middle of the kitchen. Titus sat on one side, and Eli parked his chair under the empty space on the other. Titus supposed that the family had gotten rid of the chair to allow Eli room to be at the table with all of them, but he made no comment. It was just one of those adjustments that his friend had been forced to make in the last few years.

"I guess you heard about Lorie and Jonah," Eli said.

Titus nodded. "I ran into Jonah in town."

"*Jah,* I heard," Eli said.

"So how's he doing?" Titus asked. "I mean, he says he's okay but . . ."

Eli frowned, the expression so foreign to his normally happy face. "He says he's okay, but I can see he's struggling."

Titus took a handful of the pretzels and popped them into his mouth. The taste brought back so many memories of after church and all the other events. Somebody had always brought seasoned pretzels. He'd missed them on the inside. There were snack mixes that had pretzels in them, but they didn't compare to Amish seasoned pretzels. Not by a long shot. "How so?"

"It's hard to say," Eli said. "There's not anything he does outwardly. But I can just tell. And then Sarah Yoder."

"Mandy's cousin?"

Eli nodded. "I think she has a crush on him. She follows him around all over the place and just . . . well, it worries me."

"How so?" That was another thing about Eli. He didn't worry.

"She's just so obviously crazy about him. And he seems vulnerable. It just looks like a bad combination from where I sit."

He might have a point there, but Jonah Miller was a grown man. He had joined the church and by Amish standards should be able to handle himself. What could tiny little Sarah Yoder do to Jonah anyway?

"Anything else interesting happen while I was gone?"

Eli nodded, his face pulled into a serious expression. "Lots of things. The Glicks over on Redbud Road. They bought a new pig. And let's see, the Petersheims, they built a new fence." He tapped his chin and stared at the ceiling as if trying to remember all of the momentous events of the last five years.

Titus chuckled. "I get it. Not much happens in Wells Landing."

Eli smiled. "You got that right."

It was true, and yet Titus was grateful. Maybe, just

maybe, in the slower pace of life that Wells Landing offered, he would figure out how to live again.

Abbie braced herself against the rain and dashed from the tractor toward the waiting cover. Coming to town today was a bad idea, but she didn't have much choice. She had a deposit to make at the bank, a bill to pay, and groceries to buy. Her parents had been taking care of such things. At least they had been while she was away, but now it seemed that they had forgotten the everyday things they had to do and instead relied on her to take care of it all.

She hurried through the driving rain, her goal the dry space under the awning at the post office. She had already been by the bank and the store. All of the groceries she had to buy were nonperishables and stowed neatly behind the tractor seat. One last stop and she would be able to return home, dry herself, and get on with the rest of her day. Just a couple more steps and she would be sheltered by the—

With her head ducked against the stinging rain, she didn't see what she ran into. Only that she hit something and hit it hard.

The barrier let out an *oomph* and together, she and this unseen obstacle went tumbling to the sidewalk.

By some miracle she didn't crack her head against the hard concrete, but she landed smack on top of what could only be another person. A male person if the hard muscles of his torso were any indication.

Without hesitation, she pushed herself up. An apology springing to her lips as easily as the heat crept into her cheeks. "I'm s—You!"

Titus Lambert!

"Me," he said as he pushed to his feet.

As the passersby walked around them, they stood there, squared off like two adversaries preparing for battle. Wasn't that what they were? Adversaries? Though they were both Plain and not allowed to fight even if they wanted to.

Of all the people in the world she could have run into—literally—why did she have to pick Titus Lambert? And why today of all days, when she looked like a drowned rat? Not that she cared what he thought about her, but she had wanted to be at her best when she saw him again.

She had never given a thought to what would happen after the guards had handcuffed Titus and led him from the courtroom that day. She had only registered that Titus was going to prison and would no longer be walking around free while her brother was buried next to her grandparents in the little cemetery at the edge of town.

Her parents had begged her not to attend the trial and then flat-out forbade it, but she had gone anyway, defying their wishes in order to see the punishment the judge would hand down to her brother's killer.

In the end, she had cried when he was sentenced. She had been so comforted that he wouldn't walk away without some sort of consequence and ashamed of herself for feeling that relief. That was not the Amish way, to punish and not forgive. She had said endless prayers concerning the matter, but she couldn't bring her heart to forgive Titus for the role he had played in Alvin's death.

She ran trembling hands down her dress, trying not to shiver from the wet chill or shake with anger and surprise.

"Abbie." He said her name as if it were the beginning

of a prayer, but she couldn't stand to hear his voice. Once upon a time they had all been friends—her, Titus, and Alvin. They had all been in the same buddy bunch with Mandy Yoder and Eli Glick. She would have been in the car with them that night had they not specified that no girls were allowed at the party. She had known immediately that they weren't telling the truth. She had been angry and yelled at them as they had pulled out of the drive. That was the last time she had seen her brother. He was dead, and Titus was responsible.

She clenched her jaw and tightened her resolve as she tried to push past him. They might live in the same town, but that didn't mean she had to rekindle their friendship.

She was almost past him when his hand snaked out and wrapped around her arm.

She started at his touch, then willed her pounding heart to return to its regular rhythm. "Let go of me, Titus Lambert."

He looked down at his hand as if until that moment he hadn't been aware he was touching her. He snatched it away and shoved his hands into the pockets of his jeans. He was wearing jeans, not the broadfall denim trousers that some of the men in Wells Landing preferred, but honest to goodness *Englisch* jeans.

"I just want to talk to you."

She shook her head. "Well, I don't want to talk to you." She did her best to ignore the hurt that flashed across his face. What did he expect? That he could come back to town and everything would be forgotten?

Of course! What else would he expect? That was the Amish way, forgive and be forgiven.

Forgive us our trespasses as we forgive those who trespass against us.

It had been so easy to say those words when she hadn't been wronged. When she could still eat supper with her brother every night. When her parents had been whole and healthy. Before her *dat* had started drinking. But they were much harder to follow when faced with the adversity that her family had endured. She had tried and tried, and then she had simply given up that battle. The entire town could celebrate the fact that Titus had come back. They could even hold a party to welcome him home, but that didn't mean she had to attend. That didn't mean she had to forgive him.

"Abbie," he started once again.

She tugged her arm from his grasp. "Leave me alone, Titus."

He released her. "I just want to talk," he said before she could walk away.

"You've done enough already."

With that, she turned on her heel and entered the post office with as much dignity as she could. She held her chin high in the air as she took her place in line. She would not let him steal away her anger and hurt. It was all she had left of her brother, and she needed it.

Alvin had been her twin. Her only sibling, the one person in the world who was always at her side. Even as children they were inseparable. It was as if they knew that one day they wouldn't have each other any longer and they had to make the most of the time they did have.

And Titus Lambert had taken all that away from her. It was unfair of anyone to ask her to forgive him. She wished she had that capability, but she didn't. And there was nothing anyone could do about it.

* * *

"Abbie, is that you?"

Abbie toed off her slip-on shoes and sighed. She had just walked into the door and the rain had stopped. Why couldn't it have done that while she was running errands? She pushed those negative thoughts away. She tried, really she did, but everything seemed so hard these days.

"Yes, *Mamm.*" She grabbed the bags and headed into the kitchen. She had just a few minutes to put everything away before she needed to head to the barn and start the afternoon milking. Today's chore would be a little more of a challenge considering all the rain they had gotten that morning. Mud made everything a little slower. It didn't help that with every milking she grew more and more concerned about her father. He seemed to have lost interest in everything. Life. And she didn't know what to do about it.

She took the boxes of crackers from the bags and started stacking the cans on the counter next to them.

Shuffling footsteps sounded behind her and alerted her to the fact that her mother was coming into the kitchen. Had her *mamm*'s footsteps always been that slow? Had they always dragged? She wished she could remember, but she thought they hadn't. And knowing that her mother was sliding downhill as quickly as her father nearly broke her heart in two.

She hadn't wanted to come back to Wells Landing from Missouri, but her cousin had wanted her to return for her wedding and after seeing her parents, Abbie couldn't bring herself to leave again.

Her parents had recognized that she had been having a hard time after Alvin died and they had wanted her to be able to get away from all the places that held such heartbreaking memories for her. She hadn't wanted to leave them, but they had insisted, citing that her aunt in Jamesport had needed help. So off she had gone.

No one was more surprised than her when she actually liked it there. Or maybe it wasn't that she liked Missouri as much as she needed time away from Wells Landing and losing Alvin. In Missouri she could pretend that she could return home and he would be there. That they were just miles apart. After that, it became harder and harder to make those trips back home even for the holidays. Until she waited nearly two years before returning. She had thought it would be easier, but it wasn't. Coming back to Oklahoma was like losing Alvin all over again, everywhere she went.

And if it was like that for her, she could only imagine how her *mamm* and *dat* felt.

"Need some help?"

Abbie smiled in her mother's general direction. "I can manage. But thanks."

"Did you get the soup I was telling you about?" *Mamm* asked.

Abbie shook her head. "I couldn't find it," she lied. They had can upon can of the soup at the grocery store, but she hadn't wanted to buy it. Not because her mother liked it and had requested it, but eating soup from the cans just seemed to signify that they had given up all hope of life returning to normal. Once in a while, sure, it was fine. She was worked to the bone trying to milk the cows and take care of everything else in the house; she should be grateful to accept the convenience of a premade meal. But she just couldn't. It seemed like the end of the line.

Her mother sat back in one of the kitchen chairs and propped her chin on her hands as she watched Abbie unload the grocery sacks.

"But I got the ingredients to make some similar." She did her best to make her voice sound upbeat and positive like homemade soup was the best idea in the entire world.

But her *mamm* shook her head. "That's a lot of work to go to for just a meal."

Abbie had to bite her lip to keep from responding with the first thing that popped into her head. Her mother had spent hours cooking meals for one thing or another not complaining once. It broke her heart to hear her say so now.

It's just the depression talking.

She knew that, but it didn't make it any easier. If only she knew what to do. She could talk to the bishop. But what exactly could he do to help her parents? No, that didn't seem to be the answer she needed. Maybe she needed to talk to a fancy *Englisch* doctor, one of those who dealt with emotional problems. A psychiatrist, she thought they were called. Or maybe even a therapist. That would be a good idea. But she had no idea how to find one. And no idea how to get her *mamm* and *dat* there when she did. Would they even go?

She turned back for a swift glance at her mother. She was staring out the window as if waiting for something to happen. What? It was anybody's guess, but Abbie had the feeling she was waiting for Jesus to walk down the road, coming for redemption, or maybe she was silently praying for Alvin to return from heaven. Either way, the chances of it happening right that second were pretty slim. All it did was give her mother a faraway look that seemed even less stable than when she focused on something in front of her.

Whatever Abbie decided to do, she needed to make up her mind quick and put it into motion. Her parents seemed to be slipping away by the day. Who only knew how bad they would be if she hadn't returned from Missouri?

Abbie finished the groceries, shut the cabinet, then turned toward her mother. "I've got to milk."

Mamm glanced at the large grandfather clock in the corner. Abbie knew it had been a present from her grandfather to her grandmother on their wedding day and passed down to her own mother at her wedding. Abbie had hoped to one day claim it as her own, but these days there was no time for courting, no time for singing, no time for dates and all of the fun things that she knew her peers had been engaging in while she was gone.

She hadn't given much thought to courting while she was in Missouri. She'd been too worried about repairing her broken heart over the death of her brother to give much else any thought. But even if she had, how was she supposed to marry someone from another state? She supposed in the back of her mind whether she loved her time in Missouri or not, she'd always known that she would once again return to Wells Landing. Now that she was here she had even less time for courting.

"*Jah*, okay then." Her *mamm* stood and shuffled back into the living room.

With a shake of her head and a small frown, Abbie headed to the barn.

"Are you coming with me?"

Mandy Burkholder turned as her husband approached. She had forgotten that Levi had a horse about ready to foal. He had worried all morning about leaving the mare and going to church, but in the end, his faithfulness to God had won out and they had

headed over to the bishop's house for the Sunday
service.

"You're leaving now?" she asked, hoping he didn't
realize she was stalling for time. She really didn't want
to leave right then. In all actuality, she wanted to have a
word with Titus Lambert before she left for the day. But
here was Levi wanting to go home, and they hadn't
even eaten yet.

"I feel like I need to get home to Lily Jo. I can't help
but feel like she needs me."

Of course it didn't hurt that Lily Jo had cost a small
fortune and was the mare that he had built his new
breeding program around. Well, Lily Jo and the stud
Samson, a big black horse whose coat went blue in the
sunlight and whose eyes looked like wildfire. The horse
scared Mandy so she stayed away from it as much as
possible.

Mandy hesitated, looked around at all the church-
goers gearing up for the afternoon meal, and allowed
her gaze to travel back to her husband.

"If you want to stay, you can get your parents to bring
you home. That would be good, *jah*?"

Exactly the answer she wanted. She smiled at her
husband. "If you're sure."

"I'll be in the barn if you need me." He gave her a
quick nod and headed toward their buggy. Mandy
watched him go as if she couldn't take her eyes off him,
but really she wanted to make sure that he was down
the road before she went in search of Titus.

She just wanted to talk to Titus. Just talk. But she
wasn't sure that Levi would understand. Once upon a
time she and Titus had something wonderful together.
Some might even say special. But then that fateful night
had torn everything apart. Alvin King had died. Eli
Glick was left crippled. The *Englisch* boy Blaine Carson

was gone as well. That left Titus, who was driving, to take the blame for the accident. She had been surprised to learn that he was going to jail for murder. It didn't make sense to her. But not much about the *Englisch* court system made sense to her.

Once Levi's buggy disappeared down the road, she went in search of Titus.

Chapter Four

"Hi, Titus."

Titus whirled around, recognizing the voice and yet not believing it all the same. "Mandy."

She looked the same as she had five years ago, same silky brown hair, same green eyes, same cinnamon sprinkling of freckles across her nose. Five years and nothing had changed. Five years and everything had changed.

"Where's Levi?"

She gave him a one-shoulder shrug. "He has a mare that's about to foal. He headed home to check on her."

Titus was all too aware of the eyes that seemed to settle on the two of them. He had been talking to Eli and Jonah when Mandy had approached him from behind. Now they, along with half the people still milling around the Ebersol yard, were watching to see what would happen between the two of them. Like anything could.

"You're looking good, Mandy."

She smiled. "Will you take a walk with me?"

Titus swallowed hard. "I don't think so."

She tilted her head to one side as if studying him from a different angle. "Why not?"

Titus moved toward her, snagging her arm in one hand and pulling her several steps away from Jonah and Eli. "You know why not, Mandy."

He couldn't read the look in her green eyes. It was as if a shutter had fallen between them.

"It's just a walk."

Her words were more of a challenge than a mere statement. They dared him to make more of it than what it was on the surface. They dared him to walk with her and pretend that it was nothing more.

Once upon a time he thought he and Mandy would get married. Everyone in Wells Landing thought he and Mandy would get married. Then one party, one fateful night, one car wreck, and everything had changed. Mandy had stayed by him during the entire trial. She had called every day, written letters to show her support in so many ways. But when the verdict came down, everything changed.

She visited him a few times in the jail until he begged her not to come back. She promised that she would wait for him, then two years later she married Levi Burkholder.

"*Jah.* Fine." He started walking, expecting her to follow him, not really sure where they were going or how many people were watching them. He should've told her no. He should've told her that whatever she needed to say to him could be said in front of Jonah and Eli, but he had moved away from them first. What did that say about him?

He veered to the left, still walking way faster than a casual stroll. Twenty yards and they were at the fence by the horse pasture. He stopped there and braced his arms on the top rail and hooked one foot on the bottom.

"That wasn't much of a walk."

He shook his head, but didn't turn to look at her. "I walked with you."

She sidled up close. Close, but not touching. "I miss you."

He tried not to laugh, but a sardonic bark escaped him anyway. "I can tell."

"That's not fair."

"Tell me any part of this whole situation that's been fair, Mandy. Then I can take it into town and have it bronze-plated so we can hang it over the mantel."

"What was I supposed to do, Titus? Wait for you forever?"

He sighed. She was right. He wasn't being fair. But he was right, none of it was fair. But more than anything it was in the past and now he was home. Free, at least physically. And she was married to another. "It was nice talking to you, Mandy." He walked away without a second glance, even though he thought he heard her whisper his name.

By Monday afternoon Titus felt as if his world were a fragile glass ball, like the ones that the *Englisch* put on their Christmas trees. One hard look, one drop, one small quake, and the whole thing would break into a billion pieces. Or maybe that was him.

He had heard tales of people who had been in prison for a long time. Much longer than he had. When they were released, they had trouble surviving on the outside. At the time, he thought those stories were completely ridiculous. Now he understood. He couldn't sleep at night. The room was too quiet, too dark, too big. Though he was in the minimum security facility and their cots were side by side, bunk-bed style, there was a certain close feel to the area. Not at all like what he had in the room he shared with Gabe Allen. Even though the bedroom was small by regular standards and was stuffed with two beds, it still felt large, like he was rattling around inside the universe. He felt open and exposed and scared, of all things. He wanted nothing more than to sink down into that mattress, so much more comfortable than what he had been used to for the last few years, and just sleep like a baby. Instead he jumped at every little noise, the quiet magnifying everything to near unbearable levels.

Lack of sleep, he told himself. That was all. That was making him edgy and jumpy. He would just have to figure out how to get a decent night's sleep soon and all of his agitation would melt away.

He had gone into town to run an errand for his *mamm*, volunteering himself off the farm and out of the house. Yet the minute he set foot in town he wished he was back home in the sanctuary he had made for himself there. The *Englisch* and Amish alike stared at him, some whispered behind their hands, even more were very blatant and let him know that they were talking about him. They were reliving the details of the trial, the people who died, and all the other details that had landed him in jail for nearly five years. Yet he was the only one who knew the truth. And he was not telling.

"I thought I heard you out here," Gabe Allen said, coming out of the barn, a handwritten list in one fist. "Are you going to town with me?"

Titus shook his head. "I just got back from town."

Gabe Allen shrugged and stepped up into his buggy. "And?"

Titus shook his head again. "I don't need anything in town."

"Who said anything about needing stuff?"

Titus nodded pointedly toward the list his brother held. "What about that?"

Gabe Allen laughed. "So there are a few things I need, but I also thought it might be fun to just ride with you for a while. We haven't really gotten a chance to talk alone since you came back."

That wasn't entirely true. They'd had plenty of times to talk and not once had they taken advantage of them. At night, after they went to bed, they talked for a few minutes there in the dark. Gabe Allen had been telling him about the little happenings that only seem to occur in a small town, and Titus had politely listened. But Gabe Allen fell asleep long before Titus even closed his eyes.

"Come on," he said, motioning with his head for Titus to join him. Unable to find another excuse as to why he shouldn't, Titus climbed in beside his brother.

"What's with you and Mandy yesterday after church?"

So that's what this is about. Titus didn't know what Mandy was thinking, what was in her heart, but if he was reading it correctly, there were regrets in her eyes. Regrets that neither one of them could do anything about. Regrets that he wasn't going to do anything about. He was having a hard enough time just being out of jail. He surely didn't need to complicate matters worse than they already were.

"You know Mandy."

"I know Mandy's married." Gabe Allen turned the buggy onto the road and flipped the reins to start the horse into a nice trot.

"I know Mandy's married, too."

"Just be careful," Gabe Allen said slowly.

"What do you mean?"

They jostled along a minute before Gabe Allen replied. "There's a lot of people who were a little unsure of how to handle your going to jail."

Titus thought back to the day when he had learned that Mandy had married another. "It seems she handled it in her own way."

Gabe Allen shook his head and eased the black buggy toward the side of the road. A car pulled past, and he sped up again.

"I'm not sure she loves Levi."

"I guess that doesn't matter now, does it? She married him."

He felt his brother's gaze fall on him as surely as if it were a touch. "Just be careful, okay?"

"Why do I get the feeling you're a little biased over everything that happened with Mandy?"

Gabe Allen shrugged. "Maybe I am. But I saw how she looked at you all during church. And I have a feeling that Mandy has more regrets than all of us put together."

The words knocked around inside Titus's head for the rest of the afternoon. He helped Gabe Allen gather things from the seed store to finish his project. He had taken to building doghouses. Five years ago Titus would've never thought twice about something as simple as a doghouse. Amish dogs spent the night in the main house or more likely in the barn. There weren't any special houses just for puppies. But the *Englisch* had different ideas, and it seemed that Gabe Allen had turned his summer project into a full-time business. He made all sorts of doghouses in all sorts of shapes, colors, and styles. Some were even equipped with heaters. As ridiculous as it seemed to Titus, he realized that his brother had hit on a fabulous idea.

They loaded the supplies in the back of the buggy and headed to the house.

Titus remained silent, just enjoying being with his brother after so long. Growing up, he and Gabe Allen had been practically so inseparable even their four-year age difference was not noticeable. That was, until Titus started his runaround. That didn't mean he loved Gabe Allen any less, but Gabe Allen had to find other ways to entertain himself as Titus had more of a social calendar than ever before. That time had left something of a gap between the two of them, one that Titus desperately wanted to close. He had missed Gabe Allen on the inside. He had missed them all, but Gabe Allen a little more than the rest. It seemed that his brother was more like him than he had even realized back then. And maybe by hanging out with Gabe Allen, he could find himself once more.

They pulled the buggy into the driveway and Titus noticed that his *dat*'s tractor was back. That meant *Dat* had completed whatever errand he had run, probably something to do with the stand at the market.

Titus got down from the buggy feeling relaxed for the first time since yesterday afternoon. Maybe that was what he needed, a short drive with his brother to reconnect a bit and unwind from all the tensions coming home had brought. If he had been asked before his time in jail, he would've said this should be a happy time, an easy time, reconnecting time full of love and understanding. But in truth it was nothing more than stress and tension and so many emotions he didn't know where to put them all.

He and Gabe Allen began unloading the back of the buggy.

His *mamm* came out on the porch. "Titus," she hollered. "Come in here. I need to talk to you."

Titus looked to Gabe Allen, who looked back and shrugged. "Go on," he said. "You know how she gets in times like these."

It had been awhile, but Titus remembered. His mother would get a bee in her bonnet and no one would have peace until she got it taken care of.

He gave a small nod to his brother, then headed toward the house.

But it wasn't just his mother. He opened the door to find his father waiting for him as well. The look on his face was enough for Titus to know something was wrong.

"Come in, boy. Sit down."

He didn't feel much like sitting, but did as his father bade him, perching on the edge of the chair.

Titus looked from his *mamm* to his *dat,* then back again. But neither one seemed about ready to talk. So he sat. And waited. Finally, his father spoke. "Bishop Ebersol just left."

Titus's heart sank into his lap. Was this about Mandy? He had done nothing wrong. He had talked to her out in the open, had barely laid a finger on her. It might have looked bad, maybe a little suspect. But he had not been alone with her. He had not walked out of the sight of others. He had not asked her for a buggy ride.

"Oh, *jah?*" He tried to make his voice as offhanded as possible.

"He came to talk to you about rejoining the church," his mother said. She looked to his father for confirmation.

Dat nodded, then turned back to Titus. "It's time, don't you think?"

Time? He hadn't even been back in town for a week

and his church was already demanding that he kneel and confess his sins. He needed time to get his head right. Time to figure out how to live on the outside once again. Then he could decide if he wanted to rejoin the church.

There, he admitted it. Maybe not out loud, but to himself. He didn't know whether or not he wanted to rejoin the church. He had questions. Questions that had surfaced when he was in jail. He hadn't been allowed to practice the Amish faith as he would have outside. Not that there wasn't freedom of religion in prison. There was. But the Amish church, the Amish community, the Amish religion all centered around togetherness. He had been alone in prison, the only Amish man there. No one else prayed the way he did, no one else worshiped the way he did. He went to church and the service was in English. No one sang from the *Ausbund.* The only thing that had been the same about church on the inside was God. And Titus had a problem with that as well.

The Amish were all about forgiveness. He felt their gazes on him as he walked down the street, but it was more curiosity than anything. The people of Wells Landing had already forgiven him. That was the Amish way. The problem was when he would ever be able to forgive himself.

"I don't know" was all he could manage.

His father gave an understanding nod, though Titus wondered how much he truly understood of the situation. How could he? No one could understand exactly how Titus felt other than Titus himself. And he felt adrift, like he was in the middle of the ocean in a tiny little boat with no paddle or hope of ever reaching land again. Maybe someday he would find a way that would take him home, but even then he didn't know what home was. He belonged no place. He didn't belong with the *Englisch*. He didn't belong in prison, and he surely didn't feel like he belonged in Wells Landing any longer.

"Please go talk to him," his *mamm* said.

How could he not? "Of course, *Mamm*. I'll go talk to him first thing tomorrow."

Titus had no idea what time it was when he pushed himself out of bed. The house was dark and quiet and not a sound stirred in the stillness. Every so often he could hear the squeak of bedsprings as one of his siblings or one of his parents turned over in their sleep. But then the sound faded away and all was quiet once more.

He crept down the stairs, stepping to the right of the third one to the bottom because it squeaked loudly if stepped on right in the center. Funny, but he hadn't remembered that until now.

He wandered into the kitchen, the battery-operated lights under the cabinet offering a little bit of illumination as he poured himself a glass of water from the tap. He stood at the counter drinking it, gazing out the window toward the barn. The night was as still and quiet outside the house as it was inside. How could he ever become accustomed to such nothingness in the night? The room where he slept was so open it seemed as if he was at the mercy of everything. Though there was nothing to be at the mercy of. He had suffered through the worst part of his life. He had survived. So why did he still feel so vulnerable?

He rinsed out the glass and placed it upside down in the dish drainer. Then, without thinking, he let himself out the front door.

The outside was big, but it was different. He hadn't had a whole lot of time outside or maybe it was that all the time outside he did have was taken up with sports with other inmates and trying to survive. He hadn't had a time where he could just walk out into the night all by himself, staring up at the moon and just breathing.

He dropped his hands to his sides and let himself into the horse barn. The carriage sat to the right as he walked in. The first stall contained his mother's horse, and the second one contained his sister's horse. On the other side was that ancient horse that they'd had forever and next to him the horse his father used when he took out a buggy. The stall at the very end was empty.

Titus walked inside the empty stall, standing there for a moment and taking in the small space. The barn smelled like dirt, hay, and horseflesh, such a comforting smell that it almost brought tears to his eyes. It didn't smell like sweaty men or rotting food or any of the other sins that accompanied him in jail. It didn't smell like pine cleaner or bleach and just smelled like nature.

Two hay bales were stacked in one corner. Without thinking Titus made his way over and lay down there. Hay pierced his clothes and poked his skin, but he didn't care. Somehow, there in the barn, he felt warm, secure, and of all things, welcome. He closed his eyes and was asleep in seconds.

"He's in here!"

Titus blinked awake, taking a moment to remember where he was. Last night coming out in the moonlight, walking into the barn, and falling asleep on the bales of hay in the empty horse stall.

"What?" he sputtered, and looked over toward the door of the stall.

His sister Rachel stood there, her sweet smile mixed with worry. "Are you okay?"

Titus pushed himself upright and brushed the straw from his hair. "*Jah*, of course I am."

"Why are you in here?"

He didn't know how to explain. How could he tell a twelve-year-old that it was almost impossible for him to sleep in the house? That he couldn't sleep in the quiet and the stillness? Or in the comfort and the happiness that seemed to be there? How could he explain it when he didn't understand it himself?

"I just came out here to check on the horses. I guess I fell asleep."

"Oh, Titus! Thank goodness." His mother rushed in, then turned toward the door. "Abner, he's in here!" She turned back to Titus. "You had us worried sick." She reached to help him up.

Titus accepted her hand and allowed her to pull him to his feet. "I'm sorry, *Mamm*. I didn't mean to."

"What in the world are you doing out here?"

Titus didn't have time to answer.

"He said he fell asleep," Rachel said.

"He fell asleep? How did you get out here to fall asleep?"

Titus shrugged and tried to make light of the situation. His mother had been through so much in the last five years he surely didn't want to add any more to her plate. "I was having trouble sleeping last night, so I came out to look at the moon. Then I heard one of the horses, so I came in to check on it, and I guess I fell asleep." It was almost the truth.

His *dat* arrived at the doorway, and Titus could see his other sister and the rest of his brothers behind him.

Great, the entire house had been out looking for him, and he had finally gotten a decent night's sleep.

"I'm sorry," he said. "I didn't mean to worry anyone."

His *mamm* nodded, then steered him toward the door of the stall. "No harm done," she said. "You're found now. Let's go in and have some breakfast."

He followed behind her, the words rattling in his head. Was he found now? He didn't know.

"Where's *Dat?*" Abbie looked to his favorite chair, but he wasn't there reading the *Budget* as was his custom in the afternoon.

Today she had a plan. She would somehow convince her father to help her with the milking. She had to do something to keep him interested in things . . . life. More than the newspaper.

Her mother placed one finger in her Bible to hold her place, then shrugged.

It was ironic that her mother spent so much time reading the Good Book these days and yet she found no comfort in the words there. It was as ironic as it was sad.

"I don't know. Outside I guess. I think he said something about the roof on the barn."

The roof on the barn? Surely he hadn't . . .

Just because he was on the roof of the barn didn't mean anything, she told herself as she hurried out the door. She was just worrying too much. It was to be expected. They were the last of her family. Aside from a few cousins who lived in Clarita and Missouri. Theirs wasn't like some of the close-knit families that were easily found all over the district.

She stopped short and took a deep, soothing breath as she saw her father on the roof of the hay barn.

Lord, please don't let him be drinking. Amen.

He seemed steady as he turned and gave her a small wave.

She returned it, then ducked inside the milking barn to begin her chores. It would've been nice to have him help with the milking, but if her father felt like repairing the hay barn, then that was what he needed to do. Any hand on the farm was a good hand as far as she was concerned. Whether it was construction or milking.

She spread the grain on either side of the milking stalls and led the cows into the holding pen.

Maybe this was a good sign. Maybe her father heading back to work was a preview of what was to come. Maybe he had hit his bottom and was headed back in the right direction. *Jah*, she liked that idea. He seemed steady enough, and she couldn't ask for any more than that.

She prepared the milk vats and led the cows into the milking half of the barn. As usual, the bull stayed in the holding pen and Abbie shut him in there while she hooked all the cows to the hitching posts. Then she turned on the air compressor and started to work.

Just as she suspected, it was slow going. There had been just enough rain lately to make rivers of mud. And as cows were prone to do, some had laid in the mud. Their udders required extra attention to get them clean enough to milk, but Abbie refused to calculate how much longer each cow was taking her and how much that would add to the overall total of the milking day. It was what needed to be done and it was what she would do. And that was all there was to it.

One by one she washed the udders, milked the cows, poured the vats into the sputnik, on and on and on until all twenty-five were done. Again she vowed to get some new cows. They couldn't keep living with twenty-five.

Although it would be hard to find the money to buy them, she knew it was what needed to happen. It was a vicious circle. Without cows to milk there was no money and without money they didn't have enough cows to milk. It was just something she was going to have to do. Bite the bullet, as they said, and buy more cows.

She turned off the air and rinsed out the equipment, the smell of bleach strong in the milk room. Perhaps she should go over and talk to Elam Riehl. He'd done good on his farm. Maybe she just needed a little bit of expert help to get started back in the right direction. Maybe he could help her with the situation concerning the cows. He might have some connections that she didn't have. All she could do was ask.

She sprayed down the floor of the milk room and went back out into the barn. The cows were waiting patiently for her to unhook them and allow them to return to the pasture. As they waited for her, most had laid down as lazy cows were apt to do. But she couldn't unhook them until she had their feed on opposite sides of the holding pen.

Once again wishing she had someone to help remix the silage and hay, she set about that chore. The mixing machine was loud as it turned everything together. Sometimes Abbie wondered if her hearing would be permanently damaged from all the loud noises in the milk barn, but she pushed aside those thoughts along with all the other negative ones she had these days. She had to do what she had to do and right now what she had to do was feed the cows. She took the mixture, spread it on both sides of the holding pen, then went down to the cows and started unhooking them. Down one side, then down the other, front to back, she unhooked the cows and allowed them to enter the holding pen. Once she had them inside she went back to fetch the broom and swept the droppings underneath the barn into the manure pit. She had no sooner taken it down from its nail on the wall when a loud crash sounded.

Her heart leapt into her chest. She tossed down the broom and ran for the door. It sounded as if someone had crashed into the barn. Or worse . . .

She shaded her gaze against the sun and looked over to the roof, where her father had been before. He was no longer there and in his place was a huge hole. Her father had fallen through the roof!

On the list of things that he wanted to do on Tuesday, going to talk to Bishop Ebersol about joining the church was pretty far down. Like at the bottom. But how could he refuse.

He knew if he didn't go to see the bishop, then Cephas Ebersol would come back out to the house again. It was better if he headed to the bishop's house without everyone hanging around them. This would also allow him to use the element of surprise to his advantage. He knew when he got there that the bishop was going to want to talk about his plans for the future and rejoining the church. He had always admired Bishop Ebersol, and the last thing he wanted to see on the man's face was the disappointment when Titus told him that his faith had slipped in the last five years.

So it was better this way. He could go to the bishop's house and talk to the man face-to-face without his family hovering around. Whatever conversation they had would hopefully remain between the two of them and no one else need ever be the wiser, until he decided what he wanted to do, that was. Aside from the disappointment on the bishop's face he could only imagine the heartbreak and devastation on his mother's if he decided not to come back into the church. He may have been a part of the church before, but as a whole the Amish believed that if he didn't rejoin the church, he would have no protection against the world. No protection against temptations that could swoop in and lead a man astray. And *astray* meant hell was your future. It was as simple as that.

Just give it some time, the voice inside him whispered.

It had only been five days since he had come back, and it hadn't been easy. But he knew that he was expected to rejoin the church or at least make a pledge to. Maybe that would appease his family. But more than anything, he needed to decide if he was going to stay in Wells Landing. Could he rediscover his place in the Amish community? He wasn't sure. One thing was certain though: he had to give it a try.

He pulled his buggy into the bishop's drive and sat there for a second absorbing the familiar house. It had only been a day and a half since he had been there last but coming on a non-church Tuesday was completely different from being there with two hundred people milling around, children playing, dogs barking, tables everywhere, horses, buggies, the whole works. Now there was a peace at the house that had not been there on Sunday.

He was just getting out of his buggy when the front door opened and the bishop stepped out onto the porch. "Titus." It was a short greeting, but that was Bishop Ebersol. He didn't waste words. The man was fair and honest and for that Titus was to be grateful. "I heard you wanted to talk to me."

The bishop gave a small nod. "More than that, I thought you might need to talk to me."

He wanted to do more than talk, he needed to do

more than talk. But he wasn't sure how much the bishop could help with his own problems. No one in Wells Landing could understand how he felt. No one. As much as he needed guidance from another, he wasn't sure how anyone could help him in the matter.

It's going to take time.

"Come on in the house. I'll get us a glass of lemonade, and we can sit for a while."

Titus wasn't sure who would be at the house, but it seemed it was just him and the bishop. "Helen has gone over to the quilting circle. The girls are in school. Or at work. The good life." The bishop led them into the kitchen. Titus sat down at the table and waited as the man poured him a glass of lemonade. He knew he needed to start talking, but he had no idea where to begin. No idea at all. Did he start with his lack of forgiveness of himself? Did he start with the fact that he didn't know if he could ever be a part of the community again? Or did he tell the bishop his fears of leaving the community and never being a part of the *Englisch* world?

He picked up his glass and drained it in one gulp. He couldn't do this. Not today.

"I shouldn't have come here. I need to talk. But not now." Before the bishop could answer, a large clatter sounded outside. The men looked at each other then ran to the front door.

Abbie King was on the porch, pounding on the door and dancing in place. "Bishop Ebersol! Come quick, *Dat* fell in the barn."

Chapter Five

The bishop wasted no time, jumping into action. Abbie charged toward her tractor and the bishop jumped into his, motioning for Titus to join him.

Titus hesitated only a second before climbing aboard. Abbie had already pulled into the road, and he knew that she hadn't seen him. She didn't know he was coming. Hopefully, she wouldn't be too upset when she saw him.

Like the sun dawning, an idea warmed him from the inside. This was his chance. He could help. He hadn't been able to help for so long. And now he might be able to make a difference.

He didn't live far from the Ebersols, but it was almost fifteen minutes later when they pulled down the Kings' driveway. Abbie had already parked her tractor and hopped off by the time they pulled to a stop. Titus didn't know if she had seen him and was ignoring him or didn't care that he was there. Whatever it was, she gave him no mind as she pointed toward the hay barn. "He's in there."

Bishop Ebersol started for the barn while Titus lagged behind. The run-down condition of the farm slowed his steps. He had been telling himself since he got back to Wells Landing that he would stop by to see if the Kings were willing to visit with him for a bit. He had made apology after apology so long ago, but he still was burdened with the aftermath of that one night. Could a person ever apologize enough for being responsible for the death of another?

Abbie led the way inside, with the bishop close behind. Titus ducked in a few seconds later to see Emmanuel King propped up on a hay bale, his hat sitting next to him. One leg was outstretched, and other than a small tear in the front of his shirt and the hay sticking out of his hair willy-nilly, he appeared to be fine.

"I told you I was okay," he groused as Abbie approached.

"And I told you that we needed help," she retorted.

Titus had only caught a glimpse of her at church on Sunday. She was like a ghost, appearing and disappearing, always elusive and out of his circle. Or maybe he had just stayed far enough away from her that he didn't have to acknowledge that she was there. Then he could pretend the tragedy from five years ago never happened.

Seeing her now, getting a really good look at her, he noticed the changes that had happened over the years. Gone was the carefree young girl that she had once been. Now she looked pensive, her face slightly pinched into a frown, turning down the corners of her mouth where a smile used to reside.

"I don't need no help." Emmanuel pushed to his feet, seemingly determined to stalk out of the barn. But instead, he swayed on the spot, looking like a tree in straight-line winds.

Titus rushed forward without thinking, wrapping one arm around the man to keep him from falling into a heap on the barn floor.

"Titus?" Emmanuel's voice was soft, incredulous, like he had seen a ghost. Titus supposed to most he was like a ghost from the past who no one thought they would ever see again.

"Sit down for a spell." He gently pushed the man back onto the hay bale, hoping that he would remain there. When it seemed as if he would, Titus stepped back, but not before catching a whiff of alcohol fumes.

"Are you okay?" Bishop Ebersol eased forward, his gaze roving over Emmanuel.

Abbie's father nodded. "It just knocked the wind out of me, and someone totally overreacted." He sent a sharp look Abbie's way.

To her credit she didn't so much as blush. She simply folded her arms and met his gaze.

Did she know her father was drinking? Titus looked from one to the other but could not decide.

"Maybe you should go to the hospital," Bishop Ebersol said.

Emmanuel shook his head. "I did not hit my head. I'm fine. Someone just overreacted."

Hadn't he said that before?

Titus let his gaze roam over the three people there in the barn with him. Something was going on, though he didn't know how much of it was common knowledge. Did the bishop know that Emmanuel was drinking? Should Titus say something?

Abbie's shoulders were stiff one minute and then the next they seemed to crumble. "I'm sorry I panicked, Bishop. Please forgive me. And thank you for coming."

Bishop Ebersol gave them all one last look, then administered a curt nod. "Just take care of yourself, Emmanuel. Abbie here needs you."

"*Jah*," Emmanuel said. Was Titus the only one who heard the crack in his voice?

The bishop let himself out of the barn, then turned. "Are you coming, Titus?"

What was he supposed to say?

As if she had just realized that he had come with the bishop, Abbie turned her blue eyes to him, their intensity as sharp as a laser beam.

"Of course." He tipped his hat to Emmanuel and started after the bishop.

That night all he could think about was Abbie King and her *dat*, her *dat* obviously drinking, and the poor state of their property. Something wasn't right at the Kings', and it seemed as if Bishop Ebersol might know something about it. He didn't seem shocked that the house needed painting or the roof was in such bad shape that Emmanuel had fallen through. But Titus himself had witnessed the man's reluctance to have anyone help him. Is that what it was? A matter of misplaced pride?

Or was it merely grief?

He wished he knew, maybe then he could figure out what to do about it.

"You're awfully quiet tonight," his *mamm* said, handing him the bowl of beans. June had set him up a small TV tray next to the table. Technically he wasn't at the table with them and wasn't in any violation of his *Bann*.

"Sorry," he mumbled. He didn't know what else to say. He supposed he was quiet these days, and perhaps even quieter today. But Abbie King was taking over all his thoughts. She had changed so much. He couldn't quite put his finger on what it was. She looked the same—that pale brown hair that landed somewhere to the dark side of blond. Her eyes were the color of the sky above a meadow after a rainstorm. Beautiful,

clear, kind blue eyes that almost looked unnatural in
their usual color. Why had he never noticed those eyes
before? Maybe because he had been too wrapped up
in Mandy? Or maybe because he wasn't wrapped up in
Mandy any longer he could see more of the world
around him? Or maybe he was simply a different
person now.

Definitely she was.

"No need to apologize," his *dat* said. "Just . . ." He
trailed off and for that Titus was glad.

It's going to take some time, the voice said. And he knew
it to be true. He hadn't been home a week yet. It was
ridiculous to think that things would go back to being
the same after such a short period of time. But it was
hard, so much harder than he thought it would ever be.
He wasn't sure how much longer he could stand it.

"Have you been out to the Kings'?" Titus asked. He
let his gaze fall to his mother then drift to his *dat*. They
exchanged their own look. His mother shifted in her
seat and his father cleared his throat. "No, after . . .
everything, we sort of grew apart."

It was a nice way to say it. But Titus could read between the lines. *After the accident, they didn't want to be
around us anymore.* What other shunnings had his family
endured because of that one night?

He knew that others might not consider it a shunning, but what else would you call it? Once upon a time
the Kings and the Lamberts had been nearly inseparable; now they didn't speak and it was all his fault.

He put his fork down, unable to take another bite.
Never in his life had he not eaten everything on his
plate and yet the thought of eating the rest of his meal
sent his stomach rolling.

His *mamm* looked at his plate and back up to meet

his gaze. "Are you okay? Is something wrong with your food?"

Titus shook his head, unable to speak. Somehow he managed to force himself to pick up his fork and eat another bite. He could never return to life before, and if he was going to figure out how to live his life now he had to start doing it by living.

Baby steps. One bite at a time. Then maybe one day this wound inside him would heal.

Titus hardly slept all night. He tossed and turned thinking about the Kings, Abbie, then Emmanuel's drinking. Titus hadn't seen Priscilla, Alvin and Abbie's mother, while he was at their farm, but he figured if Emmanuel was in as bad a shape as he was that she would probably be no better. He could hope for it to be different, but he wasn't expecting it.

He set the brake on the buggy and took a deep breath to gather his courage. Pulling into their drive yesterday with the bishop had been easy. Titus hadn't given a second thought to coming and seeing what needed to be done. Today was different. Today he had chosen to come. He didn't have the bishop as a buffer, and he had a feeling that Abbie King didn't want him anywhere around.

Well, too bad. He needed this. His soul needed this.

He swung down from the carriage and went to the back to pull the supplies he had brought out of the attached trailer. Just a couple of boards and a piece of decking to repair the roof.

"What are you doing here?"

He turned, the large piece of decking half in and out of the trailer.

Abbie King stood on the porch. The expression on her face was not a happy one.

"I've come to fix the barn roof." He turned back to the job at hand, an intense sense of peace coming over him. This was the right thing to do. She might be doubtful, but he knew it in his heart.

His attention focused on unloading the buggy, he heard rather than saw her march down the steps. "Titus Lambert, you put that stuff back in your trailer right now and get on down the road."

He stopped and turned to face her. "No," he said. "I don't think I will."

"You are not welcome here."

"You don't say."

She sputtered a bit, yet somehow managed to regain her verbal footing. "Titus, please leave. Your presence here is disturbing."

He grabbed the wooden toolbox from the trailer. He hoisted it out and once again turned to face the spitting-mad Abbie King. "It looks to me that you're the only one that this is disturbing."

"I'm serious, Titus. I want you to leave."

He nodded. "I can see how serious you are. But I'm serious too. I came to fix the barn and that's what I'm going to do." He turned and headed toward the out-building. "You have a ladder?"

She marched past and into the barn. She came back seconds later, dragging behind her a ladder that had seen better days, like years and years and years ago.

"That's a ladder?"

She stood it up against the side of the barn and studied it with a critical eye. "*Jah.* It's a good ladder."

Titus wasn't so sure about that, but it seemed to be the only ladder available. Perhaps a little prayer and the knowledge that he was doing good for someone would keep the thing intact while he fixed the roof.

He climbed up, careful not to set foot on the already-compromised rafters. It didn't appear that the roof had any big problems in the construction, just maybe a weak spot here and there. Emmanuel King happened to hit the wrong one. At least the barn wasn't falling down around their ears. It wouldn't take long to fix this. Then he needed to find something else to fix. Because this gave him such a good, warm feeling, he had to come back and do this again and again and again, and maybe after a while his feelings of guilt would go away altogether.

He headed back down the ladder to fetch his tool-box, then back up again to set to work.

"Fine," she yelled from below. "Fix the roof and get out of here. You're not welcome, you know."

Titus bit back a chuckle, somehow feeling better than he had in days. "*Jah*, I know. And by the way, Abbie—"

"*Jah*?" she asked.

"I'm sorry about your brother."

Her heart tripped at his statement. The last thing that she wanted to feel was empathy . . . *anything* for Titus Lambert. He was the reason for all her family's heartache. Never mind that once upon a time they had been the best of friends. She didn't want to take into account all the other things she knew, like that her brother had gotten into the car with Titus willingly that night. That they had purposely left her behind to have their "boys' night." One last hurrah before Eli and Alvin joined the church. Titus should have known better. He was the only one of them who had already been baptized. But the last thing, the very last thing she wanted to feel was empathy. She wanted to go on being angry with him and when he said things like that, it made it harder and harder for her to fuel that hate.

She shaded her eyes and took one last look at him crawling around on the roof like some *Englisch* superhero who came to save the day. Or fix the roof.

Abbie flounced back into the house. If he wanted to fix the roof, it was silly to tell him no. It was the least he could do after all the heartbreak he had put their family through. He could fix the roof. She would give him a drink of water and send him on his way. Hopefully, that would get him out of her hair for the rest of their lives. And that would be good.

She went back to the breakfast dishes, which were still sitting in the kitchen. Her *mamm* just didn't have enough energy to finish them these days. Abbie needed to do something about this depression and quickly. She wasn't sure what. She had wanted to talk to the bishop, but then her father had fallen and Titus had come over. Now here he was again.

"All things in time," she told herself. "All good things in time."

"What is that noise?" Her mother shuffled in from the living room.

She looked the same today as she had yesterday—a little too unkempt, a little too disheveled. Her dress had a stain on the front and her apron should've been changed days ago, but Abbie felt as if she were battling a dragon, trying to keep everything in the house running smooth and everything in the dairy barn running smooth, and somehow manage to keep her parents from sliding down the slippery slope of depression.

Lord, give me strength, she silently prayed.

"That's Titus Lambert." Her *mamm* slumped into one

of the kitchen chairs as if her feet and legs could no longer support her weight. "Titus Lambert is here?"

Abbie wasn't sure exactly how to answer that so she simply nodded and kept scrubbing pans.

"I never thought . . ."

She glanced back as her *mamm* closed her eyes. She wasn't sure if *Mamm* was praying or simply had endured more than she could take so early in the day.

"*Jah*, he came and said he wanted to fix the roof." She gave a one-armed shrug. "I figure if he wants to fix it, he can fix it. It's the least he could do." A stab of conscience ran through her. "Do you want me to make him leave? Is him being here bothering you?" Well, it was bothering her, but she figured she was not physically large enough to make him leave, and who was she to stop him if he wanted to work for free?

"No, no." Her mother pushed to her feet. "Titus has done nothing wrong."

Abbie whirled around to tell her mother exactly everything that Titus had done wrong, straight down to the color of shirt he was wearing today, but her mother had already shuffled back into the living room. Abbie was left standing there alone, wondering if she was the only sane one left in the world.

The sense of well-being stayed with him all the way back to his house. He hadn't seen Abbie after he'd climbed on the roof and started to work, though he could feel her gaze on him throughout the morning. She didn't come out and offer him water or ask him if he needed to take a break. That was fine with him. She didn't want him there. He didn't really want to be there. But it was something that needed to be done. The work had been a salve to his soul. It didn't make up for the wrong he had dealt the Kings. But it was an effort. And all he could offer.

But the good feeling stilled as he pulled into the drive to see another tractor parked in the side yard. He had seen the tractor before. It was one of the few blue tractors in the district, and he knew exactly who it belonged to. Levi Burkholder.

Titus pulled the buggy to a stop and got out, secretly hoping that Levi had come to talk to his father about something, but he had a bad feeling it was Mandy inside the house.

That doesn't mean she's here to see you.

Reluctantly he entered the house. The women had gathered in the kitchen. June, Rachel, his *mamm*, and of course, Mandy. She turned when he entered, smiling at him much as a wife smiles at her husband when he returns from work.

He shook the thought away. Once upon a time he had thought that sort of relationship would be theirs. But no more.

"Titus," his mother said. "I didn't hear you come in."

"I just got back." Titus moved to the sink to wash his hands. He had to reach around the many jars lined up on the counter.

"Oh?" Mandy moved close to him, appearing busy as she lined up some more jars next to him. The girls were canning tomatoes—a lot of them, from the looks of things. "Where'd you go?"

Such an intimate question. Titus scowled at her as he shook his hands and reached for a dish towel.

"To Abbie King's." Rachel smacked a hand over her mouth. The girl couldn't keep anything to herself. Not that his going to Abbie's was a big secret; he just didn't want everyone to know. Or Mandy.

His mother turned back to the bubbling pot of

tomatoes on the stove, and June bustled over to the pantry for something or other. Rachel went back to slicing tomatoes at the kitchen table. Mandy moved in close. "Why would you go over to Abbie King's?"

It was on the tip of his tongue to tell her that there had been a time when she could ask questions like that but those days were gone. She had married another and she could ask her husband anything she wanted to, but not Titus. No longer. But there were too many ears in the room with them.

"Emmanuel fell through the barn roof yesterday. I went over and repaired it." It was the truth. He just left out the satisfaction he felt in helping the family, the validation he got from doing something worthwhile. He felt like a useless piece of driftwood floating on the ocean. Nothing big enough for anything, yet still drifting. Fixing the roof at Abbie's had given him a strange sort of hope. A wonderful sort of peace. Mandy didn't need to know that. This was just between him and God.

"That was nice of you." Mandy said the words, but he could hear the hurt somewhere inside. What did she think? That he could come back and everything would be the same? Did she suppose he would never come back at all?

She moved away, and Titus grabbed a quick glass of water. Then he headed to the barn. He was much more comfortable out there with the animals than he was in the house full of people. Even though they were his family and he loved them dearly, he'd had enough of people the last five years. He was never alone, never had a chance to hold a thought in his head without incredible noise rattling all around. The barn offered peace and solitude, a place where his thoughts could dwell and thrive. The animals were nonjudgmental. Beautiful creatures of God who only wanted to help. And he wanted to help them in turn. But he had gone to prison and lost his place on the farm. They may have welcomed him back with open arms, but things had changed. Life had gone on without him. He had no job here. He had no anchor. And he was still floundering around trying to find it.

Give it time, he'd told himself so often since he'd been back. That was all he needed: time. But he was afraid that no matter what he did he would never find himself back in the Wells Landing that he knew before.

"What's for supper?"

Mandy stood as her husband came into the house. Levi was a handsome man with dark brown hair and eyes that somehow seemed exotic in their small community. He was big and strong, everything a woman could want in her husband. And he loved her. Or rather, he said he did.

"I thought we would have sandwiches tonight. I did so much today at the Lamberts'." Even as she said the name she was unable to look her husband in the eye. Instead, she moved to the refrigerator and started pulling out sandwich makings. The cheese, mayonnaise, lettuce, tomato. She loaded up her arms and took everything to the counter.

"Sandwiches?"

Guilt stabbed Mandy's heart. Levi worked hard. His job training horses was physically demanding. He raised some of the best horses in northeastern Oklahoma. And for that she was proud of him. He was a good husband, a good spouse, and a good Amish man.

But do you love him?

"I'm sorry," she said. "We just canned so many tomatoes, I lost track of time."

"That doesn't have anything to do with Titus Lambert being home now, does it?"

The biggest part of her wanted to whirl around and emphatically tell him that Titus had nothing to do with the reason she went over to the Lamberts' today. But that would've been a bald-faced lie. Titus had been the very reason she had gone over. The tomatoes had merely given her a good excuse. Yesterday she had overheard Jenny Lambert talking about canning tomatoes, and Mandy had thought it might be a good surprise for her to come help, and the trip over would also give her an opportunity to run into Titus once more.

"Of course not," she said. "I mean, I'm glad he's back in town. But isn't everyone?"

"Everyone but Abbie King," Levi said.

"*Jah*, well. Can you blame her?" Mandy would much rather talk about Abbie King than her own relationship with Titus.

She turned around to find Levi studying her. "Are you sure that's all it is?"

She gave him her most sincere smile. "Of course. What else could it be?"

But her own words haunted her for the rest of the evening. Was that all it was? Just being appreciative that Titus was back in town? But even as she asked herself, she knew there was more to it than that.

She sat in the recliner with her crocheting while Levi sat on the couch with a copy of the *Budget*. Somehow when she had imagined herself married, this was not the life she had envisioned. Her *mamm* and *dat* had nine children and their brothers and sisters had had countless more. It seemed as if the Yoder household was always full of children of one family or another. All different ages running around, playing, asking to be read to, arguing with one another, helping one another.

That was what she had wanted: a family. But she hadn't gotten that. At least not yet.

Once they had a family, what then? She bit back her sighs and sat her crocheting in her lap as she glanced over to her husband. It wasn't that she was unhappy. There was nothing wrong with Levi. She couldn't say that he didn't provide well for her. They had a beautiful house. They had plenty of money to do the things they needed to do. He had a fantastic business raising horses and was well respected in the community. So why wasn't she ecstatically happy? Was it that she just wanted a baby? Or was it more than that?

Titus Lambert's face swam before her mind's eye. His chocolate-brown eyes and straw-colored hair. He had to be the cutest boy she had ever seen. She glanced back at her crocheting and then up at her husband once more. Levi was a handsome man with his dark, neatly trimmed beard. He was clean and always went around in nice clothes. They weren't as fancy as the Lapps, but they had enough feeling of self-worth, and they did their best to represent their family's good blessings.

She picked up her crocheting once again. Levi turned the page but didn't bother to look up. "Something on your mind, Wife?"

He never called her that. Was he doing so to remind her of their relationship? How could she forget?

"No," she lied. She had a lot on her mind, but nothing worth sharing yet.

The house was completely quiet when Titus got out of bed and crept down the stairs. He didn't know why he went to bed like a normal person. Maybe he just thought his family would feel better thinking that he went to bed in a regular bed and then woke up before all of them. No one had realized that he slept in the barn. Not since that first day. No one imagined that he was out there before everyone else because he had been there all night.

He didn't want to worry them. But he couldn't sleep in the house. Something about the barn drew him in, comforted him. All the gentle sounds, creaky boards, and soft, snorting animals . . . he felt more connected to the community, the earth, and God when he was in the barn than he did anywhere else. There was something about the animals. They gave him hope. In their eyes he saw the future. Maybe not in detail, but the intelligence reflected their promise to him that there was a future. He may not know what it was just yet but it was there all the same. He let himself into the barn and down to the last stall on the left, his hay bale there where it was the day before, his pillow and his blanket, too.

He settled down, a sigh of near contentment escaping him. This was the closest to happiness he got on the outside. He still had too many ghosts and demons haunting him for much more.

He closed his eyes. Aside from ghosts and demons there were two women plaguing him as well. Mandy and Abbie. There was one thing about the inside. It wasn't nearly as complicated as relationships. Frankly, he hadn't had any, except for the people immediately surrounding him. The people who served his lunch every day, the guard who passed by. But the people he had been closest to he'd pushed away for that time. Now he was out of practice, unable to find his way back into the relationships that had been put on hold. Abbie he could understand. She might be Amish, but she was human. She loved her brother, he knew that. But if she only knew the truth . . . Yet he wouldn't be the one to tell her. He hadn't defended himself in court, refusing to delve into all the small details of that night. The big ones were the only ones that mattered. He had been driving. Now Alvin and Blaine were dead and Eli was in a wheelchair. Everything else after that didn't matter.

But Titus hoped one day that Abbie could forgive him. She'd been such a beautiful girl. In fact, she still was. But it was hard to tell with that wrinkled frown permanently between her eyes and the downward curve to the corners of her mouth. Mandy, on the other hand . . . He knew what she wanted. But he couldn't figure out why. She had made her choices. She had married another. She knew that he would come back one day. Even if he didn't know how long he could stay.

Life on the outside was much harder than he anticipated. Everywhere he went he saw Alvin and Eli. As much as he wanted to stay because of his family and the people he had loved before, he had a feeling his presence was harder on them than anyone wanted to admit.

He rolled over, pushed his pillow down a little, and tried to relax once more. He might be more comfortable in the barn, but that didn't keep his mind from racing.

No, he would stay for now. He would stay as long as he could. But if the time came—when the time came—he'd be on the next bus out of town.

Chapter Six

"Come on," Titus said. "It's time to go home now." It had been time to go home for a while, but his friends had other plans.

"I don't want to go now," Alvin said. "There's this girl—" He jerked a thumb over his shoulder and stumbled a little with the motion. They had all had too much to drink, and it was past time to head back to Wells Landing.

"Where's Blaine?"

Eli pointed toward the porch of the house, where the party was still in full swing. "He's up there."

Titus frowned. "Go get him. We need to leave."

"I don't wanna leave," Alvin protested. "You see that girl?"

Eli moved away toward the house and, Titus hoped, toward Blaine. It was getting late, and though the party was still going strong, they needed to be back on the road to Wells Landing. They should have stopped drinking an hour ago, but he had lost track of time. Hopefully, Blaine had been more diligent in keeping up with drinks and time.

Titus watched Eli tug on Blaine's sleeve, then the two of them stumbled down the stairs that led to the yard.

"All right then," Blaine said. "Let's go." He weaved toward

his car and Titus realized that of all the friends, he himself was by far the least impaired.

His stomach fell. He would have to be the one to get them home. The thought in itself was sobering. He would stop at the first convenience store he came across and load up on coffee. Surely with a lot of caffeine and even more prayers they would manage to get home in one piece. "Blaine, give me the keys."

Blaine protested, but he handed the keys to Titus as they made their way over to his sleek little sports car. It was elegant and expensive and though it was tiny, it seated four. Still, Titus felt like they were crammed in like sardines.

"Can you come get me tomorrow?" Alvin asked. "There's this girl . . ."

"There are a lot of girls," Eli said. "What are you going to do with an Englisch one?"

Alvin shot Eli a look that conveyed much more than words.

Blaine laughed and smacked him on the back. "That a boy."

"No one's going after girls," Titus said. "Now, everybody in."

Despite their reluctance, they did as he said and Titus backed the car onto the road.

Wait . . . he had been here before. This was where it all began. God had given them a second chance. He was driving. He was stopping to get coffee. He hadn't gotten coffee before, only thought about it. But maybe if he truly did it this time, they would all be saved. Maybe it would change the course of events enough that they wouldn't crash.

He blocked out the chatter around him as he searched each side street for a convenience store. It seemed like there was a QuikTrip on every corner and now that he really needed one, there were none to be found.

Yeah, that was all he needed to do, get a cup of coffee and change everything. It was perfect. A second chance, a do-over. Not everybody got one, and he was grateful.

The talk went on around him and still he couldn't find the convenience store. There was one across the divided street, but it would take so long to get there and then he would be pulling out in the wrong direction. It was better to wait for another one. But by then they were getting on the ramp to the highway that would take them to Wells Landing.

He rolled down his window a bit. The night air was cool. This had been Eli and Alvin's final wild night before baptism. It wasn't a normal practice. In fact, the elders would have them all kneeling in confession before the congregation if they knew. But they would never find out. Not if they got home safe this time. Baptism candidates had to walk a narrow line when they started classes. Titus knew. He had gone through the same classes just two years before. All the candidates did everything in their power to make sure everyone knew that they were taking their classes seriously. No one would do anything to jeopardize their standing in the community. Everyone was watching them. So why were they out taking such chances? They shouldn't have been so stupid. So careless.

"I want to go back," Alvin said.

"We're not going back," Titus said. But déjà vu stabbed at his heart. He had definitely been here before.

He hadn't gotten coffee. He needed coffee. He hadn't stopped, he hadn't changed anything.

"I wouldn't mind going back," Blaine said.

Titus glanced into the rearview mirror. Eli's head lolled against the seatback. He had fallen asleep while everyone else was chattering.

"We're not going back," Titus said.

"Who left you in charge?" Alvin pouted.

"I did." Titus said the words even as he knew that he had said them once before. Nothing was changing. How could they get a second chance if nothing was different? He had to do something. He had to do something now that would change it, but what?

"It's Blaine's car," Alvin said. "And he wants to go back. I say we go back."

From the backseat Blaine laughed. "Hear, hear," he said.

Everything was the same. Why was nothing different? If it was a second chance, things should be different.

"We're not going back," he said again. Why couldn't he say something different? He needed to say something different.

"But there was this girl," Alvin said, and reached across him and grabbed the wheel.

Everything went black.

Titus woke, a strangled cry escaping him. He was sweating. His hands trembled. His heart pounded. It'd been a dream. It was always a dream. He didn't have a second chance. No one got a second chance.

He stood and prowled around the small stall. He'd had that same dream too many times to count, gathering everyone at the party, driving home, looking for coffee, not being able to find any. They all wanted to go back and then nothing. Every time, he thought he was getting a second chance to stop the accident and save his friends' lives from being wasted by death and disability. But every time, it was only a dream.

There was no going back. Just like the book from the *Englisch* author Thomas Wolfe. There was no going home.

He barely slept a wink after he had the dream. He'd had the dream so many times those first months in jail that he had lost count. Now they came fewer and further between, but they still came. Sometimes he had the dream two or three times a week, sometimes only once. It seemed more vivid this time, probably because he was back in Wells Landing, surrounded by all the ghosts that he tried to hide from in McAlester.

There was no hiding here. There was only action and forgiveness.

He made his way to the house, acting as if he had been there the whole time. He stopped by the bathroom, washed his hands and face, and went to the kitchen. As usual, the Lambert house was bustling with activity. His *mamm* was preparing scrambled eggs. He could smell bacon that had recently been cooked and biscuits still baking in the oven. His sister June had peeled a cantaloupe, and Rachel was currently cutting it up into bite-sized pieces for them to share. The scene was wonderful and amazing and heart-wrenching all at the same time.

"Titus, I wondered where you were," his *mamm* said. She turned back to the eggs, scooping them into a bowl.

"I went out to check on a few things in the barn," he lied.

Mamm nodded, but he couldn't tell if she believed him or not.

A few minutes later his *dat* came in from the outside with Gabe Allen. Paul and Michael were right behind them.

The sisters put the food on the table as the brothers washed up. Together they sat down as a family to eat, only Titus had to sit at a small tray stand off to one side.

They bowed their heads, then his father conducted the silent prayer. Titus had no words for prayer, but in the week that he had been home, he went through the motions. He hadn't been able to pray since his first day in jail. There just didn't seem to be much to pray about, and he wasn't sure God was in jail at all. They held church services and had all kinds of prayer meetings, but if God was there he surely didn't find Him.

As everyone started to rustle around, Titus knew the

prayer was over and lifted his head. Food bowls were passed and everyone filled their plates.

"What are your plans for the day, Titus?" *Mamm* asked.

In between bites, Titus didn't hesitate to answer. "I'm going back over to the Kings' place to work."

Now where had that idea come from? He'd fixed the roof, the one thing that desperately needed repair, but hadn't thought about everything else that needed work. Yet the words slipped from his mind as if they had been there all along.

"Oh, *jah?*"

He nodded. He hadn't been sure of anything in a long time. But he knew he needed to help the Kings. Just the feeling alone of helping them was enough to draw him back out.

And it wasn't like they needed him at his own family's farm. They had everything under control. They'd had five years to learn how to work without him, and they had done it shockingly well as far as he was concerned.

Titus nodded. "They need a lot of help right now."

And I'm the reason why.

"That's a good idea," June said with an encouraging smile.

But he needed more than to simply help a family. He needed the atonement. He needed to make amends. He needed the payments for his crimes and sins, and this was the only way he could get it. The only bright spot was that it would benefit the Kings regardless of the fact that they would rather have him a hundred miles away than helping them do anything. Or rather Abbie would rather have him far, far away.

But a little slip of a girl was not going to stop him from carrying out what needed to be done. She couldn't

stand in his way. He needed to forget, and she had work
to be done. As far as he was concerned that was a good
enough arrangement for now.

"I thought I told you to leave."

"Good morning to you too, Abbie." The look in her
eyes made him want to get back in his buggy and head
back home. But he had made up his mind, and he was
going to see this through. His own family might not
need him, but this one did.

"I meant what I said. We don't need you here."

He looked pointedly at the front porch where it
sagged on one end.

"We don't *want* you here," she corrected.

He stopped unloading supplies from the trailer and
propped his hands on his hips. "Honestly, Abbie, I can't
say that I want to be here all that much either. But this
is something I have to do."

"Do you think a little bit of paint and home repair
will erase your sins?"

"Abigail Kate!"

Her attention was split as her mother came out onto
the porch.

"*Mamm,* I—"

Priscilla King shook her head and waved away
whatever Abbie had been about to say. "*Danki,* Titus
Lambert. We gladly accept any help you are willing to
offer." She headed back into the house, leaving Abbie
staring gape-mouthed behind her.

"That doesn't mean I like it," Abbie said.

Titus shot her a grim smile. "I wouldn't have it any
other way."

* * *

But that was a lie. At least he knew it himself even if he was reluctant to say it out loud. Of all of the people he wanted to forgive him, Abbie King topped the list. Even if he wasn't sure why.

They had been friends so long ago. He had lost so many friends in that accident; he didn't want to lose her, too.

Titus lugged his toolbox over to the fence and started assessing the damage. It might have been caused by someone backing into it, but more than likely it was caused by years of neglect. Five of them, to be exact.

Several of the boards would have to be replaced, but a few of them could be salvaged. He went back to the trailer to get the rest of his supplies.

There was more damage on the King farm than he had noticed at first. It would take days, maybe even weeks, to get everything in order. But time was the one thing he did have. At least until his six-week *Bann* was over and he had to reenter the church.

He used a two-by-four to prop up the fence and started to work. He had made his confession and asked for forgiveness, but he was a long way from being ready to reenter the church. That was one reason why he had asked for the six weeks. Hopefully, by the end of that time he would feel like he belonged in Wells Landing once again. But he wasn't sure what he wanted from his life. How could he come back and rejoin the church knowing all that he knew now?

The Amish community was close-knit and sheltered. These days, he was far from either one of those.

The sun beat down on his shoulders as he worked. It was hot, but the heat felt good. It made him know that he was alive. Sweat trickled down the side of his face, and he wiped it away with one sleeve.

More than alive. This was the best he'd felt in a

long time. The work wasn't hard, but it was work. It was fulfilling and satisfying as the sun warmed him and the wind blew through his hair.

"You should have a hat on if you're going to be out here all day."

He stopped hammering and straightened as Abbie came toward him, a plastic tumbler in one hand. "I stopped wearing one while I was . . . inside."

"Here." She thrust the cup at him. "It wasn't my idea. *Mamm* said I needed to bring you a drink."

He put his hammer aside and accepted the drink. It was cold and went down easy. "That's good," he said, wiping his mouth with the back of one hand.

"It's just water." She sniffed.

He met her gaze and their eyes held. "But it's still good." He finished off the rest and handed the tumbler back to her. "Thanks again."

"This doesn't mean I want you here," she said.

Titus bit back a smile. "Noted."

The grin stayed with him long after she left. What was it about Abbie King? He had known her his entire life, but even given the circumstances, everything had changed.

Maybe because he knew exactly where he stood with her. The Amish forgave, but not always from the start. There were those in the community who he knew would take a little more time to look past his transgressions and go on. But until they did, they played at the part, almost like an actor in a movie. But not Abbie. She might not ever forgive him regardless of what the Amish were "supposed to do," and he knew that she wouldn't hide those feelings. It shouldn't have been a comfort to him, but it was.

He took a step back and surveyed his handiwork. Abbie's father had come out once and thanked him for the help. The man wasn't so steady on his feet and Titus wondered if he'd been drinking again today. He had debated talking to Abbie about it, but he figured she had enough to deal with since he'd come back. But soon, maybe when she got used to his being there, they could talk about it.

Abbie King. He rolled her name around in his head. A name almost as familiar as his own. Why had seeing her come to mean so much to him?

Because she was the only one in town who treated him with all the honesty she had. And for that he was grateful.

Once again, when Titus pulled up to his house Mandy was there. The first time he could count as pure coincidence, now he wasn't so sure.

But his doubts intensified as Mandy came out of the house, a plastic laundry basket propped on one hip. "Bye," she called to someone inside the house, then skipped down the stairs.

"Oh hi, Titus," she said.

"Hi." He nodded toward the empty basket she held. "What was today's errand?"

She looked down at the empty basket, then back up at him as if she was just then aware that she was carrying it. "Your *dat* said I could add some items to the sale. I brought some of my yarn goods for your *mamm* to look at."

"You're going to sell them at our stand at the market?"

Mandy beamed and nodded. "Isn't that great?"

"Just great." But they had only sold their own goods at the market. Never anyone else's. It shouldn't matter, but it did. On some level it seemed as if Mandy was trying to worm her way into his family. He shook his head. He had to be mistaken. Mandy was married.

"See you later," she said, then hopped on her tractor and headed down the road with a jaunty wave.

Titus watched as she disappeared, then started into the house. He'd been gone for five years. And not just gone, but in prison. Perhaps he had just forgotten how things were. Surely that was all it was.

"Hi, Titus." As usual, Rachel seemed to be the happiest to see him. She raced from the other room to meet him as he came in the door. "Look what Mandy gave me." She held up a tiny crocheted dress.

"Are you sure that's going to fit?"

"It's for my doll, silly."

"You still play with dolls?"

She shook her head. "No, but I still have her, and now she can wear this beautiful dress." She pranced away leaving Titus staring after her.

His mother came out of the kitchen, her apron dusted with flour. "I thought I heard you come in."

"Are you baking?"

"Your sister wanted pretzel wraps for supper."

Titus nodded. It had been awhile since he'd had a pretzel wrap, and his mouth watered just thinking about it. "So Mandy came by again today?"

His mother smiled. "She's been such a big help this week."

There wasn't much he could say to that. He couldn't very well warn her that he thought Mandy might have ulterior motives. Not without her pointing out that he was back in Amish country now.

"Wells Landing isn't prison." He'd been told that too many times to count. Enough times that he had already started quoting it to himself. Maybe soon, he would be able to adopt the philosophy as his own.

Abbie was striding across the yard before Titus set the brake on his carriage. "Are you going to do this every day?" she demanded.

He swung down next to her, noticing how the dark blue of her dress made her eyes appear even bluer than normal. "That's the plan."

"Why?"

He shrugged. "You need help."

"Are you trying to absolve your part in Alvin's death?"

He didn't respond, only started to unload the tools he had brought for today's job.

"You're absolved. Just take your stuff and go."

"Tell me," he started, leaning on the handle of the post-hole digger, "why do you want me gone so bad?"

She stood there long enough he thought for a moment that she might not answer at all. Then she spoke, her voice quiet and solemn. "Every time I see you, I see him again. You were the last person to see him alive."

"I know that," he said as tears filled her eyes. "I think about that every day."

She seemed about to say more, then she pressed her lips together and started back toward the house.

Titus watched her go, wondering if they would ever find purchase on the slippery slope of friendship. It was an unusual situation, he knew that. But he needed more than a solution. He needed forgiveness. Though he might not ever have that, he had to try. He had to do everything in his power to make the life she had easier.

He finished unloading the trailer, then got down to work.

* * *

The sun was high in the blue sky when she came out of the house. Titus was sure he could wring out his shirt it was so wet, but the work was still more satisfying than anything he had done since he'd been out.

She flounced over to where he sat in the partial shade of the large oak planted to the side of the house. He liked the vantage point, which allowed him to see the handiwork and let him imagine what the rest of it would be like.

"Here." She thrust a plate toward him. It contained a ham sandwich, what looked to be homemade potato chips, and what he hoped was her mother's pickles.

He accepted the plate with a grateful smile. "I have a little bit of food here." He pointed to his sleeve of crackers and the slices of cheese he'd rummaged out of the refrigerator that morning. They were out of bread. He wasn't sure what to do, so he grabbed the one thing he could find.

She rolled her eyes. "You need more to eat than that."

He looked down at the sandwich, then back up to her. "Was this your idea or your *mamm*'s?"

"Does it matter?" She propped her hands on her hips, but he noticed that she didn't run back into the house.

"Will you join me?" He set the plate on the ground in front of him and patted the patch of grass where he sat.

She hesitated then flopped down across from him. He considered it a good sign.

Then she picked up half of the sandwich and took a bite. He followed suit.

He hoped that it was more than a good sign.

"Are you really coming every day?" she asked.

"Yes." He shoveled one of the potato chips into his

mouth and closed his eyes. No one took the time to make chips these days and he appreciated the extra effort.

"Is it good?"

He opened his eyes and met her amused gaze. "Very. Tell your *mamm* thanks." He finished off the rest of his sandwich, then reached for the pickle.

"*Mamm* didn't make this. I did."

He stopped. "You did?"

She nodded.

"Even the pickles?"

"Even the pickles."

He finished his bite and took another.

"*Mamm* doesn't cook much these days."

Somehow he got the impression that she was reluctant to tell him as much.

"In fact, she doesn't leave the house unless it's for church." She heaved a big sigh and started drawing random shapes on the fabric of her apron.

"I'm sorry, Abbie." She would never know how much. But there was more to the situation.

Just leave it alone.

But he couldn't. "Your *dat* . . ."

"What about him?"

He should drop it right now. It wasn't any of his business. "Is he drinking?"

"No . . . yes." A dull sheen of pain cloaked her eyes. "Yes," she said with another sigh. "I don't know what to do, Titus."

All of his fears were confirmed. "Have you talked to him?"

She shook her head.

"Have you talked to the bishop?"

"I should have never gone to Missouri." Tears welled in her eyes, then made their way down her cheeks.

"Abbie."

"They needed me, and I deserted them." She covered her face with one hand, a sob shaking her shoulders.

"Abbie, don't cry." Pickle forgotten, he pulled her close. She was warm and sweet and smelled like peaches and outdoors.

Awkwardly he patted her on the back. He wanted to wrap his arms a little tighter around her and never let her go, but those feelings were as foreign to him as an exotic island. She was Abbie, his friend, and she needed comfort from him, not romance.

She buried her face in the crook of his neck, her tears wetting his skin. He could get used to the weight of her in his embrace. She exhaled softly, then all too soon she pulled away.

"I'm sorry." She wiped at her tears with the back of one hand. "It's just a lot, you know." She swiped again, then let out a small laugh. "Of course you know."

He wanted to touch her, reassure her. But words were all he had. "It's going to be okay."

"How do you know? And please don't tell me to pray about it."

He shook his head. "I haven't prayed in a long time." Not since that first year. But he wanted it to be okay. Not for him, but for her.

Chapter Seven

The last thing she wanted to do was forgive him, but that was exactly where Abbie found herself that afternoon. Titus packed up his tools and headed for home and she could still feel his arms around her. She didn't want to forgive him. She needed her anger. It brought her comfort. But the more he kept coming over and trying to help, the harder it became to hang on to that anger.

"He's a good boy." Her *mamm* shuffled up behind her as she stared out the window. She had watched him leave; now she stood there still as if he would reappear at any minute. Not until tomorrow.

The thought filled her with a bright emotion. Happiness? How could anything Titus Lambert did for her bring her happiness?

"I hardly think he's a boy." That was another thing she had noticed. Titus had grown up in the years he was away. He had filled out, turned into a man. But the biggest change was the hard edge to his eyes.

She on the other hand felt suspended. Her time

away had only delayed her life, her grieving, her . . . everything.

"You could do worse than Titus Lambert."

Abbie whirled around, briefly noticing that her mother had taken a shower and changed clothes. These days she did one or the other, but not always both at the same time. "Are you suggesting that I should—" She shook her head, unable to finish the statement. It was unthinkable. For a number of reasons. The most important being that Titus had shown no interest in her. Besides, he was the one responsible for her brother's death.

Wasn't he?

There's a lot about that night you don't know. Wasn't that what he had said? What didn't she know and why wouldn't he tell her?

And why would it make a difference?

"I hardly think that's appropriate, *Mamm.*"

Her mother patted her on the shoulder and moved toward the door. "You should learn to be more forgiving, Abbie."

"You certainly are spending a lot of time over at Emmanuel King's."

Titus hoisted the lumber into the trailer and dusted his hands before answering his sister. "I guess." He headed back to the shed with June on his heels.

"Any particular reason?"

"They need my help."

"Oh, *jah.* I know they do. Abbie King especially, maybe?"

"What are you hinting at, June?"

"I'm not hinting at anything." She trailed her fingers

over the side of the trailer as she walked from front to rear.

He loaded the paint into the back. He had started painting a couple of days ago. He figured it would take a week to get the buildings done, if that was all he did. But from time to time he had to stop to make a small repair.

He hadn't eaten a meal with Abbie since she had shared the sandwich with him. He had secretly hoped that she would come out of the house and talk with him again, but she had kept her distance. She hadn't even come out to tell him to go away.

It was better this way. He had enough to deal with without adding Abbie to the mix.

"People are starting to talk, you know."

"Your friends, you mean?"

She shrugged. "There's been a little speculation."

That wasn't something he could control. "I saw a family in need, June. *Dat* certainly doesn't need me around here."

"You really feel that way?" Her teasing fell like a stone to the bottom of a puddle.

He nodded and braced his arms on the side of the trailer. It was packed and ready to go but he had a feeling his sister wouldn't let him out of her sight until he explained himself. "Look around, June. This place hasn't suffered one bit while I was gone. Michael has taken over my responsibilities at the market." He shook his head. "I have no place here any longer."

"No one means to make you feel that way."

"I know that. But it's there all the same."

"What about Mandy?" she asked as he climbed into the buggy. He still couldn't bring himself to drive anything with a motor.

"What about her?"

"People are talking about her, too. Well, the two of you."

"There is no two of us."

"If you say so."

"I do," he said and set his horse into motion.

So there was talk about them.

He should have expected as much. There was always talk among the Amish. That was what happened in tight-knit communities. Everyone was genuinely concerned about everyone else and talk ran around like a child after too much sugar.

There was nothing he could do to stop it, but he at least had to talk to Mandy about it. He wouldn't want idle chatter at the quilting circle to damage her relationship with her husband.

Once upon a time he had thought he would be her husband. But that wasn't to be. And though he felt certain she was putting herself in his path intentionally, he was equally sure that she hadn't thought how it might look to others.

He was still mulling over the problem when he pulled into Abbie's drive. So people were talking about them as well. That wasn't so bad. They would all find out soon enough that their suspicions were unfounded. He had too many ghosts to consider a relationship. Too many demons to put another person through that. Especially someone as sweet as Abbie King.

Maybe *sweet* was the wrong word, he thought, remembering her demanding that he get off their property. But whatever description he gave her, she deserved better than him.

As usual, no one came out when he pulled up. It was almost as if the Kings understood that this was something they needed him to do. Or maybe they recognized that he needed it too.

He set up his ladder and started to work. Normally, he enjoyed painting. It was just mindless enough that he could sink into his thoughts without making mistakes and just taxing enough that his mind couldn't wander very far. Since he had begun painting the Kings' barn he had managed to push all thoughts of prison aside and just paint.

He might be able to push the last five years from his thoughts, but Abbie wasn't so easily dismissed. Maybe because aside from his nightmares, prison was over, yet he and Abbie still had unfinished business. Perhaps they always would.

She came out of the house midmorning with a glass of tea and a frown.

"Here." She unceremoniously thrust the glass toward him.

"Thanks." She had that look, and he wasn't sure if he wanted to know what had put it there. If he was lucky it was something other than him. What if she had heard the talk that June was telling him about?

"Are you ever going to tell me about that night?"

He took a deep gulp of tea and shook his head. "Let it go, Abbie. Nothing can change it."

"You're one to talk. Out here every day trying to work off some sort of imaginary debt."

"I've got to work my way to heaven somehow."

She shifted from one foot to the other. "Church."

He shook his head before he could think better of it. "We'll see."

But she had already read between the lines. He could see it in her eyes. "Titus, I—"

"I can't tell you how sorry I am," he said, hoping to change the subject before he had to admit that he no longer belonged in the Amish church. How could someone like Abbie understand that?

"About Alvin?" She tilted her head to one side as if thinking about his point of view for the first time. "Are you really?"

"He was my friend, Abbie. And I loved him like a brother."

"Then why—" She stopped. Was she just now realizing that what happened that night was a terrible, terrible accident?

"There's a lot about that night you don't know, Abbie."

"Then tell me."

He shook his head. He would rather her put the blame on him than tarnish how she felt about her brother. If he told her the truth now, it would only make her second-guess everything she knew about Alvin. Nope, it was better this way. Besides, Abbie's knowing the truth wouldn't change a thing. "Just let it go, Abbie. It's not worth it."

She gave him a look he knew well. "Then quit bringing it up," she said, and flounced back to the house.

This was the last place he wanted to be. Titus pulled his tractor into Levi Burkholder's side yard, still wondering if this was such a good idea. He had come during the day, figuring that if Levi was home it wouldn't appear quite so scandalous that he'd come by. He had a basketful of jam that his mother had packed. It was the perfect excuse. His mother had sent him with goods to give to Mandy. Who could turn down their mother?

He set the brake and climbed down from the buggy. It was early. Another part of his plan. Chances were that Levi was home and that was exactly what Titus needed.

He loped up the porch steps. The house seemed

unusually quiet. He knocked on the door, then glanced behind him at the yard and the horse barn. Everything was very still. Perhaps no one was home. He set the box of jam on the bench next to the door and peered in the window. Nothing stirred inside the house. Had they gone somewhere? Up to the store? Or maybe to a horse show? He hadn't heard anyone in the community say. But he hadn't actually been listening, either.

He stood there for a moment trying to decide his next course of action. What had started off to be a solid plan was quickly becoming unfruitful. Perhaps he should go back home and try again tomorrow. He gathered the box and started down the porch steps. That was when he heard her.

She was singing, though he couldn't decipher all the words. It was a hymn about God, love, and understanding.

She must be out back.

He changed course and walked around the side of the house.

Mandy was hanging clothes on the line and singing her hymn, the picture of an Amish woman.

Memories slammed into him. All the times they had spent together—courting, swimming, just being together—came rushing back. Suddenly he wanted that again more than anything. The feeling was all-consuming, overwhelming, and he had to take a deep, shuddering breath in order to control it. Mandy had been his first love. His only love. But now she belonged to another. And he would do well to remember that.

"Mandy." His voice was more like the croak of a frog. He cleared his throat and tried again. "Mandy."

She whirled around, her eyes lighting up as she spotted him. Her hands flew to her head where a handkerchief covered her hair. She smoothed her fingers across it then down her faded day apron. She shifted in place, then cleared her throat. "What are you doing here?"

"I—I . . ." He suddenly felt so very awkward. Then he remembered the jam. "*Mamm* sent some jelly over."

"Thank you."

He nodded. "I guess I'll just leave this on the porch then." Why did he suddenly feel so uncomfortable? This was Mandy. The Mandy he had known practically his entire life.

The Mandy who had married another.

"*Jah*, sure." She gave a small nod and retrieved another article of clothing to hang on the line.

He had done his best not to think about her in years. What good was there? He had known that she had married another. Eli had written to tell him. And honestly he couldn't blame her. What kind of life could he offer someone now? He couldn't even make up his mind whether or not he wanted to remain in the church. He had a foot in both worlds and a hold on neither. He wasn't Amish nor *Englisch*. He was a convicted felon, a lost soul. He had nothing to offer. And though he could still remember the silky feel of her skin beneath his fingers, he knew it was better this way. But was it?

"There's been some talk," he blurted. He couldn't keep dancing around the issue. He needed to leave as soon as possible. But he couldn't come out here without telling her the reason why.

"Talk? About us?"

Titus nodded. "I thought you should know. I wouldn't want anything to come between you and Levi."

"Levi's not here."

The words crashed into him like a huge mistake. "I should go."

He turned to leave, but she dropped her basket and

rushed after him. He was halfway to his buggy when she caught his arm, spinning him around.

"I didn't say you had to leave."

He could see it all in her eyes, every minute they had together, every promise they had made to each other. And though it had broken his heart when he found out that she was marrying another, that pain didn't seem so important anymore. What he wouldn't give to go back to the day, that time, that place, before the accident. What he wouldn't give to live those days over, to change them, and to change the course of all their lives.

"I need to leave. I shouldn't have come here."

"You don't have to go."

He closed his eyes against the sweet words. "Yeah, I do. I just came here to warn you. You need to stay away from me. People are starting to talk, and I wouldn't want it to affect your relationship with your husband."

"This isn't about Levi." She released his arm only to grab his hands into her own. "This is about you and me. About us."

Titus shook his head. "There is no us. Us was over a long time ago. And us will never be again."

"It could."

"You don't know what you're saying." He pulled free of her grasp and stalked back to his carriage, ignoring her as she called his name.

He had done what he set out to do. Now all he had to remember was to stay clear of Mandy himself.

"Titus, may I talk to you?"

Titus turned as Bishop Ebersol approached the following church Sunday. How badly he wanted to say no, that he didn't want to talk. That was the truth. However, he didn't think the bishop would appreciate it.

"Of course." He fell into stride beside the bishop as they walked across the Fitches' property.

Titus had always liked the place and now it had a completely different look. Andrew Fitch had taken to living on the farm after he and his wife, Caroline, had gotten married. Abe himself had moved into town to live with his new wife, Esther Lapp, who ran the bakery just down the street from the Kauffman Family Restaurant. Titus didn't know Andrew and Caroline since they had come to Wells Landing after he had gone to jail, but they seemed to move in the same circles.

As he walked with the bishop, Titus noticed little groups of friends clustered together. Those groups had once been buddy bunches and cliques, and now their members were all married and raising their families.

Everyone else had moved on. Everyone else had continued to live, while his life had been suspended. He supposed he would get used to that idea eventually, though right now it was more than strange to see the teens he ran around with baptized with babies.

As an Amish youth he had been encouraged to taste a bit of the world so that he knew when he was ready to settle down. He had his running around time and was baptized. Two years passed and it became Eli and Alvin's time. They had done everything they were supposed to and they claimed that they were ready to settle down and join the church. After this one party. One more party and then they would be baptized. Though it was one more party and everybody's life had changed.

"I think I know what this is about." Might as well get a jump on the conversation. All the walking in silence was beginning to strain Titus's nerves. He knew what the bishop wanted.

"Have you given it any thought?"

Titus shrugged. "I don't know really. It's just been a

couple weeks and . . ." He trailed off and shook his head. How could he explain to the bishop that just being back in Wells Landing was enough to throw him for a loop, much less adding in all the commitments of rejoining the church?

"I've been talking with some of the other elders," the bishop said. Titus studied his face for any hint of what was to come but could find none. "This community suffered a great loss that night. We lost Alvin, we lost you, and we lost Eli, not to mention the grief over the *Englisch* boy. I think it would be better if we get you back in good standing in the church as soon as possible."

They could do that?

He shook his head. He was the bishop and he could pretty much do whatever he wanted to as long as the church was behind him. As far as he knew the church was ready to accept him back with open arms. He was the one who was having trouble deciding if that was what he wanted or not. "I—I don't know what to say."

The bishop walked over to the fence and braced his arms up on the rail. Church had been over for an hour or so and the festivities were winding down. The women were starting to put the food away, children were playing tag, and a volleyball game had started in one corner of the yard. It was a typical church Sunday in Wells Landing. But for Titus it felt anything but typical.

"Are you having doubts, son?"

Doubts? That word didn't come near to describing his feelings. But how could he tell a man who would never walk in his shoes what it felt like to be locked in jail with hardened criminals? How could he explain the battles he fought both physical and emotional in order to maintain his sanity on the inside? How could he ever go back to being the Titus he was before after all he had lived through?

He couldn't. It was as simple as that. He was forever changed from his time in prison and there was nothing anyone could do about it. And he couldn't pretend it never happened. Because it did happen and it was horrible, life altering, scarring. And as much as he wished that none of it had ever taken place, it had. And he was . . . not worthy.

He shook his head, but no words came out. How could he tell a man like the bishop that he wasn't worthy any longer? How could he stay here and continue to be a part of the community when he knew he could never belong?

"I need some time." That was an understatement, but perhaps the bishop would accept it.

The bishop gave a small nod. "I can understand that. But we don't have a lot of time." The bishop looked out over the field where the horses that Andrew trained and bred for others were corralled.

Titus followed his gaze, watching as the creatures frolicked in the green, green grass. They were magnificent beasts, beautiful, sleek and muscular. Titus could watch them all day. It sure beat trying to decide what to do with the rest of his life. "Surely, you can't expect me to make a decision in two weeks." He said the words though he knew the bishop would be in his rights to demand that Titus make up his mind and quick. But he hoped to buy a little more time.

"This community is trying to heal. We need to have something to look forward to as part of that healing. I'll expect your decision in a month."

Titus glanced over to those groups again, watching as the girls bounced their babies and exchanged recipes, while the men with their newly grown beards strutted around as if they knew a secret that no one else in the world did. Things had changed. Things had moved forward. And though he had changed, he was in the same position he had been five years ago. Back then he knew what he wanted. Now he wasn't so sure. And with each passing day, instead of getting an answer, he seemed more confused than ever.

He had to figure out his life. And he only had a short time to do it.

Monday fell into the same pattern as the weekdays before. He would head over to Abbie's and work on her farm. It was looking better and better every day and soon he would not have the excuse of helping her to fill his days. Then what would he do? Then he would have to decide about his life. How could a person decide something so important in just a few weeks? If the bishop had his way, he would have Titus kneeling and asking for forgiveness at the next church service.

Why not?

What better way to come back into the community than by confessing his sins and rededicating his life?

He eased down the ladder, the paintbrush between his teeth. He had the nearly empty paint can in one hand and was using the other to steady himself as he descended.

Yep, it wouldn't be long before he had everything in shape over here, and yet his guilt was not so easily assuaged.

The dreams still haunted his nights. Thoughts of Mandy and what might have been haunted his days. Only his time at Abbie's seemed to wipe his thoughts of all else. Here he could simply be. It shouldn't be that way. He should be uncomfortable and sad. But somehow coming to the farm where his best friend had grown up made him feel closer to Alvin.

At the bottom of the ladder, he removed the paint-brush from his mouth and dunked it back into the paint can. There was just a little bit left. Too much to throw away and too little to really begin a new project. Maybe he should ask Abbie if there was a door that needed a second coat. Or maybe he shouldn't worry so much about it and just start his work on the milking barn.

He had saved the barn for last. Mainly so he could stay out of her way. Or at least that was what he told himself. Abbie confused him.

Against his better judgment, he started for the milking barn. He was here to help out on her farm. He couldn't avoid her forever. Not that he had evaded her much since he'd been there. Though it seemed that she had been dodging him lately. He ducked into the barn, blinking to clear his vision as he stepped out of the sunlight.

The afternoon milking was well underway. Or at least he thought it was. There were so many stalls that didn't have cows in them he wasn't certain if she was milking or doing something else.

He did a quick head count and there were only about twenty-five cows hooked up to the railing in the stalls. There were nearly that many empty stalls as well.

He started to call out to her but with the noise of the air compressor, he didn't think she could hear him. So he continued on to the center aisle of the milking side of the barn. Four cows were hooked up to the milking machines with one empty vat in the center aisle. But Abbie was nowhere to be seen. He looked around hoping to catch sight of her. Surely, she couldn't be far.

A few seconds later she came out of the milking room pushing a large container on wheels. It was similar to the milk vats standing by each cow, but bigger.

She was looking down as she pushed the apparatus, stopping when she got next to the empty vat. Then she straightened and screamed.

"Titus!" She slapped a hand over her heart, her eyes wide. "You scared me to pieces."

"I'm sorry," he said. "I just came to see if you had anything you might need painted." He held up the paint can in one hand. "I have a little left over, and I didn't want to waste it."

Abbie shook her head, then walked over to check the status of one of the cows. Seemingly satisfied, she straightened and turned back toward him. "I don't believe so, no."

"It's okay to ask me." Titus propped one hand on his hip and waited for her answer, waited for her to change her mind. For someone who needed help so badly she was the last person to ask for it. He understood her need to get her family back together, so why wouldn't she take the help that was being offered her?

"I can't think of anything else that needs paint."

"I guess I'll put the lid back on then. I hate to waste it." He thought she might change her mind if she thought she was inconveniencing him in any way. But she continued her milking, barely glancing at him as she moved to the next cow in the line.

Titus scooted along next to her, watching as she unhooked the milking gadget then clamped it to the empty vat in front. He might not have been raised on a dairy farm but he knew enough to know what to do. He picked up the full vat of milk and poured it into the larger container. They called them something weird, but he couldn't remember what. Not that it mattered.

"You don't have to help me," she said.

"Of course I do. We're Amish, aren't we?"

"That doesn't mean you have to help."

Titus finished pouring the milk into the large vat, then moved the newly emptied container to the front of the line. "Tell me, why are you missing so many cows?"

She straightened and glanced around at the beasts. Then she took a big heaving sigh as if she had decided she would impart some great knowledge to him. "We lost a few for one reason or another. *Dat* didn't say as much but I think he sold all the new calves." She shrugged. "Now this is all we have left."

Titus took another quick count of the empty stalls. "You should have twice as many cows as you do. Well, almost."

Abbie nodded. "I know. But it's not the easiest thing." She brushed her arm across her forehead and glanced around the barn once again. "I need to buy more cows, but nobody will seem to help me. I can't leave here long enough to go take care of those things, and *Mamm* and *Dat* . . ." She shook her head. "I'm afraid to leave them alone for long." She exhaled as if she had relieved herself of a great burden.

"I saw your *mamm* when I came in," Titus said. "She's looking good. Better," he said. And she was. The first time he had seen her since he got back she looked run-down, tired, and sad. And though that melancholy look hadn't left her eyes, she still appeared to be clean and on the upswing. But Abbie's father was another matter altogether.

Abbie traded out the milking device one more time. "I worry about *Dat*."

Titus shifted from one foot to the other, not wanting to have this conversation, yet somehow feeling dragged into it all the same. With some of the closer calls the man had had, Titus knew that he was drinking. Plenty by the looks of it. On a farm, any drinking could be dangerous, but that glazed-over look in his eyes put it on a whole new level. He had already fallen through the barn roof. What was next?

But maybe if Titus could convince her father to care more about the property, then Emmanuel would quit drinking and take care of the milk cows like he was supposed to.

"Have you talked to him about his drinking?"

Abbie stopped. Her shoulders stiffened, and she dragged her bottom lip through her teeth. She closed her eyes and shook her head.

"You need to." He felt horrible bringing it up. But he could see that Abbie needed normalcy as much as he himself did. Titus needed things to go back to the way they were before Alvin died. Before he went to prison. And Abbie needed the same thing. She needed her life back, her parents back. He couldn't give her Alvin, but maybe he could give her the rest. "Do you want me to talk to him?" he asked.

She shook her head. Though she had opened her eyes, she looked everywhere but at him. The floor, the walls, the cows' rumps.

"I could talk to the bishop for you if you'd like." Heaven knew he was in good with the bishop these days. Maybe if the bishop had other things to worry about, more important souls, souls that could actually be saved and salvaged, then maybe he would forget about Titus for a while.

He shook his head at his own fanciful thoughts. Bishop Ebersol was nothing if not thorough and efficient. Titus doubted there was much that went on in the district without his knowing about it. Still, it was a nice thought. And one that would benefit everyone. Titus would have more time, and Emmanuel King would be allowed to get himself back together. No harm in that.

Abbie pinned him with her blue gaze. "No, please don't, Titus. Just don't. I'm not sure how he'll react."

"The bishop or your father?"

"Both."

"He can't go on like this, Abbie. He's going to end up hurting himself."

She shuddered, then seemed to rouse herself out of her stupor and started back up with the milking chores. She attached the apparatus to the next cow in line, poured the milk into the container, and started the process all over again. He thought she might use the time to change the subject, but instead she turned back to him with a sad smile. "We don't farm like some of the others. We don't have sharp farm equipment for him to get hurt on. I take care of the cows. That's good, *jah*? He pretty much lets me handle most things. He feeds the horses and the chickens. Things like that."

"He fell through the barn roof, Abbie."

"I know, but I made him promise he wouldn't get on the ladder again."

"I'm afraid he's going to end up hurt badly, and there won't be anything you can do about it."

Abbie shook her head, but he had a feeling it had more to do with her not wanting to hear what he had to say rather than not believing the words to be true. "Just a little more time, Titus. Just let me have a little more time. I'll figure out exactly how to say this to him."

Titus frowned. "What are you afraid of?" He knew fear when he saw it. She was terrified, but he didn't know why.

"I don't know. But I do know that if we handle this wrong, I'll never get my *dat* back."

"I only want to help," Titus said. And he did. This was one thing he had to do to help this family. He had done so much harm. He needed to give back.

"Then get some milk cows in here. If you really want to help."

He drew back, surprised by her response. "You want me to buy you some milk cows?"

"I'll pay for them, I just need help finding them. It's amazing that the men in this county will not talk to me about milk cows. I don't understand."

He couldn't help but chuckle. "Have you looked in the mirror lately?"

She frowned. "What does that have to do with anything?"

"You're as pretty as anything, as sweet as candy, and you have the eyes of an angel. You don't exactly look like the typical dairy farmer."

She slammed her hands on her hips and glared at him with those angel eyes. "That is a very sexist thing to say, Titus Lambert."

"But it's the truth. Maybe people won't talk to you because they don't take you seriously."

"Fine, you talk to them. And buy me some milk cows."

Titus managed to control his humor to nothing more than a grin. "Great. I'll start tomorrow. I say we go after lunch."

"We?" she asked.

"Yes, we. I don't have a problem finding you someone who'll sell you a cow, but you should pick out the livestock yourself."

"After lunch is fine. It's a date. You know . . . between friends."

Titus shook his head and started from the barn. It

was the weirdest date he'd ever had. And somehow he was looking forward to it. Way too much.

He thought she was pretty?

The thought shouldn't have sent such a thrill through Abbie, but it did. It warmed her completely from the inside out. Titus Lambert thought she was pretty. He thought she was sweet and had the eyes of an angel. Never before had she received such a wonderful compliment from anyone. Much less from someone she really didn't like.

That wasn't true. Once upon a time, she had liked Titus just fine. He had been her brother's friend and confidant, a steady fixture at their house while Alvin had been alive. But since the accident Titus had taken on a new role in her thoughts, going from friend to killer. But now that was changing once again.

There was more to that night than what anyone was telling her. And that confused her as well. As badly as she wanted things to be different, she needed them to be the same. She needed to be able to hate someone for her brother's death. So far she had failed miserably at hating Titus Lambert. In fact, she was beginning to suspect that she liked him more and more.

How could she hate him? He seemed to want the same thing from life that she did—an answer to how to go on without Alvin.

She finished up the milking chores and headed out of the barn. She and Titus Lambert were going out tomorrow to look at milk cows. As far as dates went, it wasn't a great one. Or even a real one. But she was looking forward to this more than she had been looking forward to anything in a long, long time. She looked down at herself in the milking dress splotched with iodine solution, mud, and other questionable streaks. More than likely she smelled like the barn and her shoes were caked with mud and stuff she didn't want to identify. And he still wanted to go with her tomorrow.

She shook her head. She was reading way more into this than what was there. That didn't mean she had to go tomorrow looking like this. She gasped and started for the house. What was she going to wear?

Chapter Eight

"Should I have gotten a driver for today?" Abbie tried to temper the excitement in her voice. It had nothing to do with Titus and everything to do with the fact that she hadn't done anything in a long time. That in itself made buying cows seem like a special treat.

Titus shook his head. "I went through a copy of the paper last night to find anybody that might have some cows."

"The *Budget*?"

Titus chuckled. "The *Tulsa World*. I don't think the *Budget* or *Die Botschaft* would do us much good at this point. Most of those ads are from Ohio and Lancaster. We need a local seller for the cows."

Abbie nodded. "I wondered about that."

Titus propped his hands on his hips, and Abbie couldn't help but notice the way it broadened his shoulders. He looked so Amish today in his black broadfall pants and sky blue shirt, black boots and straw hat. And she didn't know what to make of it. Did that mean he was staying? He still hadn't gone up in front of the church and made a kneeling confession, and he talked about *if* he stayed. She shouldn't care.

What about what she wanted? For him to leave as soon as possible. But now that he was helping her with the cows, was everything different? She pushed the thought away. Everything was different. Every day it was different, and she couldn't lie about her attraction to him. The whole thing was beginning to get tiresome.

She smoothed her hands over her black apron, trying not to yet at the same time wanting to draw attention to how she was dressed. She had chosen today's ensemble with a critical eye. Her dress was a beautiful peach color, her apron black. The sleeves had a raw edge with a small stripe of a black grosgrain ribbon sewn around. It was perhaps the prettiest dress she had. One that her cousin Miriam in Missouri had made for her special. She loved the dress. And she liked how the color made her eyes seem bluer and how it made her hair appear more brown than blond.

"You look nice today."

She stopped, her heart mid-soar. She couldn't get too excited over a little compliment like that. And certainly not one from Titus Lambert. He may not be her enemy these days. But that didn't quite make them friends, either. They had a date, *jah*, to buy cows. Nothing really. "Are we going to buy cows or not?"

Titus nodded. "I checked out a couple of places last night. I need to call a few more today. After that, I'll see about getting us a driver."

"So we are going to need a driver?"

Titus shrugged. "It all depends. Bacon Dan might have a few cows. How many are you looking to buy?"

Abbie thought about the dwindling bank account and the risk she was taking. But they would have to have more cows in order to make the farm work. And that would cost money. "If I can get a good deal on them, maybe twenty."

Titus whistled under his breath. "That's quite a bit for you to work all by yourself."

"I'm going to talk to them, Titus. I promise." Why was she promising anything to him? But it was more than a promise to him. It was a promise to herself. She would talk to her father. She would get him back on the straight and narrow. But he had to have something to walk that line for. And that was where these cows came in. So much responsibility to put on a few bovines, but that was exactly what was about to happen.

Together she and Titus walked into the shed, where the Kings kept their phone. Titus sat down in the only chair while Abbie leaned her rear against the make-shift desk.

She listened as Titus made phone calls, talked price and lineage, and tried to make her a good deal. But she lost the thread of the conversation in the rich timbre of his voice. His voice hadn't been so deep when he left. It had changed in jail, most likely from the years that had passed than anything else, but to her chagrin she liked it. Yet she didn't want to like anything about him.

That was dumb. How could she not like certain parts of him? He had come and helped out on the farm, painted almost everything except the milking barn, re-paired buildings, fixed the roof, and done countless other chores that her father couldn't seem to get around to. She supposed that had been his plan all along, ease his guilt by lending her a hand, then once everything was done he would most likely return to the *Englisch* world.

You don't know that.

He might be dressed Amish but . . .

Titus hung up the phone and turned to her. "Elmer Nolt has at least ten. He might have more if another deal falls through. I'm sure he'll give you a really good deal on them, but I say we go out and look first. Agreed?"

"Are you staying?"

He blinked a couple of times, understandably confused by her quick change in subject. "Until about supper, I suppose."

"No, I'm talking about staying. In Wells Landing."

His chair squeaked under his weight as he leaned back. He folded his arms and leveled his gaze on her. "I don't know."

The moment hung heavy between them, a little too intense for Abbie's liking.

"Do you want to?"

"I don't know." His voice rang with honesty. It was just as she suspected. He was assuaging his guilt, then he would be on his way once more. He had spent too much time in the *Englisch* world to come back now. And as her cold feelings for him melted, she would do well to remember that. She shouldn't even count on him as a friend, for the *Englisch* world would pull him away very soon.

"Are you up to going out to Elmer's tomorrow morning?" he asked, effectively changing the conversation topic.

Spell broken, she pushed to her feet. "*Jah*, sure. Do I need to get a driver?"

Titus nodded. "He lives all the way over in Taylor Creek."

Taylor Creek was just one town over and where most of the Mennonites in the area lived. There were still a few Amish houses sprinkled throughout just as there were a few Mennonite houses in Wells Landing. But for the most part, they had clustered together in the tiny town.

"I'll call Bruce," Abbie said, talking about her favorite driver. "Or should we just rent a trailer?"

"Why don't we take a look at the stock first and then decide?" He smiled, and Abbie felt another little bit of her resolve melt away.

"Are you going to tell me what's been on your mind lately or are you going to keep it a secret?

Mandy jumped as Levi's voice sounded behind her. She had been lost in thought, no doubt about that. But the last thing she could do was tell her husband about it. Not until she decided what she should do. Could do.

"Oh, just this and that. You know how busy the summers are." So it wasn't really what was on her mind, but the statement was true nonetheless. Summertime was always busier. There were always vegetables to can, jelly to make, and tomatoes to pick, aside from all the yard work that had to be done. Mandy didn't mind though. Right now she needed all the physical work she could get. She needed something to keep her mind off Titus Lambert and what could've been. Should have been.

It had been so easy to push him from her thoughts while he was gone. She had lived the last three years with Levi and hardly giving Titus Lambert a second thought. Her marriage was happy enough, she supposed. All marriages had bumps and trials. She knew as much from the beginning. But she never dreamed that after such a short time she would be wondering if she had made the right decision. The feeling was uncomfortable, to say the least. And she needed it to go away. Titus had made his feelings perfectly clear. Heat rose in her cheeks as she thought about their conversation from a few days before. She hadn't thought about the words before they slipped from her mouth. Now they brought her great shame. Her stomach fell as she remembered the look in Titus's eyes. And he was right. They couldn't remain in the Amish world and be together. She was married to another. She had tied her life to Levi Burkholder's. There was no undoing that in their community.

"There you go again." Levi's voice lacked an accusing edge. Did he not care? Or maybe she should be thankful that she didn't have an overly jealous husband. She had seen that with some couples and it always led to problems. Of course they worked it out. They were Amish, after all. But it taught her that things aren't always what they seemed. She did her best to show everyone how happy she was married to Levi. How wonderful she thought he was. Their house was beautiful, and she tried to make certain that everyone knew how grateful she was to have the blessings God had bestowed on her. On them. But now this . . .

"I'm sorry, Levi. Really I am."

He came up behind her and laid his big hands on her shoulders, giving them a small massage.

She sighed and leaned back against him. They had a good relationship. Levi was loving and caring. She would do well to remember that.

"Maybe you should get away for a couple of days. You could go into Tulsa. Maybe you and Sarah. Get a hotel room and just relax for a bit."

Mandy's eyes snapped open. "I can't do that. If I left now I would be even further behind." And it was the truth. But the last thing she needed to do was go away for a weekend. If she was in Tulsa and Titus was in Wells Landing she wouldn't have the opportunity to run into him, talk to him, look at him, see him. How could she figure out what was going on inside her head if she couldn't see him?

"Suit yourself." He pressed a small kiss next to her ear.

She needed to get over this . . . obsession she had with Titus Lambert and the past. She had made her choice, but she was going to have to learn to live with it.

If only she knew how.

"Turn right just past that tree," Titus said, looking at the paper he held in his hand. He had gotten driving directions from Elmer to help them get to the cows. He could only hope that the cows were all that he imagined.

Bruce Brown chuckled from the driver's seat. Bruce was an older man, a retired Air Force medic who now spent his days driving the Amish wherever they needed to go. He was in great demand, and Abbie had explained to Titus that they were lucky to have gotten him on such short notice. "I could have put it in the GPS, you know."

Titus shook his head. "I keep forgetting about things like that." He smiled. Bruce made the turn as directed.

"So you lived here before?"

Titus's stomach fell. He wasn't sure what was harder, the stares and whispers of the people who had known him before or the curious questions of the people who had just moved to the area. Either way, such incidents made him realize that he might not be able to stay. Anytime he got to thinking about it, something like this happened and he realized that he would never be able to live down his reputation. Deserved or not, it didn't matter. He had served five years in prison because someone had died at his hands, and that was something no one could forget.

"*Jah*," Abbie said before he could respond. "Titus thought he needed to take the longest possible *rum-springa* on record in Wells Landing. But he's back now and that's all that matters."

Bruce nodded. "Amen to that."

Had she just taken up for him? Titus wasn't sure if he could trust his ears, and he wasn't sure what to do with the warm feeling that filled him. He never imagined he would have a champion in Abbie King.

"Can't be much farther," Titus said. He felt the need to comment in some way, but couldn't find any words that seemed suitable. Best just stick to the original topic of why they were here. Milk cows.

"Yeah," Bruce said. "I've been out here once or twice. I believe that Elmer lives on the other side of Ezra Hein."

Ezra Hein? Where had he heard that name before?

Abbie turned in her seat and snagged his gaze. "Ezra is the Mennonite courting Sadie Kauffman."

Titus nodded. He wasn't sure how Maddie Kauffman felt about her daughter running off to join the Mennonites, but he supposed being close was better than nothing. It seemed that a lot of people who left the Amish felt a certain amount of comfort in the Mennonite church. Whether it was maintaining the conservative dress and traditional head covering, who knew, but that might be an option for Titus. Taylor Creek was just as small as Wells Landing and any talk would bleed from one to the other.

They drove past the mailbox with the name HEIN painted on it and a large sign that said HEIN RANCH EXOTIC MEATS AND ANIMALS. In the next pasture was a herd of buffalo. Titus stared at them as they drove past, unable to take his eyes from the magnificent creatures. They were big and lumbering, though he knew they could run like anything and were strong to boot. He twisted his head around to still look at them as they continued down the road.

"I bet he would let you come visit the farm if you wanted to," Abbie said from her place in the front seat.

Titus turned around. "That would be great. Maybe on the way back we could stop for a minute."

"Sure thing," Bruce said.

Titus gave the buffalo one last look, then turned back to the front. A couple of minutes later they came upon the mailbox boasting the name ELMER NOLT. Bruce turned the car into the drive, and Titus's heart began to pound. He was excited for Abbie. Excited to look at these cows for her farm. He just hoped that they were everything he had heard them to be.

Bruce stopped the car and everyone got out. A few minutes later an elderly man hobbled out of the barn. He wore a long-sleeved industrial blue shirt, overalls, and a straw hat. Titus had assumed that with a name like Elmer Nolt he would be Amish, but he quickly changed that assessment to ex-Amish.

The man moved toward them, one hand outstretched. "You must be Titus Lambert."

Titus nodded and other introductions were exchanged. Bruce and Elmer talked for second about the weather, then Elmer rubbed his hands together enthusiastically. "Are you ready to see the old girls?"

"Yes, please," he said.

Abbie had grown quiet. Something that Titus had noticed she did when she got overly excited. She could be loud while angry, but being excited seemed to make her pull inside herself. Maybe she was just worried like he was that the cows wouldn't end up being what they needed for her farm.

"Come this way." Elmer motioned for them to follow behind him toward the pasture.

It really was a beautiful farm. All green hills and rolling pasture, with jersey cows dotted about like sprinkles.

"Now, these girls here are currently giving milk. I've got a few that aren't ready yet. But I'll make you the deal on all of them."

Titus studied the cows. They all looked to be in good shape, but they would have to test the milk to make sure. "The other deal fell through?" Titus asked. If it truly had, then they would be able to purchase all twenty cows that Abbie wanted.

"That's right."

"Why are you selling them all again?"

Elmer jerked his thumb over his shoulder back toward the house. "The missus. She wants to move into town. Some condo or some such. She says we're getting too old to farm." He shook his head. "Bah, I'll never be too old to farm."

"How many do you have?"

"I had thirty-four total and ten calves. I got a man coming to look at those tomorrow so if you're interested, it'll have to be after that."

"No, we need the milk." Abbie finally spoke up. Somehow between the car and the cows she found her voice. "I don't need all thirty-four, though."

Elmer pushed his hat up on his forehead and scratched his head. "Well now, how many do you need?"

"I'll take twenty-five if I can get a good deal."

He grinned, flashing the gap where an eyetooth was missing. "I'll give you an even better deal if you take all thirty-four."

Titus chuckled. That was country math at its

finest. "That sounds great, but we don't have room for thirty-four."

"I know a guy if that will help," Bruce said. "My neighbor wants to buy some cows. This might just be the thing."

"Can you call him?" Titus asked.

Even as he said the words Bruce was digging his phone out of his pocket. In no time at all they had a deal on all thirty-four cows.

Titus turned to Abbie. "Are you okay with this?"

She swallowed hard and nodded.

He supposed it was a big jump from the twenty-five she already had: now they were all the way up to fifty head. It was a bit unnerving, but the logic was sound. She wouldn't be able to make anything without more cows, and she'd have to spend the money she had to get this running.

"Can I talk to you for a minute?" Abbie pinned him with her blue gaze.

Titus nodded. "Okay."

She looked at the two men standing next to them, then back to Titus. "Alone."

Titus gave a quick nod and walked with her back toward the car.

"This worries me, Titus."

"It's a big jump, I understand that. But you know this is what your farm needs."

She swallowed hard. "I know, but I can't do this alone."

"Your *mamm* and *dat* are there."

She nodded, even as her mouth turned down at the corners. "You know how it is right now."

"All the more reason for you to talk to him."

"I know. But if I make this deal right now, I'm going to need some help. More help than just my *dat*."

"I'll be there." His promise surprised him. Had he just told Abbie King that he would be there for her when she needed him?

"You mean that?" Again she pinned him with her gaze.

He shifted from side to side, suddenly uncomfortable with the situation. Could he stay? Did he want to stay?

That wasn't the question. He did want to stay. He wanted to spend as much time as he could with Abbie for as long as he could until he was forced to leave. He had no idea when that would happen, but until then . . .

"Yeah," he said. "I mean that. I'll be there to help you for as long as you need."

It'd taken longer to drive to Elmer Nolt's house than it did to decide to buy the twenty-five head of cattle. Abbie's fingers trembled as she shook Elmer's hand on the deal. She couldn't believe it. She hoped she knew what she was getting into.

Titus said that he would help her as long as she needed, but she wasn't one hundred percent convinced he would uphold that promise. But she wanted him to. Oh, how she wanted him to.

Titus promised to arrange for a truck to pick up the cows later in the week. Then they said their good-byes to Elmer and climbed back into Bruce's car.

"You still want to stop by the Hein place and look at those bison?" Bruce asked as they drove back.

"If we have enough time, that would be great."

Bruce smiled. "We have all the time we need."

Just a few minutes later Bruce pulled his car into the gravel drive at the Hein exotic animal farm. She felt a little weird just showing up, but she had met Ezra one other time earlier in the spring at the farmers' market. With any luck he would remember who she was and wouldn't think their visit entirely strange.

A young man came out of the barn, pulling off gloves as he walked toward them. "Can I help you?" The wind ruffled his streaky blond hair.

Titus took a step forward, extending a hand to shake. "Sorry to bother you. We were passing by, and I saw your bison. I had to stop and take a closer look." He grinned, and Abbie tried to remember if that was the first time he had smiled since he had been back in Wells Landing. She couldn't remember, but his grin was still a welcome sight. He didn't smile nearly often enough.

"Sure, I'd love to show you around. Ezra Hein," he said.

"Titus Lambert."

The two men shook hands and introductions went all around. "We won't keep you long," Titus said.

"Stay as long as you like," Ezra said. "I have a lot of curious passersby who stop for a closer look. Locals and tourists alike."

"We don't come here often," Abbie added. "We live in Wells Landing."

Ezra smiled, the action lighting up his dark brown eyes. "Oh, perhaps you know my fiancée, Sadie Kauffman?"

Abbie nodded. "You might not remember, but you and I met at the farmers' market in April."

"That's right." Ezra snapped his fingers. "How are you?"

Abbie thought about it a second. How was she? "I'm good," she said. And she was. Especially on the days when she didn't dwell too much on Titus, him as her partner, her brother's death, or that her brother would never get to experience the things she was experiencing now. As long as she didn't dwell, she could hold her own. That was more than she could say for her father.

"Good, good," Ezra said.

"Abbie," Titus called. "You've got to come see this." Abbie shot Ezra an apologetic smile and started toward the fence where Titus stood.

"Aren't they magnificent?"

Abbie looked at the great beasts. They were huge, way larger than she thought. And much bigger than her milk cows. That alone made them more intimidating than any animal she'd ever seen. But they did have a certain gentle beauty about them, a quiet majesty that set them apart from everything else around them.

"You thinking about getting a bison?" Abbie asked.

Titus scoffed. "Where would I put it?" He shook his head. "No, I just wanted to look at him."

She looked out over the pasture. "Are bison the only animals you keep?" she asked Ezra. She thought she heard someone in town say he had other meats as well, but she wasn't sure.

Ezra nodded to the pasture across the driveway from where they stood. It retained the ostriches, and if she wasn't mistaken, she saw some deer in the distance. "And then there are the camels."

Abbie laughed. "Camels? In Oklahoma?"

"Yeah, it's kinda crazy. I got them from a guy when I first started farming. He wanted to get rid of all of his animals, and he had those, too. He used them for brush control. That's all I do with them, but they are fun to have around when we have children come out to see the ranch."

Titus turned around, the look on his face so intense it almost scared Abbie. "Is everything okay?" she asked.

"Do you milk them?" Titus asked.

Ezra shook his head. "Two of them are females, but the third is a gelding. Like I said, they were just part of the deal to get the bison. Now the camels are more of an ornament than anything."

"Are you in the market to sell them?"

What was Titus talking about? Was he in the market to *buy* them?

She turned to study Titus. He looked serious enough as he stared intently at Ezra, waiting for his reply.

"I might be."

Titus nodded. "I read this article about how camel's milk is better for you. It's got all these nutrients in it and people are charging a lot of money for the milk."

Abbie could almost see the wheels turning in his brain.

"Those aren't milking camels," Ezra said. "They haven't been bred or anything."

"They could be, though, right?"

"I suppose. Are you serious about buying them?"

He nodded. "Very. Just give me a second." He grabbed Abbie by the arm and hustled her off to one side. "What do you think, Abbie?"

She stared at him. "What do I think? You're asking me this now?" She propped her hands on her hips. "Wait . . . why are you asking me at all?"

"I've got this idea." The light in his gaze was so bright she almost shaded her eyes. "What if we get these camels and a bull and we start breeding them. We can sell the milk and build up your farm that way."

She shook her head. "Titus, I just bought twenty-five cows."

"I know. But there's plenty of room at the farm for these."

"So you're talking about buying Ezra's camels, taking them to my farm, and then milking them?"

Titus nodded. "After a time. I mean, we'll need to get a bull and—"

"Where are you getting the money for this?"

He shook his head. "I'll worry about that. Are you in?"

"Like partners?"

He nodded. "I'll pay you a leasing fee. How does that sound?" The offer was almost too tempting to pass up. But she couldn't imagine the camels on the farm. Then again she could hardly imagine a lot of things that happened in the last five years.

"Get the camels. We'll work out a leasing agreement," she said. "But you are going to be the one who milks them."

Chapter Nine

He could hardly believe it. He had gone out with Abbie to look at milk cows and come home with plans to start a business. It was beyond impulsive, but he had taken one look at those lumbering animals and knew that there was something there.

"Am I taking you back to Abbie's?" Bruce asked as they started through Wells Landing.

Titus sat up a little straighter in his seat. "Can you drive by the library?"

Bruce nodded. "Of course, but how will you get home from there?"

He shook his head. "I don't know. I was just thinking . . . Never mind."

"I could wait for you for a while if you have a small errand to run or something."

"No, that's okay," Titus said.

He had wanted to go by the library and do some research on camels. He had taken a big responsibility with absolutely no knowledge on the subject. But somehow this crazy idea seemed perfectly normal. Why shouldn't he buy some camels? Why shouldn't he milk them for profit? He was floating around here anyway. And when the time came he could either sell them to Abbie or find another person who might want to take over whatever business it was that he got together. Maybe even Gabe Allen.

He should tell his brother about it, but somehow it seemed like it was his and Abbie's idea. Even though it truly belonged to him alone, she would forever be wrapped up in the day, and this decision.

"If you're sure," Bruce said.

"I'm sure," Titus replied. "Take us to Abbie's. I'll take care of everything else from there."

They pulled into Abbie's drive just before four o'clock. Titus knew that she would immediately begin the milking, and he had too many thoughts in his head to do something as mundane as painting today. He would need something else to do to burn off the mental energy that was backing up on him every second. He hadn't been excited about anything in a long, long time. Not even getting out of prison or coming home had brought this much joy into his life. Leaving jail had been filled with trepidation and worry. But this . . . This was the greatest feeling ever. It was new and exciting and all his.

They got out of the car and paid Bruce. "You call any time," the man said.

"We will," Abbie replied. They stood at the edge of the drive as he got into his car and started backing up.

A yell of pain rent the air. Bruce must've heard it too. He stopped, waiting to see if someone had summoned him.

Titus looked to Abbie. She looked back and over to the barn door. Her father was just coming out, though *staggering* was a better word for his gait. He had one arm clutched in the other, blood trickling between his fingers.

"Oh my." Abbie rushed toward him with Titus right behind. Her father slumped down on the wooden stool just outside the barn door, still cradling one hand in the other.

"What happened?" Bruce called.

Titus didn't bother to answer as he drew closer. Blood gushed from the wound though he couldn't discern exactly what type of wound it was.

Abbie took off her apron and wrapped it around the hand, using it to apply pressure and soak up some of the blood.

"What did you do?"

"I was sawing." Emmanuel King closed his eyes and leaned his head back against the freshly painted barn. Titus couldn't tell how bad the wound was since Abbie had wrapped her apron around it, but he knew it couldn't be good with all the blood splattered everywhere.

Bruce came up just then. "Do you need go to the hospital?"

Abbie turned to Titus as if he was the one with all the answers.

"I think so, yeah," he said.

But Emmanuel straightened and shook his head. "No hospital."

Titus could smell the liquor on his breath and knew that the man had been drinking once again. In fact, he hadn't noticed a time when the man wasn't drinking, and that had become a serious problem at the King household. From the look on Abbie's face, she realized it too.

"*Dat*, it's bad."

"No hospital."

Bruce caught Titus's gaze. "I'll stay until we know for certain he'll be okay."

Titus gave him a grim smile. "That would be good. Thank you."

They all hovered over Emmanuel King, just watching and waiting as they tried to give the pressure time to stop the flow of blood before they checked it once again. They waited five minutes and then ten. Finally, Abbie looked to Titus, then back to her father. "I'm going to check it out and if it is still bleeding freely we're going to the hospital."

"You can check it all you want, Abbie girl, but I'm not going to no hospital." Once again Emmanuel King leaned his head back against the barn.

Abbie swallowed hard to begin to unwrap her soiled apron from around his hand. She gasped when she caught sight of the wound.

It was bad. He had cut his pointer finger on his left hand nearly to the bone. The gash was jagged and deep, but also wide. As if he had cut it twice before realizing that he had hit something he shouldn't have.

"That's going to need stitches," Bruce said.

Emmanuel didn't bother to open his eyes. "No hospital."

Abbie looked to Titus, clearly and silently asking, *What do we do?* Why was she depending on him to make these decisions?

"Emmanuel, you really need stitches. We need to do something to that or it's going to get infected and not heal properly." He tried to make his voice sound like it was filled with reason. But with a man drinking what good was reason?

"I ain't going to no hospital."

Titus supposed that there were three of them and they could feasibly overpower him and get him to the hospital, yet what good would it do? What if they got him to the hospital and he refused his own treatment?

Next to him Bruce cleared his throat. "I know this is going to sound bizarre, but I was a medic in the Air Force. I could use some rudimentary first aid on that and perhaps save you the trip to the hospital. That is, if our patient is willing."

Emmanuel opened his eyes long enough to assess Bruce and seemingly liked what he saw. He gave a small nod. "I'll let you doctor it on one condition."

"What's that?" Titus asked.

"You fetch me my bottle from the tack room."

Abbie caught Titus's gaze as he turned to go into the barn. Alcohol was the exact reason why her father had gotten this injury and now he was going to drink again? Not if she had anything to say about it.

Titus's expression was solemn and unreadable, but he walked away without another glance.

"You aren't going to let him do this, are you?"

"I can't very well shove him into the car and take him to the hospital against his will." He disappeared into the tack room and reappeared a second later holding a bottle of Scotch.

Abbie snatched it out of his grasp. "This is what got him into this mess in the first place."

"And it's going to get him out of it." Titus took it back. "Trust me, without something to numb it and having it cleaned with hooch, your father will think twice before using a saw and liquor at the same time."

She wasn't sure whether to trust him or not. Then again, what choice did she have? "Fine," she snorted. "But when this is over the three of us are going to have a long talk."

Titus nodded and ducked out of the barn. Then he stuck his head back in. "We're going to need a needle and thread and then you probably want to stay clear for about half an hour."

She shouldn't be doing this. Mandy prayed half the morning trying to take her mind off Titus and yet the smallest thing would bring him back into her thoughts. She poured a glass of lemonade, and she remembered the time at Millers' Pond when they drank lemonade, sang songs, and Titus had kissed her for the first time. In that moment she felt that nothing in the world could ever be wrong. How wrong could one person be? If she ate peanut butter spread, she remembered that time after church when Titus had taken her for a buggy ride. They hit the back roads of Wells Landing, just driving. Or down to Duck Creek to have a small picnic on the mossy banks. Everything she did somehow got her around to thinking of Titus once more. And despite her continued prayers she had to see him.

Levi had gone over to Andrew Fitch's to talk about horse matters, things that she had no interest in, so she'd stayed home. She could've gone, she supposed, and visited with Caroline, but she just didn't think she could. Caroline was a wonderful person, yet seeing her with her daughter and her son made Mandy long for children of her own with such an intensity it brought tears to her eyes. But all she had done in avoiding those feelings was create other ones, ones that she had no control over.

She pulled the tractor to a stop and got out. This was the worst place she could be. It was bad enough to make pretenses to go see Titus at his family's home. She had taken it one step further and gone to see him at Abbie King's.

Everybody in Wells Landing knew that he had been

coming out here day after day, helping Abbie get her farm back into shape. There'd been some talk as to whether or not there was something going on between him and Abbie, but Mandy couldn't imagine the two of them together. Especially not after the way Alvin had died. How could Abbie look at Titus and see anything but the person responsible for her brother's death?

She shouldn't be here, though. She was being too forward, and if anyone saw her there . . . unfortunately, talk in Wells Landing was rampant. She could only hope that no one saw her or that no one saw the tractor in the drive and put two and two together. She didn't think anyone would understand.

She rubbed her hands down her apron, wishing she had taken the time to stop and change. She had on just regular clothes, nothing fancy or extra pretty. She'd been in such a hurry to come see Titus that she hadn't given a thought to what she was wearing until she set foot in the Kings' yard. Now she wished she had taken the time to look a little prettier. It shouldn't matter what Titus thought of her, but it did. It had always been about Titus. Somehow she had tricked herself into thinking otherwise, but now that he was back she knew the truth. She loved Titus Lambert.

"Mandy? What are you doing here?" Titus came from the direction of one of the outbuildings. Mandy had been so concerned about her dress that she hadn't seen where he'd come from. All of a sudden he appeared, like a vision from her dreams.

Suddenly her confidence fled and she was left standing there with no words for him. Were there words? How did she tell him that she had made the biggest mistake of her life? How did she tell him that she loved him? That she'd always loved him?

"I came to see you." It wasn't exactly what she wanted to say, but it was a start.

"You shouldn't have come here." He stopped a good ten feet from her, a frown marring his handsome face.

He wasn't happy to see her. Why wasn't he happy?

"I know that. You think I don't know that?"

His eyes flared with a dark fire. "You made your choice, Mandy. And there's nothing we can do about it."

That one word *we*. That gave her hope. If there was still a we . . .

"There has to be."

He shook his head as he wiped his hands on a shop towel. That's when she noticed the blood. She had been so wrapped up in seeing him that she hadn't noticed that he was smeared with blood.

She took a step forward, then stopped herself. "Are you okay? Where did all that blood come from?"

"It doesn't matter. It's not mine."

"But you're okay?" Her eyes roamed over him, looking for any hint of injury. Finding none, her gaze traveled back to his.

"I'm fine. We just had a little accident."

As long as he was okay. "So will you walk with me?" She needed to get him alone. If only for a few minutes. She needed to talk to him, walk with him, maybe even touch his hand. But she couldn't do that in the middle of the Kings' front yard.

"I don't think so." He shoved his hands into the back pockets of his pants. He was dressed in Amish clothes though his hair was cut like the *Englisch* in short pieces that stuck up all around. On him, it was nice. Yet she couldn't help but think that he looked more like he belonged in the *Englisch* world than he did in their tiny Amish community.

"Just for a bit?"

"Go home to your husband, Mandy."

"But—"

Suddenly the front door opened. Abbie came out onto the porch, her hands on her hips and her expression stormy. "Titus, are you coming in?"

Titus looked back to Mandy. "I should go."

He was leaving just like that? Because of Abbie King?

"She needs me."

Once again words left Mandy. Abbie needed him? She, Mandy, needed him more than Abbie ever had. She had always needed him. And she was losing him to Abbie. How could this be?

"You made your choice, Mandy."

His words echoed through her mind.

"Titus? We're waiting." Abbie disappeared back into the house.

"I have to go now."

Mandy watched, speechless, as he hurried toward the house. She blinked back hard, angry tears as she watched him disappear inside.

She needed him, but she had lost him.

Heart breaking, she climbed back on her tractor and headed for home.

Titus didn't have one minute to give a thought to Mandy and why she'd come out to see him today. He had more important matters at hand.

The screen door slammed behind him as he let himself into the house. It'd been a doozy of an afternoon. The worst was yet to come. How he had managed to get roped into helping Abbie have an intervention with her father was something he'd have to examine later.

"Titus." She was on her feet in an instant. She had been perched on the very edge of the couch waiting for him to come into the house. Her mother was sitting in a rocking chair and her father in the recliner. He had his feet up and the back pushed into a reclining position. He looked comfortable and about half asleep. Though Titus was sure he'd be awake in a few minutes. Emmanuel wasn't going to like what his daughter had to say. Though Titus couldn't blame the man for trying to rest. After all those little stitches that Bruce had put into his finger Titus figured he'd need a nap too.

Bruce had tried to get the man to go to the hospital several times during their impromptu first aid session. But Emmanuel King was nothing if not stubborn. Titus had the feeling he didn't want the news of his drinking to get all over the community. According to Abbie, Bruce was as tight-lipped as they came. He liked hearing news from people around the county, but he never repeated something he had heard.

Bruce said that Emmanuel would probably have limited use of that finger. He had cut into more than just skin, but again Emmanuel had ignored their warnings.

"Sit down," Abbie said, pointing toward the couch. He sat down next to the spot where she had been sitting just moments before. She sat down beside him.

"Is everything okay with Mandy?" she asked.

Titus could only nod.

"*Dat*, sit up."

"Huh?" He blustered like only the half asleep could.

"Sit up," Abbie repeated. Her tone was harsh and firm and totally at odds with her angelic face. But it served its purpose. Emmanuel straightened, though Titus noticed that his eyes were still a bit glazed. From pain or alcohol, he had no idea. Probably a strong combination of both.

"What's this about?" Priscilla asked.

"*Dat*'s been drinking." Abbie said. "And it has to stop. Now."

Titus supposed that while he'd been outside talking to Mandy, Abbie had been inside explaining exactly how Emmanuel had gotten his injury, because those questions weren't asked.

"I'm not drinking."

Abbie shook her head, and to her credit her voice was firm but calm as she replied. "You and I both know that is not the truth. The best thing for you to do now is admit it so that we can go on."

Part of Titus wanted to reach out and squeeze her fingers reassuringly. No daughter should have to be in the position that she was in at that moment.

"I don't know what you're talking about," Emmanuel argued.

"You can tell me lies all night, but we're not leaving until you admit that you have a problem and you tell me exactly where all the bottles are hidden."

"There are none—"

"There's one under the kitchen sink," her mother said.

Titus turned his gaze to Abbie's mother. She had dropped her gaze to her lap, studying her intertwined fingers as if somehow they held all the answers to the problems of the universe. "There's one in the upstairs closet and one in the bathroom."

Titus was shocked. He had dealt some with the addiction of others in prison, but it was a whole different world here. There wasn't a lot of space to hide anything on the inside. But out here . . .

"Priscilla . . ."

Abbie's mother shook her head. "No. I've ignored this too long. I even turned my head and allowed this. But no more."

Emmanuel stood, a deep red flush rising from under the collar of his shirt clear up to the roots of his hair. Titus wished that he had taken the time to go into town and look up interventions and addictions at the library. Maybe he could have been a little more help, but there hadn't been any time at all. More than that, he wished he wasn't there. This was not something he should be privy to. These people were having a family crisis, and it stemmed from something he had done. The thought made him squirm uncomfortably in his seat.

Priscilla stood. She was as small and angelic as Abbie, but somehow she seemed to tower over her husband, who stood a good head taller than she did. "It ends tonight, Emmanuel. It has to end now."

Titus slumped in this seat, trying to make himself as small as possible.

Abbie snagged his hand, squeezing his fingers as her parents squared off in the middle of the living room floor.

"You don't know what it's like," Emmanuel said. Then, as if he heard his words for the very first time, he bowed his head. Sobs wracked his shoulders as a keening escaped him. Titus had never heard such a sound. It was so heartbreaking it nearly paralyzed him.

Emmanuel stood like that for a moment, sobbing and crying, then Priscilla wrapped her arms around him. "Of course I know what it's like. He was my son too. But we can't go on this way. No more."

Abbie squeezed his fingers, then as if the dam broke, she released him, stood, then wrapped her parents in her embrace.

"I'm sorry, Abbie," her father sobbed.

"It's all right. It's all right," Abbie crooned.

Priscilla was mumbling something incoherent. But Titus didn't need to hear the words to understand her meaning. They had come through the storm. It'd taken awhile, but together they were going forward. And Titus wished he were anyplace but there. They were so wrapped up in one another, they didn't notice when he stood and quietly made his way to the door.

He looked back one last time at the people who had come to mean so much to him, yet at the same time he had hurt so badly long ago. Then he let himself out of the house.

More emotions than he could count swamped him as he made his way to the horse barn. He needed time, he needed space, he needed a place to think, he needed all that and more and then there were things that he didn't even know he needed, but he had to have them all the same.

He let himself into the horse barn, loving the smell that greeted him. He could stand there forever. He'd taken to sleeping in the horse barn at his parents' house, but when the camels arrived at Abbie's he felt like he should be here for them. Maybe he would just move in here. He wondered if Abbie would care.

As much as he wanted to make himself a part of this farm, he knew it couldn't be. And the question remained, when would he ever find a place where he felt he belonged?

Abbie stood at the kitchen counter trying not to count the many bottles lined up there. One by one they had emptied them down the drain. Her father had gone to lie down. She couldn't say she blamed him. He'd had an afternoon to be sure. This wouldn't be easy on them, she knew. But it would be worth it in the end. She was getting the farm back on its feet. With Titus's help it had been painted. The new cows were coming, and things were going to return to normal around their farm. She needed both of her parents alert and at least able to work in order to make their farm successful again.

Titus!

She'd been so busy she hadn't realized that he wasn't around until now.

She scooped the bottles into her arms and took them outside to the trash barrel. Then, feeling as if a dark part of her life had been disposed of, she turned and headed toward the outbuildings. His buggy was still parked at the side of the house, so she knew he had to be around somewhere.

She would check the horse barn first. He seemed to love it there. And she wondered why he didn't breed horses, given that he loved the creatures so much.

She stepped inside the cool interior. "Titus? Are you in here?"

He stepped out of one of the stalls, the motion easy and fluid, though it scared her all the same.

"Oh, there you are."

He shifted from side to side. "Did you get your *dat* taken care of?"

"*Jah*, I did." She stopped for a second, knowing she needed to say her thanks, but realizing that words were not enough. She took one step closer, then flung her arms around his neck.

He was warm and solid, steady and true. And she never wanted to let him go. He had saved her. Saved her family. And although she never thought she would say the words about him, she forgave him for the part he had played in the accident that night.

She squeezed a bit tighter, as his arms came slowly around her. She stepped even closer to him, needing this contact as much as she needed air. "Thank you, thank you, thank you," she chanted.

Then his arms were around her.

Somehow the feeling of gratitude turned into something else. Something more. Warmer, softer.

She pulled away, her arms still around his neck, but she needed to see his face.

His gaze snagged hers, his brown eyes unreadable. There was something there. She saw it, but couldn't identify it. Something that made her stomach pitch and her heart pound.

This was Titus. The Titus she had known since they started school together. The Titus who used to run around with her brother. But he was more than that. He was the Titus who took her to buy cows, the Titus who helped her father when he nearly cut his finger off. The Titus she never wanted to let go.

"Abbie," he whispered. He lowered his head slowly, so very slowly. For a brief instant she wondered if he was giving her time to change her mind. But that wasn't going to happen. He was going to kiss her. And she wanted him to.

Her fingers entwined in his hair as her eyes closed and her lips parted on a sigh.

Then his mouth was on hers. Soft, sweet, warm, with a building heat she hadn't known could exist. She was falling, falling, falling like the girl who fell down the rabbit hole in the book she had read once long ago. But how could she be falling and standing still at the same time? Because she was still there pressed against Titus, soaking up his warmth and strength to add to her own.

She hadn't known she needed it until that moment. Hadn't known she needed someone behind her, beside her, holding her steady and telling her without words that everything was going to be all right. Now that she had it, she never wanted it to go away.

He started to raise his head, but she refused, applying gentle pressure to the back of his neck where her fingers laced through his hair. Because it couldn't end. She needed it so very badly, this human connection, this bond, as unlikely as it seemed.

Then his arms were no longer around her. He stepped back. Left with no choice, Abbie dropped her arms to her sides.

She blinked a couple of times, trying to clear her thoughts even though that was not what she wanted. She wanted to go on kissing Titus, and kissing Titus, and kissing Titus until . . . Well, she didn't know exactly, but she surely didn't want it to end yet.

"Abbie," he started, then cleared his throat. "This is not a good idea."

A minute ago it seemed like the perfect idea. Now shame had formed a ball in her midsection and was sending tentacles out to every part of her. Why had she done that? Not only had she thrown herself into Titus's arms, she had refused to let him stop kissing her. What kind of girl was she?

"I'm sorry." Those were the only words she had to say. She was sorry that she had behaved badly. She was sorry that she had demanded more of him than he was willing to give. But she wasn't sorry that she had kissed him in the first place. She couldn't be sorry about something that beautiful.

"It's okay," Titus said.

Abbie shook her head. "It's not okay."

He looked as if someone had punched him in the gut. But she didn't have time to figure out the whys of that expression. She only knew that she needed to get away from Titus quickly. She turned on her heel and started for the door. Not even stopping when he called her name.

He wouldn't follow her. He couldn't follow her. It was better this way, he told himself. He called for her once, and she kept walking. He wouldn't call again. The relationship between the two of them was a disaster waiting to happen. He knew it as sure as he knew his own name. Forgiveness was one thing. They might forgive him for the part he'd played in Alvin's death, but it would always be there, simmering under the surface, that dragon beast of guilt and blame that would eat them all up if given half a chance. He couldn't put her through that. He wouldn't put himself through it.

No, it was better this way.

He waited a few minutes to make sure that she had gone into the house, then he emerged from the barn. It was time he went home. He'd done enough here today for sure. In a few days the camels would arrive, and he would decide what he would do then about their daily care.

He left for home without telling Abbie he was leaving. She would figure it out soon enough. They would figure out what to do about that kiss later. Or what not to do. For now, he just wanted a shower, a change of clothes, and a little bit of peace and quiet. Not that he would find that at home. But at least he would be home, right?

He had been surprised at how well everyone had adjusted to his coming back. Rachel no longer looked at him like he was a specimen under a magnifying glass and Michael had stopped boasting about his place at the market. Titus had quickly realized that it was a survival mechanism. His brother had found his place in the family and wanted to make sure that Titus didn't oust him from it.

Maybe Titus had been too quick to judge and think that he would be able to come home. And live. Truly live. He pulled into the drive and parked his buggy to the side. He unhitched the horse and poured her some oats.

A shower and a change of clothes. Yeah, that was what he needed. He started for the house wondering how many people he would run into and how many excuses he would have to make for the state of his clothing before he actually got to have that shower. If luck was on his side, he would make it upstairs before anyone saw him. But as he let himself into the living room, he realized that luck had abandoned him completely. His *mamm* and *dat* sat there as if waiting for him to come home.

"Hi," he said, looking from one of them to the other.

"Titus, come sit down," his father said.

His mother took one look at him and her eyes widened. "What happened to you?" She jumped to her feet as he tried to make his way to the rocking chair.

"I'm fine. It's not mine."

She eased herself back into her chair as he settled down into the rocker. He had a feeling he wasn't going to like whatever this was about.

"If you're okay, then whose blood is that?" *Mamm* asked.

He might as well tell them. They would find out soon enough anyway. "Emmanuel King's. He cut himself this afternoon, and it was quite messy." That was an understatement. They didn't need all the details. Some of those were between Emmanuel and God.

"Goodness," his mother said. "Is he okay now?"

"He will be."

"Titus," his father interrupted. No doubt the man had things on his mind. Titus always knew when his father needed some kind of talk. The frown between his eyebrows somehow puckered his whole face like he'd been eating a sour lemon. "It's time to start thinking about your future."

He had been thinking about the future, hadn't he? He'd bought three camels today with the promise to look at more. He was looking toward the future, but he didn't think that was what his father meant.

"Yeah?"

His father nodded. "I know that the bishop talked to you about your confession. Have you given it any more thought?"

"He gave me a month to think about it," Titus said. In his opinion a month seemed like a short amount of time to figure out what he should do with his life. Five years before, he'd had no doubts about joining the Amish church. He had joined and promised to live his life the way the church demanded. But not only had he lived five years away, they had been five hard years. Five years that no one in the community could ever imagine having lived themselves. There were times in the night when even to him it seemed like part of a bad dream. Like he had watched it on a movie screen and it all happened to someone else. But then there were times when it was so real and in his face he shook with the memories.

Five years ago he knew what he wanted. Now he only knew that he didn't know. Why was that so hard for everyone to understand? He had come home and he was doing the best that he could. Why couldn't they accept that for what it was and let him take his time and decide?

Because you might not ever confess. He pushed those thoughts aside.

"We feel that's a little long for this sort of decision. You had your mind made once."

He opened his mouth to say that a lot had happened since he'd made that first decision. But some things needed to be kept to himself. His time in prison was one of those things. He wouldn't explain to his father all the many reasons why rejoining the church had to be put on the back burner. "It's different now."

"Not for us," his father said.

Titus looked to his mother, but she was staring at her fingers once more. The lenses of her black-rimmed glasses flashed in the sunlight as she lightly rocked back and forth. If it hadn't been for that little glint he might not have known she was moving at all. She was upset and uncomfortable, and he wondered if she even agreed with his father at all. But this was an Amish household and the man was the most prominent figure. It had always been that way. What his father said was what they would do. And his father wanted him to join the church.

"I can't do that right now."

His father drew back as if someone had hit him. Titus knew he was not used to people ignoring his wishes. But Titus himself couldn't change what he knew in his heart.

"So you don't care that you bring shame to this family?"

Titus shook his head. "It's not my standing with the church that has brought shame on this family, and we both know it."

"You made the choices that you made. Now you have to live with them."

Titus clenched his jaw even as he nodded. His father's words stopped, but they were true. He had made his choices, and he was living with the consequences every day. And not just choices about going to that party or driving home, but choices concerning the trial and the details he felt needed to be kept secret. But his father would never understand any of that. No one would.

"Are you saying I have to kneel and confess at the next church service or get out?"

"You are the oldest child in this household. You set the example for the others. What sort of example are you setting now?"

Titus stood. "I never wanted to be an example for anyone. And I never claimed to be. I'll get my things."

Chapter Ten

He had no idea where he was going but started down the road anyway, the same backpack he'd hit town with slung over one shoulder. He still wore his bloody clothes. So much for a shower and relaxation.

But even as he walked down the road with no destination in mind, he couldn't find any anger toward his parents. They were as much victims of the situation as Eli and Alvin. They were doing their best to live their lives, follow God's plan and the church, and raise their family. The unfortunate aspect of the situation was that he was a problem.

Titus hadn't planned on being an issue, nor did he want to be an issue, but he was all the same. He kicked a rock at the edge of the road and kept walking. He headed toward town thinking maybe he would run into somebody. Maybe they could go in town and have a piece of pie at Kauffman's or a cookie at Esther Lapp's bakery. Just shoot the breeze for a little bit, but another part of him realized that his fantasy was so five years ago. The friends he had now were married and starting families. They didn't have a great deal of time to do single outings. Not unless they had been planned well in advance. His only friends who weren't married now were Eli and Jonah. He supposed one of them could take him in, but since they both lived at home how long would it be before their parents started to feel that he was being a bad influence on their families?

It wasn't fair. He hated to say those words because hardly anything ever was fair. But this truly wasn't fair. His parents were expecting him to make a decision over something that the bishop didn't expect him to make for another month. Why couldn't they wait? Why couldn't they let him think about it? That was all he wanted, a little time to make sure his head was clear, make sure his thoughts were right, and make sure he could stay in Wells Landing and live the life that once upon a time God had intended for him to live.

He had no doubts about that. Five years ago that had been part of God's plan for him. To live in Wells Landing, get married to Mandy, have babies, raise a family, build a house, etc., etc., like all good Amish men do. He had been fine with that. Happy, even. But then God's plan had fallen apart.

He shook his head. That was where the doubts came in. How could going to jail have been a part of God's plan? His mind couldn't fathom that God wanted him to suffer through all the horrors and trials he endured in prison. No man should have to go through that. But it had happened, and it had made him a different person. Now he wasn't so sure about God's plan. How did a person find God's plan once he lost track of it? He didn't know.

One thing was certain: he couldn't just walk around out here for days on end. He had to find a place to go. He supposed the most logical place would be Abbie's. He would be there in the morning working with her anyway. He could sleep in the barn. He preferred sleeping in a horse stall to sleeping in a bedroom anyway. He knew his parents thought that strange, and he'd been surprised they didn't bring that up during their little talk. That was just one more piece of evidence that showed he might not belong in Wells Landing ever again. The saddest part of all? He wanted to. He wanted to figure out a way to stay, to be a part of the community, to eat with his friends, go swimming at Millers' Pond and all the wonderful things that he had done in years past. But now everything seemed tainted with memories of Alvin and Eli whole and unharmed. There was hardly an inch of the town in which he couldn't recall a memory of the three of them.

And then there was the kiss. What was he going to do about that kiss? He hadn't had much time to think about it after it happened. Not when he never wanted it to stop. He knew he had to get out of there, get away from her in order to be able to fully examine what had happened. Then he had walked into a hornet's nest in his own house and his thoughts were still tangled.

That had been the sweetest kiss of his life. And he had never wanted it to end. For a moment in time he had forgotten who he was and the sins against him. It had only been a humble man kissing a beautiful woman. But it couldn't stay like that. Kisses meant courting and marriage and that just wasn't possible. Because when the kissing stopped they would go back to being Titus, convicted felon, and Abbie, sister of the brother he had killed.

Oh, but there for a moment he had held the world in his hands. The most precious and exquisite gift. And he cherished it, savored it, then had to let it go. It was the only way.

The hurt in Abbie's eyes nearly broke his heart, but it was better to set her straight now than allow too much time to pass in between. He couldn't let her believe that he was somebody other than who and what he really was.

No, being with Abbie was out of the question. To-morrow morning when he got up and went over there to work, the two of them could discuss what happened. She could give him an update on how her father was doing, and he could talk to the whole family about leasing the land for grazing when the camels got there. But until then he needed somewhere to curl up and straighten through the jumble of his thoughts and emotions, pick them out one by one to set them up in the line where he could identify them, label them, and hopefully control them. But he needed time to do that. Time and some place to stay.

He came to a turnoff.

Eli's house. It was the only choice he had, really. He would go to Eli's house, stay with them for a night, then figure out what he was going to do tomorrow. For now, he just needed a place to bed down and get his thoughts in order. Surely, Eli could give him that.

Eli's mongrel of a dog could bark loud enough to wake the dead. Beau was a good dog though strange-looking. Part heeler and part hound dog, he had floppy ears, one blue eye and one brown, and a variety of spots covering most of his body. He barked as Titus approached and continued until he recognized who it was. Then he gave one last woof and wagged his tail until Titus got close enough to scratch behind his ears.

"Hey, Beau, where is everybody?" Beau had no answer, so Titus continued on to the house. Maybe there was somebody inside, though Beau's barking should have warned them that somebody had come up.

He was almost to the porch when the door opened, and Eli rolled out. "Titus!" Eli's green eyes lit up like the traffic lights in town.

"Hey," he started.

"What's wrong?" Eli frowned.

Titus shook his head. "I need a place stay for the night, maybe a couple," he said.

"Trouble at home?"

Titus adjusted the strap of the backpack on his shoulder. "You could say that. I just need to find a place to stay for a while."

"You want to talk about it?" Eli asked. "Come on in the house. We can talk inside."

Eli rolled to the door, expecting him to follow. Titus did, only to find his sister standing there.

"June!"

She was the last person he expected to see. From the wide-eyed look she gave him, the feeling was mutual. "What are you doing here?" they said on top of each other.

Eli cleared his throat, and they swiveled their attention to him. "I guess I should explain."

Titus nodded, even as his stomach began to hurt. What else could go wrong today? Was the bottom of his life just destined to fall out?

"June and I have been dating."

Titus turned to his sister. "I thought you were in love with someone else."

She smiled but rolled her eyes. "Rachel is a darling sister, but she has a big mouth. I told her that on purpose."

"Why all the secrecy?" Titus asked. There had been a time when courting couples kept their intentions a secret, but these days, word of who was dating whom usually got out. Unfortunately, keeping the courting a surprise until the wedding was published was a tradition that was falling by the wayside in a lot of Amish communities. Titus had no feelings about it one way or the other, except that his sister was standing there trying to hide her relationship with a guy who had been like a brother to him. He wasn't sure how he felt about that, her keeping their courting a secret.

"Wells Landing is small," Eli said. "We figured a lot of people might not understand, and we knew you'd be coming home soon. We just thought we would keep it on the lowdown until things settled down a bit."

Titus snorted. "Down-low."

Eli shrugged. "Whatever."

Titus turned to his sister. "So no one knows about this but us?"

"Why do you look upset, Titus?" June asked.

"Because I am." This day had been entirely too much. And if anyone had the right to get upset at this point it was definitely him.

"There's nothing to get upset about." June crossed her arms and glared at him. He knew the look well from when they were children. But he wasn't budging off his stance.

"I don't know how I feel about this."

Eli was his friend. *His* friend. He thought things were good with them. Now he found out that Eli hadn't been telling him the truth. Lying by omission. Wasn't that just as bad?

"It doesn't matter how you feel about it," June said. "It is what it is."

"We hoped that we would eventually get your blessing," Eli said.

Blessing? The word went through Titus like a sword. Who was he to give blessing on anything? He might not approve or even like the idea of his best friend and his sister dating, but he had nothing to say in the matter. June was a grown woman and could do pretty much whatever she wanted. Eli was grown-up as well. It was their life and not Titus's. But he couldn't help but feel that sting of betrayal.

"I've got to go." Titus turned for the door.

"Titus." Eli started after him.

But he kept walking, not stopping until he reached the threshold. Then he turned and looked at his friend. "I just want to know one thing. All these years and all these letters you wrote and you never once thought you should tell me that you were in love with my sister?"

"I'm sorry," Eli said.

Titus looked at them both. "Me too." With that he let himself out of the house and started back down the road again.

He really had no other choice. There was only one other place for him to go. And that was Abbie's. The thought filled him with both dread and excitement. Dread that he would have to deal with his emotions concerning their kiss quicker than he wanted to and excitement about everything that lay ahead of them. That was another reason why they shouldn't muddle through their relationship with fickle things such as kisses. Weren't Eli and June proof of that? He and Abbie needed to keep their heads straight. They had business matters.

He kept walking even as he heard the rumble of the tractor coming up behind him. It didn't matter who it was, though he was afraid it might be someone he knew. Someone who would want to talk, ask questions.

The tractor pulled up even with him, but he refused to look at the driver.

"Titus!"

June.

He should've known she would be the one to come after him. It would've been too hard for Eli to drive a tractor. Titus didn't even know if he had a tractor he could drive. Or maybe they thought June had a better shot of talking him out of being so angry.

Well, he wasn't buying it. He kept his head down and his feet pointed north. Even as she continued to drive beside him.

She called his name again. Had she not figured out by now he wasn't stopping? June pulled a little bit ahead of him and cut him off, turning the tractor sideways in the road in front of him.

"Titus!" she hollered, climbing down with the engine still running.

Hurt and betrayal still burned within him like a blue flame. He walked around the tractor and kept going, June hot on his heels.

He couldn't hear her footsteps over the engine and was surprised when she grabbed his arm and spun him around.

"Just give me a minute to explain."

He nodded toward the tractor. "I wouldn't leave the tractor like that."

"Please," she begged. "Just get in the tractor, and I'll take you wherever you want to go. Please, just hear me out."

This was June. His closest sibling. He never remembered a time in his life without June. Hurt and betrayal aside, he gave a nod. "Okay."

Together they walked back to the tractor and climbed

aboard. June turned back to him before putting it into
gear. "Where do you want to go?"

Did he have much of a choice? "Abbie's."

"Abbie King?" June asked in disbelief.

Titus could only nod.

Titus's kiss was all she could think about. It was the
most spectacular kiss of her entire life, and she had
embarrassed herself beyond hope.

*Lord, please don't let him be so upset with me that he never
comes back.*

She needed him. She needed his help. And he had
camels arriving, of all things. She wasn't sure what he
was going to do with those, but surely he would return,
at least to get them. And the minute he did, she was
going to apologize profusely. Even if it cost her more
embarrassment. She had to tell him the reasons behind
her rash impulse.

She shook her head at herself. What was she going
to say to him? That she'd lost her head? She wasn't
thinking clearly? None of those answers would suffice.
The truth of the matter was she was thinking clearly
now, and if she could repeat that kiss, she would do it in
a heartbeat. What did that say about her?

"Alvin, forgive me," she said, looking at the blue sky
above her. If he was in heaven listening, she hoped he
understood.

The sound of a tractor drew her attention toward the
road. She turned in time to see June Lambert pull into
their drive. Titus was standing next to her.

She refused to believe that it was some sort of sign
and simply waved as she waited for them to draw near.

So much for apologizing profusely. She surely didn't
want June to know what happened between her and

Titus. An apology would have to wait for a little bit longer. First thing, she'd find out why Titus had come back. His work was over for the day.

June shut off the tractor and hopped down, Titus close behind her.

Abbie waved again as they drew close. "This is a surprise," she said.

June shot her a grim smile, then rolled her eyes toward her brother. "Is there someplace Titus and I can talk?"

Abbie nodded slowly. That wasn't exactly what she had expected June to ask.

"The horse barn?" Titus asked. "Can we talk in there?"

Once again Abbie nodded. Then she watched a bit dumbfounded as Titus wrapped his fingers around his sister's arm and tugged her toward the horse barn. At least in their haste no one noticed the deep red flush she knew burned in her cheeks. That heat alone was enough to set fire to her apron, but thankfully, neither one of them had seen it. Or at the very least they hadn't commented on it. But it seemed that there was something going on between the two of them. Abbie shook her head and started for the house.

Titus crossed his arms as June settled down on a hay bale. She patted the place next to her in invitation, but he shook his head. "Talk."

Why was he so angry? He felt his emotions were over the top, yet he could do nothing to stop them. Yes, he was hurt. Yes, he felt betrayed, but his actions seemed harsh. Yet still those emotions burned inside him like a bonfire.

"About two years ago I started going over to visit with

Eli." She shrugged. "I knew he was still writing to you, and you had stopped writing to us—*Mamm* and *Dat* and the family. So I thought maybe he might have some news from you."

Titus gave a quick nod. "Go on."

"Well, I mean you can't just go over to somebody's house and say, 'Have you heard from my brother? No? Thank you. Good-bye.' So I took a pie. We talked for a little bit and figured out that we have a lot in common."

"Just like that?"

He hated the dreamy smile that came over June's face. "Just like that. He's kind and sensitive and caring and forgiving and—"

"Is that what this is all about? Forgiveness?"

"Why would you say that?" June was on her feet in an instant. "You're the only one around here who can't forgive."

Titus shook his head, his jaw clenching. "You have no idea what I can let go."

June seemed to wilt before his eyes. She retreated back to the hay bale. "You're right. I don't. And I won't even pretend to. But what happened between me and Eli . . . it was perfectly natural. And it has nothing to do with you."

The words stabbed him. Maybe that was the problem. They had formed this relationship, and he wasn't involved in it at all. His best friend and his sister had left him out completely.

"No one knows about me and Eli. And we want to keep it that way for a little bit longer."

Reluctantly, Titus agreed. "If that's how it has to be."

June smiled. "I would very much appreciate it. *We* would appreciate it."

He jerked a finger over her shoulder. "Can I tell Abbie?"

June stood and tilted her head to the side as if

studying him from a different angle would give her more insight into his thoughts. "What's going on between the two of you?"

"Nothing." But he couldn't meet her eyes when he said the word.

June chuckled. "Never kid a kidder, isn't that what the *Englisch* say?"

He shrugged, though he knew the *Englisch* saying well. "I don't think there can be anything between us."

"Why not?"

"Do I really have to answer that?"

June laid her hand on his arm, the air around them turning suddenly serious. "Why don't you let her decide? Instead of making these decisions for yourself?"

She let herself out of the barn, and a few minutes later Titus followed her.

He hung around inside the barn long enough to make certain June had left before he came out. He didn't know why, but he didn't want to watch her leave. Maybe it was that knowing look in those blue eyes.

"There you are." Abbie hopped off the porch and met him halfway across the yard. "I thought you were done for the day."

Titus shook his head. How much should he even tell her?

"I need a place to stay. I was hoping maybe I could stay in the barn."

His stomach sank as she shook her head. "You can stay in the house."

"The barn's fine, really."

"Titus," she started.

But he cut her off. "I'm more comfortable in the barn, Abbie. Please don't make me explain."

The ghost of tragedy floated through her expression,

then she pressed her lips together and gave a nod. "Suit yourself."

"I appreciate that. I'll pay you some sort of rent or something."

She propped her hands on her hips. "You will do no such thing. You have helped me get this farm back in order and helped me get my family back on track. The least we can do is give you shelter."

He didn't bother to point out that it was his fault that her family had fallen apart to begin with. Neither one of them needed reminding of that. "And what happens when the camels get here?"

"Titus, I don't believe that three camels will take up that much pasture space. Now stop being difficult and just accept somebody trying to help you in return."

Is that what he was doing? Being difficult?

"Okay," he finally said. "Thanks again."

She smiled, and he was certain it lit up the world. "My pleasure."

Somehow Abbie managed to avoid being alone with Titus until after dark. She had been a little worried about having him in the house, eating dinner with them, but everything seemed to be going quite well. Titus sat at the table with them, her family unconcerned about any *Bann*.

After they ate, her father excused himself to lie back down. His new vows to quit drinking were taking a bit of a toll on his overall well-being, but Abbie knew that with time the withdrawal would lessen and eventually smooth out into normalcy again.

As her *mamm* settled down in the recliner to read her Bible, Abbie finished the dishes and acknowledged that she had delayed the inevitable as long as she could. She needed to go talk to him, and she needed to do it now.

She let herself out of the house, taking the trash around to the trash barrel before beelining over to the horse barn. It seemed to be his favorite place, and if he was sleeping in the barn it only made sense that he would be there now. The door was half open. "Titus?" she called, stepping inside.

"Back here," came his muffled reply. She walked down the row of stalls until he called out once again. "Last one on the left."

Abbie was surprised that he was literally in the last stall on the left. She peeked inside, realizing it was where he intended to sleep. "You've made a bed in here?"

"Yeah." Titus looked down at his bed and back up at Abbie. He held something in his hands, though she couldn't see what it was from her angle. Some sort of piece of paper. Maybe a picture . . .

"I don't understand. Are you sure you don't want to sleep in the house?"

"I'm sure. This is just fine." The air grew silent and thick between them. "I can't sleep in the house. The rooms are too big. It's too quiet and it . . ." He trailed off, losing the ability to accurately describe how he felt.

"So you sleep in the horse stall at home, too?"

He swallowed hard and nodded.

A little bit of Abbie's heart nicked off. Was that what prison had done to him?

"This feels more . . . secure to me."

All Abbie could do was nod. She waited a heartbeat, then changed the subject. "About this afternoon," she started.

He took one last look at the picture he held and put it back into his pocket. "Abbie, don't."

She raised a hand. "No, let me finish. I was out of line and wrong. And I'm sorry. I have no excuse for my behavior."

"You think you need an excuse?"

She nodded. Not only had she acted way out of character for herself, she had acted in a shameful manner for an Amish girl. She had not been raised to be so forward with boys. "I'm sorry if I embarrassed you."

"I'm not embarrassed," he said. "In fact, that was the best kiss I've had in at least five years."

She laughed, then hoped it was meant as a joke. "I'd really feel special if you said ten years."

"But if I admitted that it would be like saying you are a better kisser than Mandy." A playful light twinkled in his brown eyes, and she knew he was teasing her.

"Am I?"

"I don't think I should answer that question."

"Why? Is there something still between the two of you?" She shook her head. "Forget I asked that. I should never have asked. It's none of my business."

"She's married," he said.

Abbie could only nod. Mandy Burkholder might be married, but any fool could see the way she looked at Titus whenever he was around. "I don't think she cares much about that these days."

A red flush rose into his cheeks. "I don't know about that, but I do know that it matters to me."

"Are you sure you don't want to come in the house to sleep?"

"I'm sure."

She cleared her throat. "Do you want to talk about what happened with your parents?"

"It doesn't matter."

"Apparently, it does if you're sleeping in my barn."

He gave her a rueful smile. "Let's just say we have a difference of opinion on when I should kneel and confess."

Abbie felt a little spring of hope in her heart. "Does that mean you're staying?"

"Maybe I should say 'if.'"

"I see."

He took a step toward her. "You don't understand. They don't understand."

"Why don't you try explaining it to us?"

His eyes dimmed. "Like it matters."

"It does matter. And if you don't try to explain it to us, how can we ever understand?"

His expression grew fierce. "No one will ever understand what I went through. No one will ever understand why I have the doubts that I have. I may or may not get past it all. I'm not sure I can do it in a week or a month. Maybe not even in a year."

"Is that what they want from you? For you to kneel and get back into good standing with the church?"

"The bishop gave me a month. My parents aren't giving me that long. They think I'm a bad example."

He spat those last two words as if they were poison.

"For what it's worth, I don't think you're a bad example."

"For what it's worth, I appreciate that."

"If you change your mind about the house . . ." she started.

"I won't."

"Well, then good night." She turned to exit the stall but his words stopped her in her tracks.

"For the record," he started. "You are a much better kisser than Mandy."

Chapter Eleven

Those words shouldn't have thrilled her but they did. And they stayed with her all through the next day as they prepared for the camels and the cows to arrive.

"How are you going to pay for all this again?" Abbie asked as they strung a new fence in one corner of the pasture. Titus felt it was best to keep the camels separate from the cows, at least until they got used to one another. Abbie thought it should be a permanent arrangement, but she didn't say as much to him. They would cross that bridge when the time came. Especially if bull camels were anything like bull bovines.

"I've got a plan," he said.

She hoped it was a good one. Not that she doubted him, but she had heard what he agreed to pay Ezra for the female camels. Bulls had to be even more expensive. Titus had just spent the last five years in jail. How could he afford such things?

"What do they eat?"

"Grass and stuff, like cows."

"That's good."

He looked up from his task. "Why is that?"

"Because we've got that and it's free."

"Are you worried about money?"

She braced her hands on her hips. "I am always worried about money."

He grinned and went back to reinforcing the fence post. "After we get this rolling, you won't have to worry about money anymore."

"And what do we do until then? No, wait. You have a plan."

"I'm going to talk to my *dat* about a loan. He wants me to stay in the area. Maybe he'll think this is a good investment, along with plenty of reason for me to stay in Wells Landing."

She refused to get her hopes up that he would stay and she wasn't about to examine the reasons why she wanted him to.

"What about my *dat*?" she asked. "He would be a good partner. And you are already here."

"I thought you and I were partners."

There went her heart beating all crazy again. "We are, but this is really his farm. And he's forgotten more about dairy farming than I will ever know."

Titus seemed to think about it a minute. "Good plan."

Abbie smiled at the compliment. Everything seemed to be falling into place. She just hoped it stayed that way.

He had been rash and impulsive and now he had to pay for it. At least he was going to have to do some mighty smooth talking to make his plans a reality.

After the way he left his parents' house he wasn't excited about returning so soon and certainly not to ask for money. But it was what he needed. And a lot of it.

He had spent the morning at the library researching everything he could about camels.

He had learned how to work a computer in prison and could maneuver his way on the Internet. He found article after article concerning the benefits of camel's milk in children with ADD and autism and those people who just wanted a natural alternative to cow's milk. Titus wasn't sure exactly why drinking camel's milk was that much different from drinking regular milk, but he did get the impression that since camel's milk could be sold in its raw state, it had no levies against it with the government. It could be bought raw whereas raw cow's milk in most states was illegal.

So the New Age hipster who wanted raw, all organic, etc., found that in camel's milk. He also learned that it was selling for upward of eighty dollars a gallon, which in itself was mind-boggling. He supposed it was because there weren't a great many camel dairy farms in the country, especially when compared to how many traditional ones there were. Even so, one thing became abundantly clear to him. He was going to need money for his bull. And he was going to have to wait almost a year before he could make even the first step toward selling camel's milk, and he was going to have to go organic in order to remain competitive.

He raised his fist and knocked on his father's door. Then he felt ridiculous for standing outside on what was essentially his own front porch and let himself into the house.

"*Mamm? Dat?*" He had borrowed the Kings' buggy to drive over here, strangely enough preferring the slower pace of a horse and carriage over the motor of a tractor. The horse and buggy reminded him to slow down and take everything in. Or maybe he didn't need reminding, it was something that he needed to do. He needed to soak up every minute that he had. That was one thing prison taught him. Time was precious.

Plus, he hadn't driven anything with a motor since that night and the thought of driving a car or even a tractor made his hair stand on end. No, a buggy was much better for him.

"Titus." June came from upstairs, a laundry basket propped on one hip. "What brings you here today? Are you moving back in?"

He shook his head. "Is *Dat* around?"

She inclined her head toward the front door and in the general direction of the yard. "He's out in the barn."

"Thanks." He started for the door.

"Titus." June stopped him before he stepped out into the warm sunshine. He turned to face her. "I'm sorry about the other day."

He nodded, then let himself out the door.

His footsteps grew slower the closer he got to the barn. The last thing he wanted to do was ask his father for money, but starting a camel dairy farm was the first thing that had given him any sense of the future in a long, long time. And he was afraid his father was going to tell him no. Not that Titus could blame him. He had messed up his life. He had gone to jail for five years, then showed back up and refused to follow the family rules. Now he wanted money? It would serve him right if his father laughed in his face. But there was no getting and starting that dream until he asked. So ask he would.

He stepped into the dark interior of the barn, looking from side to side to see if he could find his father. He was nowhere in sight. "*Dat?*" he called. "*Dat!*"

"Why are you hollering?"

Titus whirled around to find his father standing behind him in the doorway of the barn. "I thought you were in here."

His father nodded. "I was." He moved past Titus and toward the tack room, machine pieces in his hand.

That was one thing about his father that Titus always remembered. He loved to tinker with the engines on the tractors and other machines. Titus had a feeling that if his father had not been born Amish, he would've been a mechanic of some sort or another. It was amazing to him how life turned out different from what he had thought.

"You need something?"

Titus followed him into the tack room and watched as he started repairing an engine sitting on the flat-top wooden table there.

"I came to talk to you about a loan."

"This wouldn't have anything to do with those camels you bought from Ezra Hein, would it?"

Shock filled him. Titus had no idea why he was shocked. His father somehow found out about everything that went on in the community. "Yeah, it would."

Dat pulled out a chair and slipped on his magnifying glasses, starting to attach the various pieces back together as he talked. "I thought as much. They don't come cheap."

How did he know that?

"How much do you think you're going to need?"

"The best I can figure, somewhere close to thirty thousand. That's on the high side," he backpedaled.

If his father was surprised at the amount he didn't show it on his face. He held up an engine piece to the light, examining it from all angles before he dropped it back down to the table and screwed something else onto the top of it. "And you want a loan for that amount?"

"I would, yes."

His father slipped his glasses onto the top of his head and turned back to face Titus, looking at him for the first time since he had walked into the barn. "And if I give you this loan how are you going to pay it back?"

"I've got a business deal going on with Abbie King right now."

That did shock his father. His eyebrows rose nearly to his hairline. "Oh?"

"I'm helping her on her farm. She's going to be partners with me in the camel farming. It's going to take us a year at least to get up and running. But I did some research today, and we're going all organic. *Dat*, you wouldn't believe it. This milk sells for unreal amounts. We'll make our money back in the first year if not sooner. That is, the first year that we start selling milk. They both seem to be in good breeding shape. I think he said they were about four years old. I still need to get a bull—I found a good one in Kansas—and another female. I figure three is a good start. And we get those bred and on their way. It takes about twelve months to have a baby. With any luck, we'll be selling milk this time next year."

His own excitement surprised him, but *Dat* merely nodded. "Okay."

Titus felt like shaking his head to make sure his hearing wasn't going. "Yeah?"

Dat smiled. "Yes. I think this would be good for you, Son. You've had a tough go of it, and I think some direction and responsibility would serve you well."

Titus couldn't believe his ears. Sure his *dat* wanted him to have responsibility and direction, but he just couldn't figure out how it was worth thirty thousand dollars to him. "I'll pay you back. You know that, right?"

His *dat* just smiled. "I know you will, Son. I know you will."

* * *

Titus's excitement grew with each mile on the way back to Abbie's house. His *dat* would loan him the money. They were on their way. Now he just had to figure out how to take care of the situation at the Kings' so that everybody would come out on top.

Abbie rushed out onto the porch first thing when he pulled up into the drive.

"Well?" she called across the yard. He barely made it out of the buggy.

"Hi to you too, Abbie. Yes, it is a lovely day. Thanks."

"Titus Lambert, I've been sitting here chewing on my fingernails waiting for you to come home. Now what did he say?"

Titus started to unhook the horse. "He said yes!"

Abbie jumped in the air. "Yippee!"

Titus let the horse back into the pasture and hurried over to join Abbie on the porch. "You didn't talk to your father yet, did you?"

She shook her head. "No, I promised I would wait for you."

He liked that. They were in this together. Partners. Though he was doing his best to ignore the fact that she called her house his home.

"Let's go." Together they walked inside.

Abbie's *mamm* was standing at the stove stirring a big, bubbling pot of what smelled like chicken and dumplings.

The temperature outside was in the low nineties, and it was way too hot for chicken and dumplings. But next to fried chicken, it was his favorite food. And he hadn't had good ones in so long.

His stomach growled in appreciation. He could sit down and eat right now, but they had more important things to do.

"Hey, *Dat*." Abbie snagged her father's attention. "Can you come talk to us for just a bit?"

Her father folded up the paper and set it to one side. "*Jah*," he said, pushing to his feet. Together they walked to the kitchen table and sat down. Abbie's mother cast a quick glance over her shoulder but turned back to the dumplings.

"What's this about?" Emmanuel asked.

"It's about a business partnership," Abbie said.

"I see." He looked from one of them to the other. "What kind of business partnership?"

"Titus, you tell him," she said. "You are better at it than I am."

"Does this have anything to do with those camels?" Emmanuel asked.

"Yes," Titus said. "I read an article when I was in . . . prison." Oh, how he hated that word. But at least these days he could say it out loud without cringing. "It was about how this family was treating their son's autism with camel's milk. It was really interesting, and it stuck with me all this time."

"And then we went to look at the cows and we saw that Ezra Hein had some camels in his pasture." Abbie shifted in her seat and shot Titus a smile. "Go on, you tell it so much better than me."

"That got me to thinking about maybe having dairy camels here. Why not? Camels are resilient, and they can withstand the heat and the cold that we have here. And the milk is selling for an unreal amount."

"Eighty dollars a gallon in some places," Abbie added. "Tell him, Titus."

He was beginning to wonder if she was going to let him get the story out at all. "I went to visit my *dat* today and got everything started. I need a bull and another female. We'll have to breed them and wait the year of gestation. Then after that we'll be able start selling the milk."

"After we get all the inspections and everything, of course," Abbie added. "And we're going to go all organic. Tell him, Titus."

Titus laughed. "I am trying to tell him, Abbie, but you keep jumping in. You want to tell it or do you want me?"

She turned a beautiful shade of rose that clashed horribly with her green dress. "I'm sorry. I'm just excited."

"We both are." Titus turned back to Emmanuel. "The problem comes in with paying my *dat* back in the first year and trying to get this operation up and running. I believe there's a lot of money to be made in camel's milk, but in the meantime we have twenty-five new milk cows out there and a dairy farm to run."

"*Jah*," Emmanuel said. He folded his hands in front of him, and Titus noticed that they were steadier today than they had been in a long time. It seemed that Emmanuel was coming out on the other side of climbing on the wagon. It wouldn't be long before he was completely back to the man he had been before. "So what is your proposition? And what is all this partnership about?"

"You know that my father wants me to get back into good standing with the church, but I'm not ready yet." *I don't know if I'll ever be.* "That means I need a place to stay. So I propose that I keep my camels here, and help you with your farm. We get my business started and when it's up and running, then you will be my partner in that as well."

Abbie bounced in her seat. "Say yes, *Dat.* Please."

Emmanuel turned to study his daughter. Titus wondered what the man saw when he looked at her. A lot of different things than his own thoughts, he was sure.

Titus saw an incredible woman who was doing everything to fight for her family. A beautiful soul who managed to love throughout tragedy and a hard worker who would stop at practically nothing to find success. He couldn't have asked for more than that in a partner.

Business partner. That was all she would be, his business partner.

"Does this mean you're going to stay?" Emmanuel asked.

"I'm quite comfortable there in the barn," Titus said.

Priscilla turned from the stove. "Titus Lambert, you cannot go on sleeping in the barn."

"I'm fine, really."

Emmanuel shook his head. "I didn't mean here at the house. I meant in Wells Landing. Does this partnership mean you're going to stay here for a while?"

Of course that was what he meant. How could Titus leave Wells Landing and maintain his half of the partnership? Then he realized what Emmanuel was really asking. "I don't know when I'm rejoining the church." Or if. He managed to leave that last part unsaid. But he knew Abbie could hear it in his words.

It was so easy for everyone else to tell him what he needed to do and how he needed to do it. It was easy for the baptized to tell him that he needed to be reinstated. But he was still trying to piece together all the shards of who he was before and somehow make them into who he was now. Once he became a complete person, he hoped his thoughts would be clear. The past would be righted, and he would know what he was supposed to do.

And for all their talk about God's will, he still hadn't figured out how God's will fit into anything. How was he supposed to kneel and confess his sins until he knew these things for himself?

That was one thing that most people forgot. Too many people were leaving the Amish faith these days, and he'd heard the bishops in other places were concerned about the dwindling members. Even the baptized members decided that they might not be able to live the Amish life any longer. That was why Bishop Ebersol had cut him a break and hadn't demanded that he rejoin the church as soon as possible. He just wanted Titus to know that he was welcome. As hard as it was for Titus to take, he had been accepted back into the community. That didn't mean he could rejoin the church. Not yet anyway. Maybe not ever.

"That's fair enough," Emmanuel said.

Titus studied the man's expression, trying to figure out if there was any hidden meaning behind his words. With all the pressure he seemed to be getting from all other sides of the confess-now camp, he was surprised that Emmanuel seemed unconcerned with his life decision. But what was that thing about looking a gift horse in the mouth?

"Everyone ready to eat?"

Titus's stomach rumbled in response.

"I'll take that as a yes," Priscilla said. Everyone laughed, then went to wash their hands for supper.

Titus and Abbie walked into Kauffman's Family Restaurant late the next afternoon. They had just enough time for a slice of pie and maybe a cup of coffee before they headed to the farm for the afternoon milking.

"Hey," Sadie Kauffman greeted as they approached the counter. "It's good to see you both." *Together* remained unsaid. Though Abbie heard it all the same. "Booth for two?" Sadie asked.

"Yes, please," Titus answered.

"Follow me."

Abbie jumped as he placed his hand at the small of her back, guiding her in the direction Sadie walked. Abbie knew that they were taking a big risk eating together in public, but how could she ever convince Titus that he belonged in Wells Landing if everyone turned their back on him? She knew that wasn't the reason they were avoiding him, but the result would still be the same.

"Do you want to see a full menu?"

Abbie shook her head. "Just the pie list."

Sadie slapped one on top of their menus. "A word to the wise," Sadie said, "Cora Ann has been experimenting with anise and cinnamon."

Titus chuckled. "Thanks for the warning."

Sadie smiled. "Anytime." She headed back toward the waitress station.

"It's strange seeing her dress that way," Titus said. Abbie turned to look at her. It was strange to see her in what looked to be very conservative *Englisch* clothes. She had on a black skirt that almost reached the floor and a short-sleeved sweater with a modest neckline. Only the tiny white prayer covering pinned over her bob was an indication that she was anything more than an *Englisch* girl who was concerned about modesty.

"It is," Abbie agreed. "But she seems happy enough." She turned back to Titus. "I guess that's what love will do for you."

"Yeah," Titus murmured. But his thoughts seemed to have shifted from Sadie and her newfound love to something else. He picked up the pie list and started reading it silently.

Abbie did the same. She ran through the entire menu twice, then looked up. "I'm thinking chocolate chess pie. What about you?"

He gave a nod. "That should be safe from cinnamon and anise. I think I'll go with coconut cream."

As if by magic, Sadie reappeared. "Are you ready?"

They gave her their order for pie and coffee, and she scooted away to get it.

"Is this really going to work?" she asked.

His gaze jerked to hers. "What are you talking about?" The look on his face was almost laughable. He seemed even a bit panicked.

"This camel farm. Are we doing something absolutely crazy?"

"So what if it is? Other people have made a go of it and done just fine. I don't know why we shouldn't too."

She studied him for a minute. Is that what this was all about? Taking a chance and feeling alive again? The thought of his using this experiment to make himself feel a part of something again was about as dangerous as a propane tank and an open fire.

"Why shouldn't we do this?" Titus asked.

"But is this what you want?"

He acted like it was. Even said that it was. And as much as Abbie wanted to believe him, she had a niggling doubt that this was just part of his integrating back into Wells Landing. Her family needed this, and they needed him to be committed to it if they were going to commit to it. So why did she have these doubts?

"Of course I want this. I started it, didn't I?" He picked up one of the napkins Sadie had left on their table and started to fold it like a fan.

Abbie tilted her head to the side trying to get a better angle and perhaps to see him in a different light. Or maybe just to see some of the things that he hadn't shown everyone else. "Are you going to rejoin the church, Titus?"

He stopped folding the napkin and sat back in the

booth's bench seat. "Why is everybody so concerned about when I'm going to rejoin the church? Why is the whole community dependent on my decision? Is my coming back going to tear the whole district apart if I don't rejoin the church?"

Abbie drew back at his harsh tone. "Many people are worried about you."

Titus's rigid posture crumpled like an onion skin in a tornado. "I'm sorry," he started, but he stopped as Sadie brought over their coffee and slices of pie.

She slid them expertly in front of each one of them then tucked the tray under her arm. "You need anything else?"

"No, thank you," Titus said.

"I'll be back to check on you in a little bit." Sadie turned to leave, and Abbie was left alone with Titus once more. Well, as alone as they could be in Kauffman's Family Restaurant.

"I guess I'm sort of touchy," Titus said.

"Why?" Abbie asked. "No one is expecting any more from you than you can give. Except for maybe your *dat* and your *mamm* and your family." She smiled. "But the rest of us are perfectly happy just to have you back."

"I seem to remember not so very long ago someone who wasn't so ecstatic that I had come back to town."

She could feel the heat rising from under her dress, up, up, up, until it filled her whole face. "I'm sorry about that. I was just—"

"Hurt? Devastated? Bitter?"

"I'm Amish, Titus. Not perfect."

He looked up at her, his brown eyes so serious. "I know that."

They sat that way for a moment, gazes locked as they each weighed in on this new level of their relationship.

The moment was broken as Titus picked up his fork

and cut off a bite of his coconut cream pie. He chewed once, twice, then stopped.

"What's wrong?"

He swallowed, then licked the corner of his mouth where a dab of meringue clung. "What does anise taste like?"

"It's like licorice almost."

"I'm not sure about it with coconut."

"Cora Ann put anise in the coconut cream pie?"

"I don't know," Titus said. He forked off another bite and held it up to her. "You try it."

Abbie looked from the bite on his fork to him, then back to the bite again. Surely, it wouldn't be too bad if they allowed her to serve it in the restaurant. Reluctantly she leaned forward and opened her mouth for the bite of pie.

It was rich and creamy, sweet and light, everything that coconut cream pie should be. But she didn't taste anything out of the ordinary. "It tastes fine to me. Are you sure you tasted anise?"

Titus laughed. "No, I was just teasing."

"Titus Lambert, you are bad."

He grinned and took another bite of his pie. "Some people say that I'm good."

Abbie laughed and cut off a little sliver of her own pie. Chocolate chess was one of her all-time favorite pies. With buttermilk being a quick second and pecan in third place year-round but at the top of the list come November. But this time was different. It tasted like . . . not anise.

"Here." She forked up a bite and held it out for Titus to taste. "You try it."

He looked skeptically at it, then back to his own pie. "I'm good."

"You try this. I tried yours."

"There wasn't anything wrong with mine."

Abbie shot him a look. "There's nothing wrong with this, either. Just taste it and see what you think."

He looked like he was about to refuse again right up until the time that he actually took the bite.

"Is that cinnamon?"

Abbie took another bite and let it wallow around in her mouth to get a better sense of its taste. "I think it is."

"It's good." Titus pulled her saucer a little closer to him to get another bite of her chocolate chess pie spiked with cinnamon.

"You have your own pie." Abbie pulled it back, but not before he got a sizable chunk.

"Hi."

They had been playing and not paying attention to the world around them. So much so that Mandy Burkholder had walked up without either of them noticing until she spoke.

Abbie stopped trying to get her pie saucer back from Titus and politely greeted her friend.

"So, how are you doing, Titus?" Mandy asked.

Abbie studied Mandy as she talked. She looked terrible. She hated to say that about anyone, but Mandy looked like she hadn't slept in days. Dark circles underlined each eye with purple smudges that made her appear almost bruised. Her clothes hung off her shoulders as if she hadn't eaten anything decent in a long time—even though she was sitting in a restaurant.

She glanced behind Mandy. Sarah Yoder and Hannah Glick were sitting at a place across the way.

They must have come in to have an afternoon slice of pie like she and Titus had.

"I'm good," Titus said. "Are you okay?"

If a man could tell that she didn't feel good or didn't

look good, then Abbie was certain everyone could see
that Mandy was clearly suffering.

"I'm fine, *jah*."

Maybe she was pregnant. That would account for the
sleepless nights and weight loss. Not everyone gained a
ton of weight especially in the first months of pregnancy.
She had heard family members and friends talk about
such things. That would surely explain the wounded
look about her. But what would account for that sadness in her eyes? Her green eyes normally sparkled like
jewels with an almost impish light. Now they appeared
old and beyond sad. Closer to . . . depressed.

Abbie hardly listened as Titus and Mandy talked for
a minute.

Mandy was depressed.

What would she have to be depressed about? Unless
those marks under her eyes were really bruises.

No, her pregnancy theory was a little more feasible.
Abbie had known Levi Burkholder for as long as she
had known Mandy and Titus. He was kind and gentle.
And though it was possible, it just didn't seem probable
that he would raise a hand to his wife.

She pulled herself out of her own thoughts and focused her attention on her two companions.

"Can I come out and see them?" Mandy asked.

"Of course," Titus replied. But his eyes told another
story. Abbie could see that he didn't want to tell her it
was okay. But what was he supposed to say?

Mandy's face brightened with a smile that seemed
both frail and hopeful. "That would be fantastic."

"Mandy," Sarah called from across the restaurant.
"Your fries are getting cold."

Mandy turned back around, still smiling at Titus. "I'll
see you next week, then?"

"Next week would be great."

Abbie watched her go, then turned back to Titus. "Something's wrong."

He shrugged and took a sip of his coffee. He looked out the plate-glass window at someone as they passed by on the sidewalk. She knew stalling tactics when she saw them.

"You know something."

"I don't know anything." He turned around, his gaze settling on her. It was serious and steady, but if he thought he was convincing her that he was telling the truth, he was wrong, wrong, wrong.

"Is she pregnant?" Abbie asked.

Titus scoffed. "How would I know that?"

"I don't know, but it seems like you know something." She allowed her gaze to roam over his face, looking for any cracks in his expression, anything that might tell her why both he and Mandy were acting so strangely.

Aside from the fact that he and Mandy had been engaged until he went to prison, and she married another man two years later. That had to be awkward the first couple of times they met up again. But it didn't seem as if Titus was mending a broken heart. No, that wasn't it. "Is Levi mean to her?"

Titus's scoffing intensified. "Would you listen to yourself? This is Levi Burkholder we're talking about."

Abbie sat back in her seat. "Right." Levi Burkholder was a fantastic man. Even if he had taken advantage of the situation, stealing Mandy away from Titus, he was a gentle and caring person. "So what's wrong with her?"

"Maybe she's having a hard time with me being back in town." Titus sighed.

"Really? I mean, she's married." She had moved on long before Titus had so why would she be upset if he'd been back in town unless . . . "She's still in love with you."

Titus reached for his wallet. "You think she is."

"And you don't think she is?"

He fished out a ten and some ones and placed them on the table. "I think she's confused."

"I suppose." But this put a whole new spin on things.

"Are you ready to go? We need to get home and do the milking."

As much as she wanted to continue their conversation, Titus was right. They had cows to milk. "*Jah.*" She grabbed her purse and stood as Titus caught Sadie's attention. He indicated the money he had left on the table.

Sadie nodded. "Thanks for coming in," she called.

Titus waved, then held open the door for Abbie.

"We still need to talk about all the things we found out at the library."

"We can talk about them when we get home," Titus said.

Abbie nodded and stepped through the doorway onto the sidewalk. The entire time she could feel someone's gaze burning through her. And she had no doubt whom it belonged to.

Chapter Twelve

Two days later the cows came to the farm in a large trailer pulled by an equally large truck. Only the kiss that she had shared with Titus gave her more of a thrill than looking out into the pasture and seeing all the new stock there.

But the camels were something different altogether. They arrived in an open trailer, their backs swaying above the red-painted slats.

She had seen them on Ezra's farm, but she had forgotten how large they were. She had been so excited about the cows that she supposed her thoughts had been taken up with that instead of Titus's camels.

"They're bigger than I remember." And sweeter.

One big cinnamon-colored creature lumbered out of the trailer, looking around as if she hadn't a care in the world. She batted her long lashes, chewed a piece of cud, and allowed Titus to lead her into the small corral that Abbie and Titus had created for them. They would need more pasture space and soon, but this would do for now.

One by one Titus led them into the pasture while Abbie watched in awe. They were really going to do this.

Titus paid the driver, and the man left.

"This just happened, right?" she asked.

"Of course. Why?"

"I can't believe we're going to be partners."

He smiled. "Is that a good thing or a bad one?"

"Definitely good."

His grin widened. "I think so too."

She glanced over to where the camels were moving around, learning their new space. She frowned.

"What's wrong?" he asked.

"Are you really going to milk them?"

"Yep. And you're going to help me."

Abbie shook her head. "Partners or not, I am not milking camels."

"What would you do if you thought you made a really big mistake?" Mandy asked the question as nonchalantly as she could, not once taking her eyes off the bowl of purple hull peas she was shelling. She and her cousins Sarah and Libby were sitting on the porch whiling away the afternoon as they shelled the peas.

"I suppose you should talk to the bishop," Libby said.

Sarah nodded. "Or confess in front of the church."

"It's not that kind of mistake," she said.

"Then I suppose you should go to the person you feel you wronged and apologize to them," Libby said.

"No, it's bigger than that. Bigger than confessing at the church. Bigger than it all. The biggest mistake ever." She felt a little like she might be overreacting, but she couldn't help it. The longer she stayed married to Levi the more she doubted the choice she had made. And the worst part of it all was he hadn't done anything wrong. He was kind and loving and caring.

The only crime he had committed was that he wasn't Titus Lambert.

"Stop talking in riddles. What have you done?" Libby asked.

"I—I—" She shook her head, unable to finish. How could she tell them her deepest darkest secret? She hadn't told anyone how she felt and to say the words aloud . . . It was almost more than she could stand.

"Does this have anything to do with Titus Lambert coming back to town?" Sarah looked up and pinned her with her gaze.

Mandy swallowed hard but was unable to go through with the lies she needed to tell. "Yes."

"What?" Libby screeched. "What do you mean it has something to do with Titus?"

Mandy shook her head. "No, no, no, no, no. It's just that I've been thinking lately that perhaps I should never have married Levi." There, she said it. And once it was out, it didn't seem like the monster that it had been inside her head. Still, the words were big and heavy and cumbersome to carry around with her all the time.

"News flash," Sarah said. "We're Amish. And we get married for life. That's just how that works."

Relief forgotten, Mandy dropped her head in her hands as the sobs bubbled up inside her. "I know. I know, and I don't know what to do."

Soothing hands reached for her. "It'll be okay," Libby said.

"No," Mandy cried. "It won't ever be okay. It will never be okay again. I made a huge mistake when I married Levi. I still love Titus, I've never stopped loving Titus."

"Then why did you marry Levi?" Sarah asked.

"I felt like I had to do something. I didn't know

when Titus was coming back. Then Levi convinced me that Titus wouldn't be the same person he was when he left."

"I'm sure he's not," Libby said. "Have you talked to him lately?"

"I talk to him every chance I get. I guess some parts of him have changed, but deep down he's the same Titus. And every day that I'm away from him my heart breaks even more. It was bad enough when he was in jail, but now that he's here I just can't stand it."

"How does he feel about this?" Sarah asked.

Mandy sniffed. "He says that it's over, but he's lying to protect me. I can see it in his eyes. He still loves me."

Libby grabbed Mandy's hands into her own. She squeezed her fingers tight. "Now listen to me, Mandy. We all make mistakes, every one of us. Some are bigger than others, but we are Amish and you will not be allowed to get a divorce and remain in this community. You know that."

"I know." Mandy sobbed.

"Then you need to get over this infatuation or whatever you would like to call these feelings you have for Titus and work on your marriage. You need to make it work. Otherwise the two of you will have to leave everything behind. You'll have to go live in the *Englisch* world. And I don't think you're prepared for that."

Mandy hiccupped on a sob and managed to pull herself together.

"Well, I say if you love him, you should do everything in your power to make him love you back," Sarah said.

"Look who's talking," Libby returned. Everyone in town knew that Sarah was in love with Jonah Miller. But Jonah had been in love with Lorie Kauffman. Right up until the time she left with the *Englisch* boy Zach Calhoun. Yet even with Lorie out of the picture, Jonah still didn't seem interested in Sarah. It was as heartbreaking as it was ironic.

Sarah looked hurt only for a moment, before she pushed the expression from her face. "There's no need to be mean. I'm just saying that if it's true love, you shouldn't let it slip through your fingers. Not for anything."

Not for anything.

"Do you really think so?" Mandy asked Sarah.

Libby squeezed her fingers once more. "Don't listen to her. You have more than true love at stake here." She tugged on Mandy's hands until Mandy turned her attention back to Libby. "This is about God, the church, about your entire life. You can't throw away everything for a boy."

"He's more than a boy." This was Titus Lambert. These two girls knew above anyone else how much Titus meant to her. She had been heartbroken, devastated, when he had gone to prison. She had vowed to wait for him and yet she hadn't. She'd broken her own promises. Didn't that count for something too?

"I don't like that look on your face, Mandy," Libby said.

Mandy pulled herself from her thoughts. "I made a mistake," Mandy said. "Should I have to live with that for the rest of my life?"

And what about Levi? She might not love him with the same intensity that she felt for Titus, but he was a good man, and he had been good to her. Didn't he deserve better than a wife who loved another?

Sarah set her bowl of peas aside and looked at each of them in turn. "One day, what is supposed to happen will happen. You have to believe that if you believe God has a plan for us all."

Mandy shook her head. How could she decipher all

of this into bite-size chunks? She had no idea. But the whole thing seemed bigger than all of them put together.

"I just want to do what's right," she said, her tears starting anew even though her sobs had softened a bit. The main thing was she had to figure out what to do, and she had to do it soon before the whole situation drove her over the edge.

Abbie looked down the row of cows in the milking barn as a sense of pride filled her. She had done this. She and Titus. Now they just had to get the cows milked and the milk into the vat so the money would start coming in.

Her new cows were already dairy cows with good milking histories. She knew they would pay for themselves in no time at all. But the thing was she had to get them all milked.

Titus had gone to Kansas early that morning to check on a couple of camels. She couldn't be upset that he hadn't made it back in time for the evening milking. They had a partnership, but there would be times when one or the other of them had to miss chores.

If it took her two hours to milk the cows when there was twenty-five, then it would take her close to four hours to get fifty of them milked. She should've gotten an earlier start, but as usual on the farm there was too much to do and not enough time to do it.

She and her *mamm* had gone out to the garden and weeded through what needed to be cleaned. They picked what was ripe and took them inside. They had enough tomatoes to can a batch, but that would have to wait until tomorrow. She looked down the row of cows again and this time her pride was mixed with dread.

"Are you going to milk those cows or not?"

She whirled around. Titus stood in the doorway of the barn. She lifted her chin. "Titus! What are you doing back?"

"We made good time is all."

"Did you buy us a bull?"

He grinned. "He'll be delivered in a couple of days. So are you going to milk or what?"

"Not by myself. I mean, you're here now."

"Does that mean you want me to help?" he playfully asked.

Abbie smiled. "Are you offering?"

"Maybe."

"And what do I need to do to convince you to help?"

Titus tapped his chin thoughtfully. "Let's see . . . If I spend two hours of my time helping you milk the cows, then I think I should get two hours of your time back for something that I want to do."

Abbie shook her head. "Oh no, I am not helping you milk those beasts. They are huge and scary and—"

Titus started laughing. "First of all, we're not ready to milk them and secondly, they're not that much bigger than the cows. And the fact that they are taller than the cows makes them a lot easier to milk than these old girls."

"I'm still not doing it."

"What if I said this isn't about milking camels?"

"Then why do you need two hours of my time?"

Even in the dim light of the barn she could see the spark in his brown eyes. "I don't know. Maybe a picnic?"

A picnic? Her heart gave a hard thump. A picnic was an awful lot like a date. Is that what he was doing? Asking her to go on a date with him?

Don't read too much into this.

But even as the practical side warned against getting her hopes up, she wanted to go.

"How long has it been since you've done something fun, Abbie?"

"Since I left Missouri."

"Then I say you're long overdue."

How could she say no to that?

She stuck out her hand to shake. "You've got yourself a deal. But you're cleaning their udders."

She shouldn't have been nervous, but she was.

It's not really a date.

This was just all part of Titus's efforts to ease his own guilt for the part he played in Alvin's death. She just had to be certain that she didn't read more into it than was there. But it had been so long since anyone had paid any attention to her. It had been so long since she'd been on a date or even had thoughts about going on a date.

It's not really a date.

"Are you ready to go?"

"*Jah.*" Was that her voice, all crackly on the end like she had some kind of cold? She cleared her throat. "*Jah.*"

"Let's go." He waited for her to get into the buggy and climbed in beside her. That was something about buggies—you couldn't sit right next to anyone without bumping into them unless they were the size of a five-year-old. Abbie both dreaded and relished each bump in the road that pushed her a little closer to Titus.

She loved riding in a buggy, though most people traveled through the week on a tractor. It was hard for two people to go too far in a buggy. Plus, her *dat* had the tractor in the field right now. And though she hated to admit it, she enjoyed riding next to Titus. "Where are we going?"

"It's a surprise."

She nodded. "Millers' Pond?"

He shot her a look. "You sure do know how to deflate the moment."

She laughed. "There's not a whole lot of places to go around here that we can reach by buggy and have a picnic."

"Sure there are. We can have a picnic anywhere we want."

"You can't. Most of this land here is private property. People will chase you off."

He shook his head. "Not in Wells Landing, they won't. You and I both know that. It's one of the greatest things about this place."

"And you're still thinking about leaving it?"

He considered. "I don't know. And I don't want to talk about it today. We're supposed to be out having fun, not contemplating life decisions."

But that was the thing. With the Amish, dating was a life decision. People didn't date willy-nilly. Most people dated one person, maybe two, and then got married. She and Titus were some of the exceptions. Titus had gone to jail, and she had gone to Missouri.

"Okay then. What can we talk about?"

He thought about it a second. "Puppies."

She laughed. "Puppies?"

He shrugged. "It seems like a safe enough subject to me."

"Okay then, let's talk about puppies."

He hit a bump, and she brushed against him once again, both hating and loving the thrill of it. She straightened and cast a sidelong glance at him. "Did you do that on purpose?"

"What are you talking about?" But the light in his eyes belied his innocence.

"You did that on purpose so that I would bump into you."

"Why, Abbie King. That sounds suspiciously like an accusation."

She shot him a look. "It was an accusation. What's gotten into you today?"

He grinned. "I don't know. Just kind of excited about the deal with the camels. Aren't you excited about your cows?"

"As much as I hate to admit it, yes. I'm excited about my cows."

"Why wouldn't you want to admit something like that?"

"I don't know. It sounds sort of sad, doesn't it? I mean, I'm twenty-three years old and the highlight of my year is getting new milk cows."

"There are worse things."

She grew silent as he said the words. There was a lot worse out there. "Thank you."

"For what?" he asked.

"For helping me get the cows that have been the highlight of my year."

He smiled. "You're welcome."

They rode in silence for a bit, then Titus turned down a side road.

"This isn't the way to Millers' Pond." She sat a little straighter in her seat and looked out the window.

"Hmmm, I must be mistaken. Let's see where this takes us, *jah?*"

His grin was infectious. What could she do but agree? And she wanted to. She wanted this afternoon with him more than she had wanted anything in a long time.

Well, with the exception of one more kiss and she wasn't making that mistake again.

Abbie looked around trying to decide where they might be headed.

"Quit trying to figure it out. You're going to ruin the surprise."

"So this is still a surprise?"

"It will be if you don't ruin it."

She folded her hands primly in her lap. "Fine. I am now on my best behavior."

A few minutes passed before Titus turned again.

"This is where Merv King lives."

"Any relation?"

She shook her head. "I don't think so. Is that where we're going?"

"You'll see."

But they drove past Merv's mailbox without stopping. On the far side of his house stood a crop of trees. Titus slowed the buggy, then pulled onto a dirt road she had never noticed before.

"Has this always been here?" She turned in her seat to get a better look as he got out of the buggy and unhooked the gate.

"As long I can remember. Drive through for me, okay?"

She did as he asked. Titus shut the gate behind them and got back into the carriage.

Abbie twisted her head to look up at the sky and the towering trees. "I don't remember seeing this before."

Titus chuckled. "It's amazing what you don't notice when you live someplace your entire life."

"You've always lived here. How did you know it was here?"

"We used to come down here when we wanted to be alone."

"You and Mandy?" The words were choked as they left her lips. She didn't want to think about him and Mandy. She only wanted to think about right now. But how long could that last?

"Me, Alvin, and Eli."

"He never told me about any of that."

Titus grinned. "Maybe your brother didn't tell you everything."

"Maybe not."

Titus pulled the buggy to one side and set the brake. "We'll have to walk the rest of the way." He slipped from the carriage and tethered the horse to a nearby pine tree.

"Is it much farther?" she asked as she climbed down to stand next to him.

He reached into the back of the buggy and pulled out a to-go sack from Kauffman's.

"I thought I smelled something yummy."

He smiled. "One of the things I missed the most."

"Fried chicken?" she asked.

He started toward the almost-concealed path among the trees. "Is that just a wild guess or did you remember that was my favorite?"

Abbie picked her way cautiously next to him. "If I tell you that I remembered, does that get me an extra piece?"

"If you tell me that, you can have anything you want."

Her heart tripped over itself and her feet tried to follow. She managed to catch her fall before she embarrassed herself.

"Are you okay?"

"Y-yes," she stammered.

They started going downhill.

"Watch your step."

She had to turn sideways to keep her footing.

"Be careful," he cautioned. "I promise. It's going to be worth it."

In no time at all they were at the bottom. The ground leveled off and a strange noise met her ears.

"Are we close to a highway?"

"How far do you think we've walked?" He chuckled.

"I don't know." It sure sounded like the roar of tires on asphalt to her. "If it's not a road, then what is it?" As they walked, the sound grew louder.

"Come this way, and I'll show you." He held two saplings aside so she could enter another cluster of vegetation. She really couldn't call them trees. It was more tall weeds and bramble. Still, she could see that the area they were entering was filled with trees a little farther in.

She ducked through the growth. It was darker due to the canopy of vines that grew overhead. And it was cool, like a fresh spring day.

"Almost there," he said, once again taking the lead.

He wound them through the underbrush as the roar grew louder. He led her down another small incline, this one covered with moss. At the bottom was a beautiful waterfall.

"Oh, my goodness," she exclaimed.

The fall of water was no more than four feet across. It ran over a fallen log before crashing down into a small pool below. One end of the pool narrowed until the whole thing became a crystal-clear stream. Mossy banks, green ferns, and large stones rounded out the perfect alcove.

"You like it?"

"It's beautiful," she breathed. "Why would you ever go to Millers' Pond if you could come here?"

He shrugged. "Have you ever done something special every day?"

"No, if I did, it wouldn't be so special any longer."

He snapped his fingers. "Exactly."

She wandered a little closer to the water's edge. "So you didn't come here that often to keep it special?"

"Yeah."

And he had never brought Mandy here. Abbie wondered if he'd ever brought a girl here at all. But she wasn't about to ask. She kicked off her shoes and stood on the moss with her bare toes cushioned against the softness. Then she turned back to Titus. "Thank you for bringing me here."

"Thanks for coming with me."

He couldn't take his eyes off her. She was the prettiest thing standing there with the waterfall behind her and green all around. An earth angel. That was what she looked like. An angel who had fallen from heaven and landed here just for him.

Except she wasn't his and most likely she never would be. That still didn't keep him from wanting to spend time with her.

"Are you hungry?" Food was a safe enough subject. At least for now.

Abbie nodded. "We should have brought a quilt."

Titus moved close to her on the bank of the small pond and plopped down on the moss. "You don't need a blanket around here."

She shrugged and dropped down next to him. It was true. The ground was soft, the moss cushioning everything on it. She wiggled herself into a comfortable position as Titus started to unload their sack.

There was nothing like Kauffman's fried chicken. It had to be the best he'd ever tasted. And he had missed it on the inside. They had fried chicken from time to time, sometimes twice a month. But it wasn't like this. He inhaled deeply. Not at all.

"Are you going to sit there smelling it or can we eat?"

Titus handed over the paper container of chicken. "That's mighty sassy talk for a girl who's afraid to milk a camel."

"You're not going to start on that again, are you?"

He pulled out a container of coleslaw and one of mashed potatoes. That was another thing that no one did like Kauffman's. Their potatoes were the best.

He fished out the container of gravy before answering. "Maybe."

"Well, don't." Her sweet smile took the sting from her words.

"You need a plate and fork?" He pulled out the paper plates and the plastic forks and placed them between them on the ground. Abbie picked at a piece of chicken and waited for him to get his potatoes. He passed her the container, then scooped out a helping of coleslaw.

Once they had their plates full, Titus bowed his head and Abbie followed suit. He knew praying was expected before they ate, but he still had no words for God. He waited what he hoped was an appropriate amount of time, then lifted his head.

"We are partners, right?" he asked. Somehow when he said that word it sounded much more intimate than people who shared a common goal involving camels and cows. But there it was all the same. He cleared his throat.

"We are."

"Good," he said, brandishing a perfectly golden chicken leg. "Because I was reading on-line at the library the other day and you have ninety seconds once you start milking a camel to get the milk. That means two people have to milk the same camel at the same time."

He didn't even finish before she started shaking her head. "No. Way."

"We can't hire someone just for this. It'll take too much out of our profits."

"Then you can just learn how to handle the camels yourself." She leaned in a bit closer. "They scare me."

"You're afraid of them? They are as gentle as lambs."

"Really big lambs." She shook her head. "I heard they spit."

"That's not true. They don't spit. They're gentle animals. And aside from having to milk them really fast, there's not much you should have to do except take in the profits."

She tilted her head to one side. "It seems like you did a lot of research."

He took a big bite of chicken and nodded as he chewed. Best chicken ever. "They're very interesting creatures."

"Good. They really scare me." She took a big drink of the tea he'd brought them to drink, then her eyes grew wide. "What about the milking machines? Why couldn't we milk them with the milking machines?"

"I thought about that, but I can't find anything about it on-line. I think camel farmers like to milk by hand."

"What difference does it make as long as you have the milk?"

"Good point. It's just a lot of these farms that I was looking at sell directly to the customer. All their websites deal with organic foods, the foodstuffs that they feed the camels, things done by hand, just stuff like that. These things are all a big deal when it comes to camel's milk."

He could see it in her eyes. It was bad enough to think about milking camels with the milk machines, but to do it by hand was almost more than she looked like she could stand.

"I don't know, Titus."

"What's there not to know about?"

"You don't find them the least bit scary?"

He took a bite of his corn bread then shook his head. "Not the least bit. Especially not the ones we have now. They were hand raised, as they say. They have been living with humans for a long time. Probably their whole life. They're used to getting human attention. They like treats and rubs and things like that. Kind of like a horse." He was right proud of himself for coming up with that analogy.

Abbie frowned at him. "Maybe," she said. "But I'm not going to try to milk a horse."

He acted as if he were considering the idea.

She playfully smacked him on the arm. "Would you be serious?"

"I am being serious." And suddenly those words were true. How had she gotten so close to him? They hadn't been sitting near each other when they first sat down. Now she seemed to be so close he could lean in and kiss her with hardly any effort at all. Well, no effort to get there but after that . . .

He leaned in a bit closer. He wanted to kiss her so bad he could almost feel her lips under his. What was the harm in one little kiss? He shouldn't do this. He was only trifling with her feelings, playing with her with no real intentions of seeing a relationship through. He had too much to deal with to add a girlfriend to his list. And that was what she was. Girlfriend material. A wife in the making. And he wasn't sure how long he would be around.

He straightened. "Abbie, I—" But he wasn't sure what to say after that.

She gave him a small smile and though it shone in her eyes, there was still something a bit insincere about it. "Oh, Titus. You think too much." She grabbed her tea and took another long sip while he sat there trying to figure out what had happened.

He had almost kissed her, thought better of it, and now she was chastising him for thinking too much. He wasn't sure how that made sense.

"Too bad we didn't think to bring our swimsuits," Abbie said, gazing toward the waterfall.

"I thought that might be a little risqué, swimming out here with no one else around." Actually, it sounded like a fine idea, and he wished now he had rethought his chivalrous attitude.

"I guess you're right." She finished her meal, and together they gathered up the trash and placed it back into the brown paper sack.

"Now what?" she asked.

"Cloud watching."

The look on her face was nothing if not skeptical, but without a word she turned around and lay back on the mossy bank. She folded her arms behind her head to keep from smashing the back of her prayer *kapp*.

Titus lay down next to her and watched the clouds float past overhead. "See anything?" he asked.

"What exactly are we looking for?"

He turned his head in her direction. "Has it been so long that you don't even know how to cloud watch?"

She turned her head to look at him. "And you haven't?" The moment started to grow intense so he turned back to stare at the sky. "No. I used to dream about doing stuff like this every day on the inside." It was getting easier to talk about his time in prison. Not that he could share all of the experiences with anyone, not even Abbie. But as each day passed it became more like a dream he had a long time ago instead of his recent nightmare.

"Are you happy to be home, Titus?"

Home? He was happy to be out and free once again, but whether or not he was home was still up for debate. "Yeah," he finally said. It was better to say that and act like it was home rather than to have to explain how he felt.

"You really staying?" she asked.

He wished he knew the answer to that. "I did go into a business partnership with you."

"And my *dat.*"

"That's all I have, Abbie."

"You could turn *Englisch* and still be in partnership with me. Things like that might be allowed."

Or maybe not since he had already joined the church and would be placed under the *Bann.* "It's all I have, Abbie."

She grew quiet for a second, then pointed to the sky. "Right there. Doesn't that cloud look like a hippopotamus?"

Titus could see a change in subject when it was handed to him. "I don't think so. It looks like a freight train to me."

"A freight train? I think you should have your eyes checked. That is clearly a hippopotamus."

He chuckled and searched for other things in the clouds. It sure beat trying to figure out what to do and whether or not he was home.

The sound of a tractor pulling into the drive brought Titus's attention from the book he was reading on camel breeding.

The Kings had gone to the grocery store, and he had

opted to stay at home and read while he waited for a package delivery. A few days ago Emmanuel had ordered new seals for the milk vats. They were expected to arrive today. But not Mandy.

"Mandy? What are you doing here?"

"I was hoping to talk to you. Alone."

He marked his place in the book, a little unnerved by the tone of her voice. He hadn't noticed the other day until Abbie pointed it out to him, but Mandy looked terrible. She looked unhappy, miserable even. And more than her eyes held a bruised look. Her whole demeanor seemed to be beaten.

If that was the case, then he definitely wanted to hear what she had to say. Why would she come out here to tell him that? It didn't make sense. "Is everything okay at home?" he asked her.

She jerked her attention from her hands to his face.

"Oh, Titus." Her voice wavered on the tears that were about to fall.

He stood from his place on the porch and loped down the stairs to pull her into his embrace. He didn't know what had happened, but she needed comfort.

They had known each other for so long. How could he not offer that to her? But then as quickly as he hugged her, he let her go. It was so easy for him to forget that she was another man's wife. When he left town she'd been his, and he just hadn't gotten used to the idea that it was no longer true.

"I'm sorry." She dabbed her eyes with the hem of her apron. "I don't know what's gotten into me lately."

He didn't know how to ask. How did a person go about asking if her husband had hit her? The best way was probably to just dive right in and ask. "Mandy, does Levi hit you?"

She'd been staring off into the pasture, most likely

searching for the camels that he recently put there. Everyone seemed to be a little bit curious about the camels. He wasn't sure why; it wasn't like they'd come from India or anything. They came from Taylor Creek.

"What?" Her tears dried in an instant and a bark of laughter escaped her. "Levi wouldn't hurt a fly."

He didn't doubt her words one bit. But he had to ask. "I'm sorry I felt I had to ask that, but we've just been worried about you."

"We?"

He nodded. "Me and Abbie."

Her laughter turned to tears, and he wondered if she was about to have a breakdown. She seemed so fragile. But he couldn't take her close and try to comfort her. That was not allowed.

"Oh, Titus. I don't know what to do."

"Come." He motioned for her to go up onto the porch and sit on the bench there. Once they were settled, he took her hand into his, then promptly dropped it back into her lap.

"I can't stop thinking about you." She wilted with the confession, as if she'd been carrying the burden around for far too long.

"Oh, Mandy." Titus pushed to his feet and walked to the far end of the porch. From where he stood he could just about see the female camel he hoped to build the entire program around; from everything he'd read, she was the perfect camel for breeding and milking. Just looking at her filled him with excitement. She was his future. He turned back to Mandy. "You're married." He might forget himself from time to time and accidentally touch her, but that was one fact he would never forget. She had chosen another over him. "You love Levi."

She dabbed her eyes again. "Do I?"

Titus leaned his rear against the porch railing and

folded his arms. "Quit talking in riddles, Mandy. It's getting us nowhere."

She took a deep shuddering sigh. "You know how it is, Titus."

"No, I don't. I have no idea. Would you like to tell me why you came here today?" Once upon a time he thought he would marry Mandy. They would live happily ever after, have a farm, raise kids, and everything was going to be perfect. But then fate stepped in, and it didn't work out that way. Not for either of them. Except from where he was standing, it seemed that Mandy had perfection pretty much down to an art. She had a beautiful house and a wonderful husband. What more could she want? "Are you saying that you don't love him?"

She stood and came closer to him. He held up a hand to stay her progress. "I'm saying that I never should have married him." She took another deep breath and he got the feeling that she was girding up for something. "I should have waited for you like I promised. I want to be with you, Titus."

His heart thumped painfully in his chest. "You can't love me, Mandy. You're married to another."

"Why can't I? The *Englisch* do it all the time."

"We're not *Englisch*."

"We could be. If we left here, we could go live in Tulsa."

"What would I do with my camels?" It was a silly excuse, but he wanted to derail her before she passed a point they both would regret.

"Then we could go to Taylor Creek. Buy a farm there. I could get an *Englisch* divorce and—"

He shook his head. "Then we would be placed under the *Bann*. You would be an adulteress. We could never see our families. You aren't prepared for that."

"I don't want to live my life without you."

"You have no idea what it's like to be away from your family the way I was. And I was only gone for five years. A *Bann* would be forever."

"Don't decide right now. Just think about it," she begged. "Promise me you'll think about it."

He wanted to tell her no. How could he think about something that would tear both their lives apart forever? He was just now getting his life back together.

But her eyes held a fragile light and her lips trembled. She looked so close to falling completely apart that he couldn't push her off that ledge.

"Of course."

For the next two days he could think of nothing but Mandy's proposal. How easy would it be to just walk away from it all? No more worrying about making sure every step of his life was in line with the church. No more worrying about whether or not he was good enough, or forgiven, or even able to live the most conservative lifestyle as he had growing up.

Every time he saw Mandy it was like stepping into the past. They would have had a good marriage, one filled with love and happiness. He just knew it. Why couldn't they have that now? Of course it would have to be in the *Englisch* world. They had already determined that. And as much as he didn't feel he belonged with the Amish any longer, he didn't feel that he belonged with the *Englisch* any more.

His thoughts chased one another in a circle in his head like a dog chasing its tail. He wished he had someone he could talk it over with, but there was no one. Eli wouldn't understand, nor would Jonah. Or his *mamm.* Or his *vatter.* And definitely not the bishop. So he was left mulling over the problems in his own head, unable to grab any thoughts and hold on to them for long enough to make it stick. Could he do it? Could he be away from his family forever? He didn't know. He did know that he was tired of walking the line every day, feeling like he was on display. He only had a couple more weeks before his deal with the bishop expired. He knew that the bishop wouldn't press the matter. But he felt obligated just the same.

Once he said his kneeling confession, he would be wholly welcomed back into the church. But he knew in his heart that no one would ever truly forget what happened. And everyone blamed him. Everyone blamed him, and he had done nothing to change their views. What good would it do, really, to tell the whole story of what happened that night? It wouldn't bring anyone back. It wouldn't get Eli the use of his legs again. And it wouldn't take away any of the time Titus had spent in jail.

It wasn't a matter of caring about Mandy or maybe even loving her. She had been his one first love. How could he not still care about her? And he knew, *Englisch* or Amish, they would have a beautiful marriage. It all boiled down to could he live without his family? Could they integrate into *Englisch* life without too many trials and tribulations? Could he live with himself knowing he had taken another man's wife?

One other question rose again and again like cream rises to the top. Did he want to?

He pulled his buggy to a stop in front of the bakery and hopped out. He had been waiting all morning for his chance to get away without Abbie noticing, but finally, and thankfully, her mother asked for help with the laundry. With her out of sight, Titus was able to hop in the buggy and come to town. He wanted tonight to be special. It was Abbie's birthday. Abbie and Alvin's. He had asked her a couple of days before if she was going to do anything special and she told him no. They didn't really celebrate her birthday much these days.

To Titus, that was tragic. Alvin might be gone, but Abbie was still here. She was still here and doing her best to be everything she could, both son and daughter to her parents. If nothing else in the world, she deserved a cake on her twenty-third birthday.

Esther Lapp was nowhere to be seen as he let himself into the small shop. He stepped inside and took a deep breath. The smells of yeast and sweets laced with brown sugar made his mouth water.

"Hi, Titus. I have your cake ready." The woman behind the counter was a pretty, thin blonde. She had sparkling hazel eyes and one dimple in her right cheek, which showed itself when she smiled.

Caroline Fitch. They had met at church. Or rather he had met up with Andrew Fitch, Caroline's husband. Both were newcomers to Wells Landing, having arrived there after Titus had gone to jail. Neither one of them looked at him with the same amount of skepticism that some of the other residents of Wells Landing tried to hide from their eyes. Neither one of them had memories of Alvin King or Eli not in a wheelchair. Neither one of them seemed to care anything about his past or the events that led up to one wild night in September. If only everyone else in the district looked at him like they did . . .

"Does it look pretty?"

Caroline smiled, revealing that dimple once again. "Of course. I did it myself."

She pulled the cake box from the cooler and took

it over to the counter space next to the cash register. Unlike the display cases, which were nearly shoulder height to him, this one came up just above his waist. They could look at the cake with ease.

Pretty was just not even the word. It was exquisite. Just like the girl he had bought it for. Soft buttercream frosting made a background for purple pansies. They were scattered all over the cake, more heavily on the left side. In that flowerless section on the right, Caroline had written HAPPY BIRTHDAY, ABBIE in the same color of purple as the darkest part of the petals. The flowers on the cake were so perfectly shaped they looked like real flowers. He had to resist the urge to reach out and touch one to see if it was indeed frosting. He had no idea it would be such a masterpiece. Now he had to wonder if Abbie would actually cut the cake after seeing how lovely it was.

"I'm glad you like it," Caroline said. "Is there anything else you need?"

Titus shook his head. He was going over to the dollar store to get purple napkins, forks, and cups along with a bottle of that nonalcoholic champagne. He wanted everything for Abbie's birthday to be absolutely perfect. Maybe they would even have a banner that he could hang up and some balloons. That would be terrific.

"No, I think this'll do it." He paid for the cake and headed for the door.

He couldn't think of anyone who deserved this beautiful cake more than Abbie King.

"Thank you," he called, and let himself out of the bakery.

Holding the cake in front of him as if it were about to break at any moment, he managed to get it to the backseat of the buggy. He wished he had thought to bring a box or something else to put it in to help stabilize it. He would just have to take it slow on the way back to Abbie's. He didn't want anything happening to that cake.

He made short work at the dollar store, gathering all the things he needed for Abbie's party. Even purple balloons with matching ribbon streamers.

The Amish didn't do a great deal for birthdays. Sometimes birthdays went without celebration for two or three years, but he didn't think that was the case with Abbie. They had lost her brother in a tragic accident and as twins they shared that same birthday. But to Titus, it just wasn't fair that Abbie had to give up any celebration of her day because they had lost her brother.

He gathered everything into the buggy and headed back to the farm. He couldn't stop the grin on his face as he drove. And he was thankful to have something else to think about besides Mandy and running away to join the *Englisch*. He had no idea why he was so tempted, other than life seemed to be so complicated these days. Joining the *Englisch* world would solve that. No one there knew that he just got out of prison. No one there had ever heard anything about them at all, just that his name was Titus Lambert and he used to be Amish.

You still are Amish.

He shook the thought away. He would not allow any of that today. Today was all about Abbie, and he was going to make sure that she had the best birthday ever.

"Is that Titus?" Abbie looked over to where she was hanging clothes on the line to the buggy pulling into the driveway. He was in the buggy, yes, and was driving, that was true. But how did he manage to get the horse hooked up and leave the house without anyone noticing? And why did he have a big black sack?

She shook her head. Probably some new thing for the camels. He was so obsessed these days with making sure that everything was organic and certified organic and a bunch of other things that she had no idea how to decipher. He said it would make their milk more valuable. She bowed to his expertise and research. He definitely knew more about camels than she did. But his fascination with the animals was almost laughable.

Still, she did enjoy having them on the farm. It always put a smile on her face to see them in the pasture. They batted their long eyelashes and otherwise seemed not to care that they had moved to a new farm in a new town. Yet there was an intelligence in their eyes that told her they knew things had changed.

She went back to hanging clothes and tried not to think too hard about Titus and his camels. It was the one thing that she knew could keep him in Wells Landing. But at the same time she understood that he could move the camels whenever he chose. Only she knew the struggles that he was going through with his decision over repenting. Every day she prayed that Titus would find peace in his heart. More and more she wanted to pray for him to stay. And to stay with her. But she couldn't find it in herself to ask for such a selfish thing. More than anything, she wanted Titus happy. He needed peace, he deserved love, and he should have forgiveness. But the problem wasn't with the community forgiving him. It lay in his forgiving himself.

"Abbie," Titus started. He stood in the back doorway,

a smile on his face along with a look like the cat who ate the canary and the cream.

What was he up to?

"*Jah?*"

"Can you come in here for a second?"

She looked down at the basket, which held only a few more items. "Can I finish this laundry first?"

"Sure." He gave the doorjamb a quick pat, then disappeared back into the house. Abbie wondered if it had something to do with what was in that black garbage bag he had brought in. Only the camels got him that excited over anything. But at least he was finding some joy. That was the main thing.

Abbie finished the clothes, picked up the basket, and headed back into the house. She sat the basket in the laundry room just off the back porch and made her way to the kitchen.

But she was not prepared for the sight she saw as she stepped inside.

"Happy birthday!" Titus called, his smile infectious. Her *mamm* and *dat* sat at the table looking a bit shell-shocked, but Abbie couldn't bring herself to worry about them right then. Her heart was filled to bursting with joy.

He had done this for her. Purple balloons were tied to the back of her chair. Two presents sat off to the side, one square and the other one small and flat. In the center of the table was the most beautiful cake she had ever seen, and it had her name on it. He had done all this for her.

"Come on in here. You've got to blow out the candles."

Abbie stopped. She and Alvin had always shared a birthday cake. This would be the first time in her life that she blew out candles without him.

Alvin, I miss you so much. I hope you're happy and safe wherever you are today. Happy birthday.

She made her way to the table as Titus began to light the candles. Thankfully, there were only twenty-three on there, but there was enough to create quite a flame.

"You have to make a wish," he said. "Then we'll have a piece."

She looked at the cake. "It's too beautiful to eat."

Titus chuckled. "That's what I told Caroline, too. But she assured me that it tastes even better than it looks."

Abbie smiled. "In that case, it must taste absolutely amazing."

She could do this. She could blow out candles without her brother. She could.

"Make a wish," Titus said.

Abbie closed her eyes and wished for the one thing that she wanted most of all. *I wish for Titus to find happiness.*

How could she wish for anything else when he brought her so much joy since he'd been in Wells Landing? If anybody had asked her last year if she would feel this way about Titus, she would have called them a liar and probably not nicely at all.

Her parents seemed a little preoccupied.

"Do you want to open presents first or eat cake?" Titus asked.

"It's almost too pretty to cut," she said.

"I knew you would say that." He went to the kitchen drawer and pulled out a knife to slice the cake. But he wasn't very good at it and some pieces were quite larger than others. He served them all a piece on the tiny lavender plates and passed them around.

Abbie took a bite of the cake and closed her eyes. "This is delicious."

Everyone nodded, but she couldn't help but believe that her parents didn't seem to be enjoying the moment as much as she was. And she wasn't even sure she was enjoying it as much as Titus.

He seemed so pleased with himself that he had remembered her birthday and had this party for her. It was beyond special, more than thoughtful. No one had ever done anything like this for her before. And though she wished Alvin were sitting there by her side at the table, she was glad to have the three people with her who were there.

"And I've got nonalcoholic champagne." Titus held up the bottle for them to see, then poured them all a glass.

After everyone was finished, Titus gathered up the plates and took them to the trash as Abbie tried to determine which present to open first. She grabbed the biggest one. It was a square cube about eighteen inches all the way around. She had no idea what it could be.

"Open it," Titus urged.

She started with the purple bow, releasing it only to tear the wrapping paper. Most all the gifts she received in her life had been in gift bags, so it was something of a special treat to actually unwrap presents. She opened the box and pulled out a pair of slippers. Brown slippers that looked a lot like . . . "Camels' feet?"

Titus laughed. "I found them on the Internet. They will keep your feet warm this winter."

Abbie shook her head. "I bet they will."

Titus's expression fell. "You don't like them?"

Abbie put the slippers back in the box, then turned her full attention to Titus. "I love them. Thank you." She hadn't meant for the moment to turn so serious but somehow it did.

He stared back at her, his gaze steady. "You're welcome."

The moment hung suspended between them, then Titus broke the connection. "Open the other one."

She picked up the second present and held it in her hands. It was the right size for a book. Her fingers trembling, she tore up the paper to reveal the cover. "*Pride and Prejudice* by Jane Austen?"

"I remember how you used to always read," Titus said.

Her mother and father nodded.

She used to read all the time, going around with faraway places in her head. But she hadn't had time to read in such a long while. She had read a little bit while she was in Missouri. But she hadn't had time for it since she had returned to Oklahoma. There was too much to do on the farm these days to spend a lot of time doing anything other than farming. But now Titus was there . . .

"Thank you," she said.

"I read it in prison and thought it was good. While I was reading it, I kept thinking that you would really like it."

"You read this?"

He blushed. "Yeah."

"Maybe when I finish, we can talk about it."

He smiled. "I'm looking forward to it."

She couldn't say it was the best birthday party of her life, but it ranked high on the list. A beautiful cake and the wonderful man who had arranged it all made it so very special. Not to mention the thoughtful, if not maybe a little silly, gifts. Her parents had been less than enthusiastic about the festivities. Part of her felt sorry for them. They were trying so hard to get over Alvin's death.

She stopped those thoughts. They had been doing better recently. It was as if Titus's jail term had suspended their grieving. These days, they seemed to be going through the steps a little easier than before. Still, she hoped that his celebration hadn't set them back. Her father's hands were growing increasingly steady as time went on. Her mother was almost back to completely the same person she had been before the accident. It was the most difficult thing to do, find the way after the loss of a loved one. Especially in such a tragic accident that everyone agreed could've been avoided.

She pushed the barn door to the side and stepped inside. "Titus?" She didn't wait for his answer before she started back to the horse stall he had claimed as his own. It was almost a little scary to her that it looked so much like a jail cell. She had seen something on TV at some point maybe in town, maybe during *rumspringa*, she couldn't remember. It had shown the inside of a jail cell with little pictures tacked to the walls and the person's personal objects all lined up. Exactly how Titus had his stall. And she had to wonder if he was either unable to get out of the prison mindset, or if he was still punishing himself for his part in Alvin's death.

"In here," he called.

"What are you doing?" she asked as she stepped inside.

"Just writing a few notes."

He sat his notebook to the side on the hay bale that he used for a bed. "Is everything okay?" he asked.

She stirred herself out of her thoughts. "*Jah*. Everything's fine. I just wanted to come out and say thank you again for the party."

That small, crooked smile made her heart beat faster. "You're welcome, Abbie."

"So what are you writing?"

He looked back to where his notebook lay facedown on the hay. "Nothing. Just a list of things."

She smiled. "Camels again?"

He continued to stare at the notebook, then turned back toward her, his brown eyes serious. "No."

"Titus, is everything okay?" Just an hour ago they had been inside laughing and celebrating. Well, she couldn't say her parents were much on the celebration part. But she and Titus seemed to be having a good time.

"Yeah. It will be."

"Is that for the bishop?" Sometimes Bishop Ebersol had wayward souls make a list of things they needed to work on, things they needed to change, a better plan to follow their baptism vows. She'd done something similar in her baptism classes. Maybe that was what the bishop had asked him do in order to be accepted back into the church. The bishop was nothing if not innovative when it came to his members.

"No." Titus said the word as if that was all he was about to say. Then he let out a sigh. "I'm trying to decide if I can stay here."

Her eyes widened. "Here as in on this farm? Or here as in Wells Landing?"

"Here as in with the Amish."

She shook her head. "What are you thinking, Titus? Why would you not stay here?"

He had talked for a while about leaving and whether or not he could, but she thought it was all just talk. He loved his family and he loved the community. She could tell. He had sat for the past two church Sundays with his face in his hands as he asked for forgiveness from the congregation. Everyone had already forgiven him.

"Why do you keep beating yourself up over this?"

He stopped. "That's good coming from you. You weren't ready to forgive me at all."

She shook her head. "That's not it at all. I was hurt. And I was wrong. I can admit that. But now you're thinking about leaving? I can't understand that."

He propped his hands on his jean-clad hips. She had seen him in them before, but hadn't gotten used to him dressing in such an *Englisch* manner. But since his first church service back, he had started to dress Amish. Every day, showing his faithfulness and his rededication to the church. This was a setback if she had ever seen one. "You don't understand, Abbie."

"Then why don't you explain it to me?"

He shook his head.

"What are you afraid of? Anything you confess now will do nothing to bring Alvin back. I've already forgiven you. Everybody has forgiven you. The problem is you can't give yourself."

"I was the one driving!"

She shook her head. "Everyone knows that, Titus. If you want to shock me, you have to come up with something better."

"It was Alvin."

"Quit talking in riddles, and tell me what you need to say."

He shifted from one foot to the other, looked down at his notebook as if it held the answers, then turned back to meet her steady gaze. "Alvin wanted to go back and see this girl at the party. But we had already started home. We were late, and I was tired. I had a little to drink, but not nearly as much as they had.

"I already felt bad about it. I mean, I was baptized. I should've never been there. I should've never taken them to this party. I don't even know why I let them talk me into it." He looked up at the ceiling of the barn as if somehow the answers were written there. "I think Eli was passed out in the backseat. Blaine was next to him on Alvin's side of the car. Alvin wanted us to turn around and go back to the party. I kept telling him no. Finally, he reached across and grabbed the steering wheel to turn us around."

Goose bumps broke out all over Abbie's arms. She eased into the stall farther, brushing past Titus as she slumped down onto the hay bale. "Alvin was responsible?"

"I was never going to tell you. I mean, what good would it do to tell you this now? It won't bring him back. It won't bring Blaine back, and it won't give Eli back the use of his legs."

She shook her head. "I don't understand," she whispered. "If you had told them that in court, you might have never gone to jail."

Titus eased down next to her. "At the time, I thought I deserved it. I couldn't tell the truth because I was just as responsible. I was the oldest one there. I was the one baptized into the church. I should've told them that it was not acceptable. There were no last hurrahs before baptism. Everyone in the community would be watching us. But I allowed them to go. I went with them. I even drove them."

"Blaine Carson was a bad influence on all of you, huh?"

"Not really. Blaine didn't talk anyone into doing

anything. At least not anything they didn't want to do. Blaine was just as much a victim. He had too much money and too much time on his hands. I never did figure out why he liked hanging out with three Amish boys."

Abbie had never thought about it that way. "So you went to jail to be punished for what happened?"

"I was punished for what happened. Blaine's family felt I was responsible, and I doubt my telling them about Alvin and his need to go back to that party would have changed anything. It would've been my word against their attorneys'. And who are they going to believe? I'm already in trouble for driving drunk, being underage, and barely having a driver's license." He shook his head. "The whole situation was wrong from the beginning. I had no defense for myself."

She reached out and ran her fingers down the side of his cheek. Such a handsome face, even with its worry lines at the corners of his eyes and the small, wrinkly frown on his forehead.

"It's not your fault, Titus," she said. "Nor was it Alvin's. Not entirely." She scooted a little closer to him, needing this shared moment with him. Never in her wildest dreams had she imagined that Alvin was the one who sent them into the crash, but she knew her fun-loving brother. And she trusted Titus. Responsible or not, he spent five years in prison to pay for a crime that was nothing more than an accident. A horrible, tragic accident.

"Abbie."

She looked into his eyes, for first time noticing that amid the sadness he held there, there was still a little bit of love, too. Love for her? She had no idea. But one thing was certain. Somehow she had fallen in love with Titus. Or maybe she had been in love with him all along.

Before, he had belonged to Mandy. Then he had been off to jail. Now he was back and trying to decide if he was going to stay.

"Please stay, Titus."

"I wish it was that easy, Abbie." He closed his eyes for a moment as she ran her fingers over his cheeks once more. Down the jawline and back up again.

His eyes snapped open as he caught her hand in his. "You don't know what you're getting into. It doesn't matter if I stay or if I go, if I live here or in Taylor Creek, none of that truly matters. All that matters is I've hurt so many people. I don't know if I can continue to hurt them this way."

"How can you say that? You just told me that Alvin was the one who pulled the car off the road and into that tree."

"And if I hadn't been drinking, my reflexes would've been quicker. If I'd been a more experienced driver, I might have known how to handle it correctly. If I'd been a better friend, I wouldn't have let them go to that party. I would have made them stay home."

"Why are you taking the weight of the world on your shoulders?"

He stopped and pulled away. "You took on this whole farm by yourself. Without my help, it would have taken you years to get back on track."

"I know that. And I thank you for it. And that's why you can't leave."

He shook his head. "I made a deal with our *dats*, and I'll see that deal through. I just don't know if I can stay in the church."

"Oh, so the deals with the *dats* have to be honored, but the deal with God you can break?"

"It's not like that."

"That's sure the way it seems."

"You have no idea what I went through."

That was true, she didn't. But she could see the horror in his eyes, the memories and the reflections of things she could only imagine. "You have no idea what it's like to walk in my shoes."

She stood. "You're right. I don't. And I probably never will. Most of the people who live in this district, in this town, will never experience what you have. So stop expecting us to know how it feels and start telling us, or start getting over it."

"What do you think I've been trying to do for the last few weeks?"

She shook her head. "Titus, you and I both know it's going to take a lot longer than weeks."

"That's all I got. I have to repent this next church Sunday. If I don't, I'm under the *Bann* permanently or at least until I can figure things out."

"Don't you see you're talking yourself in circles? Okay, go *Englisch* and see how quickly you're placed under the *Bann*. Will that help you figure out what you're doing with your life?"

He stared down at the hay-strewn floor. "There's more to it than that."

She waited patiently for him to explain.

"Mandy's thinking about leaving her husband. She wants me to go with her. We can live *Englisch*, not have to worry about any of this stuff. No one would know what I've been through, no one would know what happened in jail. No one would even need to know that once upon a time I was born Amish."

A sword of jealousy stabbed her heart. "Do you still . . . love her?" Somehow she managed to get the words past the huge lump in her throat.

He shook his head. "I don't know. I don't know if I'm more in love with the idea of being able to go back in time and suspend those years in prison or if I love her still."

"Don't you think you should figure that out before you start excommunicating yourself from the church?" She wanted to jump up and down and rail against him. Tell him how stupid he was being. He couldn't go back to that time before. Mandy had married another. It was one thing to turn *Englisch*, but something else entirely to run off with another man's wife. The rules for a *Bann* varied from time to time, from person to person, from family to family. He might be able to suffer a *Bann* and come back and even eat with his family provided that they set up a separate table for him. There would be ways around all the little rules that the bishop didn't always enforce. With Titus there would always be the hope that they could bring him back into the fold. For that reason alone she knew Bishop Ebersol would allow him to come back. Getting Titus back into the church would be the most important thing when compared with losing him completely. But if he left with Mandy, there would be no coming back.

"That's a big decision, Titus. Huge." She prayed the hurt in her eyes didn't show. Or that he didn't notice the way her voice broke when she said the other woman's name. How dumb could she be, going and falling in love with Titus Lambert?

He looked back at her and smiled, one of those sad smiles that didn't reach his eyes. "I ruined your birthday."

"No, you made my birthday wonderful. This was the best day I've had in a long, long time. Since Alvin died."

"That's what I wanted."

"For what it's worth, I hope you stay." Abbie turned on her heel and left the barn.

* * *

He watched her go, his heart heavy in his chest. The beats felt sluggish and he wondered if it was just the stress that caused such a sad rhythm.

Abbie hadn't deserved any of what life had handed her. She had lost her brother and dragged her parents back from the pit of depression. She managed to get the farm back in order after they had allowed it to go into disrepair. She bought milk cows and went into business with him raising camels. She was as good as they came. And she didn't deserve the way he had treated her. He should've never kissed her that day.

She had just looked so sweet and angelic. He wanted a little bit of that innocence for himself. He had lost his long ago. Unfortunately, he saw the world with jaded eyes. And being back in Wells Landing showed him just how world-weary he had become.

Thomas Wolfe may have said you can never go home again, but Titus didn't think he meant this. Was Titus just wanting everything to be different? Or did he just want to step back in time? With Mandy at his side, it would feel more like five years ago. Would he be able to pretend those five years had never happened? What would he do if he did?

What would he do if he couldn't?

The next morning Abbie went out to milk the cows as usual, not surprised to see Titus waiting for her in the barn. He must've been up for a long time, spreading the feed and bringing the cows into the holding pen.

"Good morning."

He nodded in greeting, and the two of them set to work.

She hated to admit that they made a good team, and she would be sad if he left. What would she do without him? Not just on the farm, but in general. She had come to depend on him so much as a friend and a companion, as a business partner. And yes, she had thought about him in other terms. A more permanent partnership. Now she realized that was all just silly thinking. Titus Lambert had too many ghosts around him for him to see past it all.

Lord, I just pray Your will be done. You know my feelings for Titus, and You know the terrible things that he feels he's done and suffered through. Things that I can't even begin to understand. Lord, please help him make the best decision. I'm very concerned for his soul and his well-being if he chooses the path he's leaning toward. You're the only one who can help him. I pray that You do. Show him the way. Show him the line. And if that way doesn't lead back to me, please allow it to lead him back to Wells Landing. Back to the Amish. Amen.

With the milking done, they went to the house to wash up. It was almost seven o'clock, and her *mamm* was putting breakfast on the table. Thankfully, she didn't look too scattered from the night before.

"Are you hungry?" *Mamm* asked.

Titus nodded. And within moments they were all seated around the table.

"Where's *Daf?*"

Her mother frowned and glanced up toward the ceiling. "He's not feeling very good this morning. He decided to stay in bed for a little while longer."

"I sure hope he's not coming down with something," Abbie said. Like birthday-itis.

Her mother shook her head. "I'm sure it's just a twenty-four-hour bug or something like that. He'll be right as rain in a little bit."

After they ate, *Mamm* rose to do the dishes while Abbie and Titus headed out to finish the chores. They fed the horses and gave all the animals fresh water.

Water for the dogs, water for the chickens. They fed the ducks, slopped the hogs, and kept going until every creature had been tended. It was just after nine o'clock.

"I think I'm going to run into town," Abbie said. The thought had come to her in the middle of the night. She wanted to do something special for Titus.

Hopefully, he would remain there and in two weeks he would become part of the Amish church again. It was a special day and Titus deserved something special to wear. She would run to the town to the fabric store and get him some material for a new shirt. She would make it for him while he wasn't looking and present it to him on the next church Sunday. She was certain she could brush aside any questions he might have, telling him it was something she was doing for her father. But she would make the shirt for Titus and he could wear it to his church meeting. He would look fine and handsome as he accepted his baptismal vows for the second time.

"Let me get my hat, and I'll go with you."

Not exactly what she had in mind, but how could she tell him no? She surely didn't want him getting suspicious. "*Jah*, sure." She nodded toward the house. "I'll just go tell *Mamm* where we're going."

"I'll meet you back here in five." Titus started for the barn as Abbie made her way back to the house. "*Mamm*, Titus and I are going to town. You want me to pick you up anything while I'm there?"

Her mother came out of the laundry room and shook her head. "No, thank you. We're fine."

She stopped and studied Abbie for a bit.

Abbie shifted in place under her mother's scrutiny. "Is something wrong?"

Her mother shook her head. And, to Abbie's dismay,

tears rose into her eyes. "No, everything's fine. It's just that you've grown into a beautiful young woman."

Abbie blinked back tears of her own. "Oh, *Mamm*."

Before a simple request turned into an out-and-out blubbering girl moment, Abbie shook her head. "We'll be back in a little bit."

Her mother nodded and ducked back into the laundry room. "Just be careful."

"We will." Abbie made her way back up to the tractor to find Titus waiting for her. He wore his straw hat, black pants, black shoes, a pale green shirt, and black suspenders. He looked so much like the quintessential Amish man that she had to wonder why he even entertained the idea of leaving the community.

Couldn't he see that this was where he belonged? She would just have to show him. Not even for herself, not even because she had fallen in love with him, but for him. The main thing was he needed to be back in the fold of the community, and in the loving arms of his family. The only way to do that was through the church. Somehow she needed to show him how much the community needed him, how sad they would be if he wasn't there any longer, and all the things he would be missing if he decided to run away with Mandy.

They hopped on the tractor with Abbie driving and headed into town. They bounced along, the roar of the engine making conversation nearly impossible.

"Are you really thinking about running away with Mandy?" Abbie took her attention off the road ahead for the briefest moment.

He turned to look at her but didn't answer.

She turned her gaze back to the road.

Why did he think this was even an option? So he made a few mistakes. And they were big mistakes, she admitted that. But how could leaving everything behind make any of it all right? He was being handed a second chance. Time to start over in the community that loved him. Why couldn't he see that running away with Mandy would be the worst possible thing he could do?

"Where do you want to go first?" he asked.

Well, that was her answer. If he wasn't going to give her an answer, that meant he was still thinking about it. And if he was, why didn't he tell her? The only answer she had was because he wanted her to talk him out of it.

She had lain in bed so many nights thinking about him and everything that had happened. On more than one occasion she tried to put herself in his shoes. She tried her best to understand what he was going through. As much as she tried, it was next to impossible. But she did have a little bit of understanding of how he felt. Running away with Mandy would be like stepping back in time. She understood that. Going to Missouri had been the same for her. For a time, she could be happy, but that happiness was a farce. Because it didn't make her face the things that she needed to address. In Missouri she could pretend like her brother was living at home in Oklahoma without a scratch. In Missouri she could pretend that he wasn't in the graveyard. But when she set foot back in Oklahoma she had to admit that her brother was gone forever. And each time she left for Missouri, coming back got harder. But she knew that staying in Missouri wouldn't be healthy. So she'd come back to face her loss and found that the people she was closest to were suffering even more in her absence. She should've never done that to her parents. She might've been the one to be able to stop them from falling into such hard times. Thankfully, they pulled themselves out of it. Her mother looked better and better every day; her father had stopped drinking.

And his finger was healing nicely. If she were to leave again, it would start all over. Is that what Titus wanted? She didn't think so.

"Abbie?" he prodded.

"What?"

"You're a million miles away."

She shook her head. "I'm sorry. I was just thinking about something. What did you want to know?"

"Where are we going first?"

She really just needed to go to the fabric store. It hadn't been that long since she'd made a trip to town. But with any luck she could talk him into getting a piece of pie at Kauffman's later.

"I just need to go to the fabric store."

"Are you making a new dress?" he asked as she pulled the tractor down Main and chugged toward the line of stores on the other side of Abe Fitch's furniture store.

"I hadn't thought about it, but a new dress would be nice." She had made a new dress when she had returned from Missouri. She'd been way too busy trying to get the farm back on its feet to think of much else, but here it was nearly August and a new dress would surely be nice.

"I need to buy some shirt fabric. Want to help me pick it out?"

He rolled his eyes. "Do I have to?"

"Oh, you," she said with a laugh. "Come help me pick up the fabric, and I'll buy you a piece of pie at Kauffman's."

He seemed to think about it a second. But only a second. "You've got yourself a deal."

He didn't want to say that the fabric store put him on edge, but the fabric store made him . . . antsy. Once he set foot through the doorway he wanted to go back out again. He didn't understand how girls could look at the same fabric over and over again.

"Which one do you think?" Abbie held up two colors of green. One was dark, the color of olives. The other was lighter and more akin to the color of the pale moss that grew on the side of the trees next to the waterfall.

"They're both nice." It was the best he could come up with. He should have no say in the fabric choice for someone else's shirt. This had to be the bottom of his list of things he wanted to do in any given day. The only benefit of picking out material for someone else's shirt was that he was with Abbie.

"That is not an answer."

"It's the best I have, Abbie. If you wanted somebody to give you a valid opinion on shirt material, you should have had your *mamm* come too."

Abbie shook her head, then took the bolt of fabric from the shelf. She held up the dark green in front of him, then the light green, critically studying each one as she did so.

"How is that helping?"

"I'm just trying to get a feel about how each color would look on him."

Titus resisted the urge to roll his eyes. He was with Abbie after all. Wasn't that the most important thing?

She had come to mean so very much to him in the last few weeks. More than ever, she was beginning to mean more to him than anyone ever had. Even Mandy in those days when he thought that he would marry her.

Abbie was the kindest and most beautiful person he knew. And she was obsessed with him and his decision whether or not to leave the community. And Mandy. Was that something he wanted to do? Not at all. But he couldn't explain to Mandy or Abbie that he had to keep that option open. He slept better at night knowing that if he failed he would have something else, somewhere he could go. Someone he could turn to. But if he stopped kidding himself for just a moment he would know that he couldn't leave Wells Landing with Mandy. He didn't even want to leave. He wanted to stay right where he was with Abbie. Working on the farm, raising camels, milking cows, and all the other things that they had been doing the last few weeks. His time on her farm had meant more to him than any other time in his life.

But what if he didn't make it through? What if something happened that tainted her opinion of him forever? What would he do then? How would he survive if that happened?

"I think the darker," Abbie said.

Titus sighed. "Good choice."

Abbie laughed, and he knew that he could get used to that sound. He hadn't heard it near enough in the past few weeks, even as the sound of his own laughter was becoming more and more frequent. That's what they both needed. Time to learn to live, time to learn to love, time to learn to be together. That was all that he wanted.

Abbie grabbed the bolt of green fabric and one of white, then headed for the counter.

Titus followed behind. If he stayed where he was, there was a pretty girl in his future. Things were looking up.

She should stay away. She should stay away. She should stay away. Abbie chanted as she walked to the barn. This was the last thing she should be doing, coming out here after dark to visit Titus. But somehow with him out here and everyone else in the house the night seemed long. Five o'clock came mighty early in the morning, but here she was headed to the barn to see what he was doing.

She should turn around. What if he had already gone to sleep? What if she woke him up by coming into the barn? But her mind didn't seem to be in control of her feet. They just kept walking until they took her all the way inside.

"Titus?" She didn't raise her voice very loud. If he was asleep she didn't want to wake him. So she tried to make it carry just far enough that if he was awake he would hear her and come out.

There was no answer. He was asleep. She turned to head back to the house and almost ran into him. "Titus!" She smacked a hand over her heart as if that alone would stop its thundering beat. "You scared me."

His hands reached out to steady her. "I'm sorry. That wasn't my intent."

"What are you doing?"

"I just went out to check on the girls."

She smiled at his affectionate name for the two female camels. They had another one arriving next week along with the bull. And of course the gelding they had gotten from Ezra Hein as well.

"Is everything okay?" she asked.

"Fine," he said.

She looked down at his fingers where they wrapped around her arms. He could have released her at least a minute ago. But instead, his thumbs had begun to trace a little pattern on the skin just under her sleeve.

"Titus?"

His gaze was centered somewhere around the underside of her jaw. He seemed to be in another world, barely aware that he was touching her. "Hmm?"

"You can let me go now," she said. *Unless you don't want to and then you can hold me forever.* But she bit back those words, keeping her love for him a secret. How could she confess her feelings if he was still thinking about running off with Mandy? It was one thing to live with the knowledge that she loved him, and quite another to admit it to him only to be turned over for another.

He lifted his gaze to hers, as if just then realizing that she was there, he was touching her, and they were standing way too close.

"You can let me go now." She coughed. Why did it suddenly seem so warm in the barn? *Jah*, it was nearly August and the temperatures soared into the hundreds often, but the sun had gone down and the nights had cooled off into the tolerable range. So why did she feel as if she'd been blasted with the desert air?

"Why did you come out here, Abbie?"

She supposed that was the true question. Why had she come out here? Better yet what could she tell him was her reason for coming out here? That she wanted to see him? Though she couldn't think of a valid reason. That she needed to talk to him? About what? The camels! She could ask him about the camels, but she had no question about camels that he hadn't already answered. That left only one possible explanation. "I wanted to see you."

"Why?"

It was her perfect opportunity. She could tell him how much she cared about him, how much she had grown to need him in these last few weeks. She could tell him the entire contents of her heart. How it had been hard to forgive him, how she couldn't stop herself even if she wanted to. But none of those words seemed to be enough. Or maybe she just wasn't ready to take that chance. She needed to know that he was staying, that he was going to be in Wells Landing forever.

Once she knew that, she would be more comfortable confessing her feelings. She wanted nothing more than to tell him how much he meant to her, how she was glad they were partners, and how she valued that partnership. But until she knew his intentions, she couldn't open herself up to that kind of pain.

"Oh, Titus," she whispered. It seemed as if that was enough.

"I'm going to kiss you."

Her heart pounded. "You are?" she asked. "You didn't tell me that before."

"I want you to know now. I want you stop me if it's not what you want. I want you to tell me that we only have a business arrangement. That I'm the reason your family has suffered for the last five years and will probably continue to suffer in the next five and beyond."

"I can't."

"Abbie," he sighed, before slipping in to capture his lips with hers.

Somehow his hands had moved from her arms to cup the underside of her chin. He held her in place, not allowing her to step away from him. Like she would have.

She had been waiting for Titus Lambert her entire life. Not just these last years. But long before that. She just hadn't known it until he had returned. She hadn't known that God had intended him just for her.

Titus raised his head, his dark eyes unreadable. "Go back in the house, Abbie."

She shook her head.

"Go back in the house." The warm light in his eyes had turned into a warning. And she understood its meaning.

He had lived by a different set of rules for a long

time. He might look like an Amish man, but he had lived a different life, walked with a different set of values, and held a different sort of rules of conduct. She wasn't in any danger from him, but she understood his meaning. She needed to go back into the house and save them both from the temptation.

Reluctantly she took a step back, tucking her head and breaking his intense stare.

"Good night, Titus."

"Good night," he said.

She made it all the way past him before she took off running, heading for the house as fast as her feet would take her.

Chapter Thirteen

Titus pulled the buggy into his parents' drive surprised to see the familiar blue tractor parked there. It was Friday. And in just two days he would go before the church, say his confessions, and everyone would vote on whether or not he would be allowed back in. Just the thought made his heart pound a little bit faster. But he knew it was something that had to be done. And as much as he felt that the members of the congregation would welcome him back with open arms, it was that small niggling of doubt that whispered in his ear and told him he wasn't worthy.

He set the brake and hopped down. He had come over to have supper with his parents, just one last time, before the *Bann* lifted. Titus wasn't looking forward to sitting at a separate table. But he knew that it was what had to be done. And after Sunday none of that would matter anymore. He had made his choice. He was staying in Wells Landing.

Perhaps it was a good thing that Mandy was here. He hadn't wanted to crush her spirit the other day so he told her that he would think about the two of them together. But to run away with her to the *Englisch* world?

Today was as good a day as any to tell her that would never happen.

He loped up the porch steps and entered the house. He'd have to go out and unhook the horse in a minute. But for now he felt it best to get the worst part of his night over with. It would just save him from having to find her and tell her later.

"Titus!" Rachel ran to him and threw her arms around him, nearly knocking him down with her enthusiasm. Of course she had always been that way, but these days she was a lot bigger. Where once he had swung her into his arms and spun her around, now he could only return her hug squeeze for squeeze. "Where is everybody?"

Rachel looked behind her toward the empty kitchen. "Out back. *Dat* is grilling hamburgers."

"I thought I smelled the grill."

She grabbed his hand and tugged him through the house.

Titus's mouth watered with the thought of grilled hamburgers. How long had it been? Way too long.

"Did you see Mandy's here?"

How could he have missed that? "Yeah, I did."

"Her husband's gone to a horse show so *Mamm* said she could stay with us."

Nothing like friends and neighbors to take care of one another. But of all times, why did it have to be now, at his dinner with his family? He shouldn't be so selfish, but he had a bad feeling that Mandy was starting to take advantage of his parents' good nature in order to sway them to her side when the time came.

He and Rachel walked out onto the back porch and down into the yard. His *dat* had set up a picnic table surrounded by several lawn chairs. Someone, most likely

Gabe Allen, had brought out the horseshoes and set up the stakes at one end of the yard.

June caught sight of them and hurried over, her smile full of secrets. "You should look behind you."

Cautiously Titus turned. A large banner had been pinned to the back of the house. WELCOME HOME, TITUS! The letters were red, obviously hand-painted, most likely by Rachel. The thought warmed his heart. He had found his way home. It'd taken weeks, and it would take many more, perhaps even years. But all he could do was stay here and try. He had another reason to want to stay. Abbie King. If he had known that this was going to turn into a party, he would've invited her. But then Abbie and Mandy at the same party? He shook his head. That was not a good idea.

"Did you do that?" He glanced down at Rachel. She smiled and nodded her head, apparently pleased with her part in his homecoming party.

"Thank you. *Danki*," he said. He was back in Wells Landing, back with the Amish. He had better start acting like it.

Michael jogged over and grabbed ahold of one of Titus's hands, pulling him toward the grill. "*Dat* needs your help."

It was on the tip of Titus's tongue to tell him that *Dat* had never needed help barbecuing before, but instead he turned to June.

"And did you do that? Tell him to include me?"

She gave him that secret smile again and a small shrug. Yes, she was behind it. But these things just went to prove that his family cared about him. They loved him, and they had missed him. Things might be different, but he was back. And their feelings for him were still the same. Maybe he wasn't so unworthy after all.

He allowed Michael to drag him over to the grill. His *dat* gave him a smile in greeting, then flipped the burgers and sprinkled them with his secret concoction. He never had told anyone what was in it. And Titus knew that once he found out he would definitely be back in the fold. Then again that might take more than years.

Mandy was pitching horseshoes and only gave him a wave as he came up.

He wondered what that cost her. She had practically thrown herself at him every opportunity she had, but tonight was not the night for that kind of behavior. And he would have to put off telling her his plans until after supper. Even though his family had thrown him the party welcoming him back into the community and into the church fold, he wouldn't believe that Mandy took it seriously until he told her himself.

"I really didn't need help," *Dat* said.

Titus inhaled appreciatively. "I know, but the sentiment was right."

His father grabbed the spatula from the hook at the edge of the grill and expertly flipped the burgers, sending the flames shooting through the grate as the drippings hit the hot coals.

"I'm proud of you, you know." His father spritzed the burgers and for a second Titus wondered if he was hearing things. Had his father just told him he was proud of him?

He studied his *dat*'s face. *Dat* sat the spritzer bottle down and wiped his hands on his cook's apron, then turned to face him. "I'm glad you're home."

"I'm glad I'm home, too."

The evening was everything a party should have been. They laughed and celebrated, ate, enjoyed one another's company, and had cake. June and Rachel had made him a cake welcoming him back to the community. It was his favorite kind. Lemon cake with lemon frosting and strawberries on the side. How long had it been since he'd had that? So long. But looking at the cake they made for him he thought back to the cake that he bought for Abbie. The only thing that would make tonight more perfect would be Abbie at his side. But that could be misconstrued as a real date, and he wasn't ready for that. He knew that he loved her. And he felt sure that she had strong feelings for him as well. But dating among the Amish was a slow process. It was one of the many reasons why Amish marriages seemed more solid than the ones in the rest of the world. It wasn't because they didn't have problems. It wasn't because they didn't have issues, sadness, or tragedy. The difference was that they did everything in their power to work things out. When a guy and a girl had known each other their whole lives and dated for a full year before they married, things were different when those tragedies hit. Much different than for those couples who had just met.

He glanced over to Mandy from the corner of his eye, careful not to reveal that he was looking at her. She had rushed her marriage with Levi. They had dated not quite a year and then they got married. She hadn't given herself time to grieve over her relationship with Titus and instead jumped headlong into another. That didn't mean her marriage couldn't be saved. It didn't mean what she had with Levi wasn't worthy and it didn't mean that it couldn't be strong once again. She just had to want to make it work.

It was just beginning to get dark when they stood and started gathering up plates and other dishes from the back. His *dat* and brothers had gone to put up the games they had taken out, and the girls, his *mamm* and sisters, had taken the dishes into the house. Somehow Titus found himself alone with Mandy.

"Your family really did miss you, Titus." Mandy clasped her hands behind her back and rolled onto her heels. The light was just different enough that he couldn't make out her exact expression. She looked a little wistful and yet happy all the same. As if it made her happy that his family cared so much for him and was so happy for his return, but sad that he had to return at all.

"It's time."

"So you're going to do it?" The words were so quiet he barely heard her over the chatter of the crickets.

"Yeah, I'm going to do it. I'm an Amish man, and this is where I belong. And you're an Amish woman. You belong with your husband." He had barely finished the sentence before she started shaking her head.

"I've made a mistake, Titus. Don't you realize that?"

"The only mistake is thinking that you and I ever had a chance. You are married now. You're Amish, and marriage is forever. The best thing to do now is to make sure that your marriage works."

"How do I do that? I love you." She took a step closer to Titus.

He braced his hands against her arms and held her in place. "You don't love me," he said. "You love the idea of me. You love the idea of the past." He shook his head. "I did the same thing, Mandy. And I'm sorry that I may have given you the wrong impression. But we can't go back to the past. We have to live now and the future that we have. Your future is with Levi. And mine is not with you."

Guilt swamped Titus as Mandy clamped a hand over her mouth. Tears rose into her eyes, and she shook her head as if she couldn't believe what he was saying. Truly, there was no way to let her down easy. He had tried that before to no avail.

"Mandy, I—"

As quickly as she fell apart, she pulled herself back together, at least halfway. Her eyes were still filled with tears, but she sniffed and smoothed down her apron. "Would you be so kind as to tell your mother that I'm going to go home now? I appreciate her hospitality."

He wanted to stop her, but it was better this way. His own heart heavy, he watched her walk away, around the side of the house. A few minutes later her tractor started, and she was gone.

"Was that Mandy I just saw leaving?" June came out of the house, laundry basket in hand. She would use it to carry the rest of the cookout things back into the house. It was a good system.

"Yeah," Titus said.

"Is everything okay?" June asked.

"No, June. Everything is not okay. I spent five years of my life in jail. I lost my girlfriend to another man, and I'm in love with the sister of the man I killed. I wouldn't say anything is okay."

She blinked at him, surprised by his tone, and he immediately regretted his harsh words.

"I'm sorry. I'm sorry."

"You're forgiven," she said. "I know this is hard on you, Brother. You shouldn't go borrowing trouble."

"I didn't want any of this," he said. Each day he had to readjust his thinking, and each day it seemed as if he had found his footing on a matter. Then something happened to rip it out from under him again.

It's going to take time.

But time was one of those things he didn't have much of these days.

* * *

Mandy wiped the tears from her cheeks as she turned down the driveway that led to her house. The house she shared with Levi.

What a fool she had been. She'd thought Titus still loved her. But he had stopped. And she had thrown herself at him.

She pulled the tractor to a stop beside the house and cut the engine. She sat there for a moment listening to the tick as it cooled and the crickets as they called to one another. In the distance, a mourning dove called to its mate. What was she going to do now?

Dear Lord, please forgive me. I've made so many mistakes in my life. A few weeks ago I thought the biggest mistake I had made was marrying Levi, but that's not right. The biggest mistake was thinking I still loved Titus. Please help me, Lord. Help me keep my thoughts straight and pure. Help me be the best wife that I can be. To be the wife that Levi deserves. Amen.

She raised her head, a sudden peace descending upon her. She had married Levi. She had made her choice. Why had she married him? He was a good and decent person. He'd been nothing but good to her in these last three years. The problem wasn't with him or their marriage. The problem was with the fact that she hadn't been able to have a baby yet. She just wanted a baby so badly. All of her other friends had already had babies, started their families. Why couldn't she?

She got down from the tractor cab and started toward the house. She should've come home while it was a little lighter outside. She never liked to come home when it was this dark, especially knowing that the house was empty.

She opened the door and stepped inside, the second thought shining inside her. She didn't like being by herself. Why was she? Why couldn't she go to Levi? Why hadn't she gone with him to begin with?

She switched on the solar-powered light and looked around the house. She was already bored. There was nothing to do here. And she would much rather be "bored" with her wonderful husband than bored at home, all by herself and trying to make relationships where there weren't any.

She shook her head. Why hadn't she realized this before now? She grabbed a flashlight from the top of the refrigerator and headed out to the barn. Levi would be in Arkansas for another day. It was just a three-hour drive. All she had to do was get herself a driver, head over there tomorrow, and she could spend the night with him there. How surprised would he be when he saw her? Plan in place, she picked up the phone and started to dial.

Titus was still smiling when he pulled up in front of the house that evening. His parents had tried to talk him into staying overnight, and he had thought about it. But the more he thought the more he realized he needed to start his own life. And that life was with Abbie King. Tomorrow was Saturday, the last day before he made his confession in front of the church. He would kneel in front of them and tell them of his sins and the part he played in Alvin's death and Eli's accident. He would go before them and tell them that he had truly seen the error of his ways. He did not want to be separated from the church any longer. He couldn't stand to be separated from God. And he wanted to dedicate his life back to the Lord and walk in the ways they had been taught.

His heart pounded a bit too hard at the thought. But

it was just nervousness. How many people messed up on a daily basis? More than they could count. He didn't have to be perfect. He just had to realize when he made his mistakes. Wasn't that what the bishop was always saying? Titus knew what mistakes he had made and though they were beyond correction, he knew that he would never make them again. He had come back from prison a different and changed man, but with the help of his family, his church, and his community, he would be able to overcome anything that life threw his way.

There was a light burning in the front room of the house when he drove up. But he knew that Abbie left that one on in case her father came downstairs for a snack.

Titus had been really proud of Emmanuel lately. He had bounced back from their intervention and somehow managed to pull himself together. In fact, since Abbie's birthday celebration he had been happier than Titus had ever seen him. Titus had been worried about the birthday celebration. He had been concerned that it would be too hard on her parents, but his feelings for Abbie had won out above any others. More than anything, he wanted her to be happy. It was her birthday and she needed to celebrate.

He started into the barn, wondering if Abbie was still awake. She was most likely up in her room reading the copy of *Pride and Prejudice* that he had bought her for her birthday. She could do nothing but talk about Mr. Darcy for days. When he bought her the book, he never dreamed he would have such competition.

He smiled to himself as he rounded the corner and headed down for his stall.

"Titus?" Abbie poked her head out of his stall. "Is that you?"

His heart warmed to see her there. "Abbie, I thought you'd be in bed by now."

She shook her head. "I just wanted to make sure you got home okay. Did you have fun at your parents'?"

He nodded. It had been a good time visiting with his family, a wonderful welcome home party, and he cleared things up with Mandy. He could only hope that she did as he suggested and went back to her husband. The poor man didn't even know that she was contemplating leaving Wells Landing with another.

Abbie stared down at her feet and shuffled in the hay as if suddenly uncomfortable. "Tomorrow," she started, "I thought we might go into town for a bit. Would you like that?"

"What do we need from town?"

She shook her head and stared at some point behind his right shoulder.

"Nothing. I thought it might be fun to go into town and maybe eat together, just you and me. We can go to Kauffman's. Or even just go to Esther's and have a cup of coffee and a muffin. Whatever you would rather do."

He smiled. "We'll do what you want. Sounds good?"

"I'd like that very much."

She moved past him for the barn door and it took every ounce of willpower he had not to pull her back to him and just hold her close. She was the reason he had the courage to take his vows back to the church. She was the reason that he had something to look forward to. And she was the reason that he knew he could stay. He watched her go to the barn door, somehow managing to keep his hands at his sides.

She turned at the door and glanced back at him. With a small wave she let herself out of the barn.

* * *

Maybe this wasn't such a good idea. Mandy looked around at all the trucks and trailers parked in the fair-grounds parking lot, but she didn't see Levi's. He had hired a driver for the event, the same guy he hired for all these types of shows. Then she spotted it over in one corner of the lot. She had let her driver go as soon as they got there, and for a moment she panicked just a bit thinking that she might not be able to find Levi and would be stranded in Arkansas.

She started toward his trailer in one corner of the lot. It was a large horse trailer, plain compared to the others in the lot, but Levi said it was good and sturdy and that was all that mattered, to get the horses to and from the shows and auctions. He was as passionate about his horses as Andrew Fitch, though they worked in slightly different areas. Andrew trained buggy horses and the like, while Levi raised the big Belgians used to pull wagons and farm equipment. They might all use tractors in the area to do their farming, but the Belgians had other uses as well.

The closer she got, the quicker her steps became. Why had she never thought of this? How could she have been so blind?

She just prayed that he was in his trailer and not out in the arena. She would never find him among so many hats. Of course not all the hats were Amish, most were cowboy Stetsons, but there were enough Amish that it would be hard to find him. And she needed to find him. She needed to tell him the truth. As much as it hurt her, as much as she knew it was going to hurt him, if they were going to have a chance at this marriage they had started, they needed to begin again with a clean slate, so to speak.

She heard a door slam and looked up as he came around the side of his trailer.

He stopped, blinking hard as if the sun were playing tricks on his eyes. "Mandy?"

Her feet flew into a run, and she plowed into him, wrapping her arms around him and holding on tight. He wasn't much for public displays of affection, most Amish weren't, and his arms were slow in coming up around her and hugging her in return. Then he placed his hands on her waist and set her from him. "What are you doing here?"

"I came to be with you."

A frown of confusion puckered his brow. "I thought you were scared of the horses."

She nodded and swallowed hard. "I am, at least your horses. They're just so big. But maybe if you teach me more about them I won't be afraid."

"Why would you want to know more about them?"

"Because I've been wrong. So terribly, terribly wrong. And I need to make it up to you. I need you to know how much I care. And I need to feel close to you."

He reached up and smoothed a hand over the edge of her prayer *kapp*. "I'm glad you're here."

And that was all she could ask.

She had cried so much she almost couldn't breathe, but she had to tell Levi her story. She had to tell him about the doubts that she'd had, the problems that she had faced, and the mistakes that she had almost made. Then she had to pray that he would understand, that he could forgive, and that he too wanted the second chance. A second chance he hadn't even known they needed.

"I hope you can forgive me," she said, using the tissue to wipe her nose. This was supposed to be a special time, make-up time. But she had to tell Levi the complete truth. And she had to do it now before they went one step further.

They had gone to eat dinner at the restaurant next to the hotel where Levi was staying and came back up into the room to get ready for bed. But then the story had started spilling from her like sparkling water from a bottle that had been shaken too vigorously. She had wept and sobbed as she told him the truth. He hadn't made one comment, not even now as he sat on the bed opposite her, his hands clasped between his knees and his eyes intently studying his fingers.

"Why are you crying?" His words were so matter-of-fact that her heart sank to her lap.

"Because I'm sorry. I'm sorry that I hurt you, I'm sorry that I hurt us. I just made a mistake, and I hope you can forgive me. But if you can't . . ."

"Why wouldn't I forgive you?"

She gave a one-armed shrug. "Because I don't deserve it."

Finally, Levi moved. He knelt on the floor by her feet and took her hands into his. "Let me tell you the truth. I knew when I asked to court you that you had given your heart to Titus Lambert. But I knew as time went on that you would eventually get your heart back. And when you did, I wanted to be the person who got it the next time."

She started to speak, but he placed two fingers over her lips. "Just hear me out. Okay?"

Mandy nodded.

"I think our marriage has been good. All I could ask for was time enough to make you really love me before Titus got out of prison. I did everything in my power to make that happen. And when I heard he was coming home I prayed and I prayed that God would see us through."

"What are you saying?" Mandy asked.

"I'm saying I'm not surprised that this happened. I knew how you felt about him, and I was worried that something like this would happen. That somehow he would get your heart back." He gave her a small smile. "Wells Landing is not that big. Did you really think I wouldn't hear what was going on?"

She shook her head. "Nothing happened, Levi. I promise. And I'm so ashamed. You are the best man I know, and I'm so grateful to God for getting you for me. I was blind there for a while, but now I see the truth."

Levi squeezed her fingers in his. "You are the love of my life, Mandy. I knew that I'd been given a second chance with you when the man you were supposed to marry was sent way, and I wasn't about to squander that chance. But I also knew that with a chance came the risk that one day he would come back and try to claim your heart for his own again."

"But he didn't."

"I just need to know one thing."

Tears welled in her eyes. "Anything."

"Are you here today because you love me or because he refused you?"

She shook her head.

"The truth, Mandy."

Her voice caught on a sob. "Would you believe me if I told you it was a little of both?"

"I would like to, *jah*. But I might need a little more explanation."

"I was ready to run away with him. I figured I'd made the biggest mistake of my life. I guess it was different not having him here when I decided to court you. You know what I mean? Maybe if he'd been in town and I had seen him every day and decided that I didn't want to be with him, then you and I started courting, it would've been different. But he wasn't here and since I was not faced with him, he was just pushed from my thoughts and then when he came back, I was so confused.

"You were always gone, and all my friends have babies and I just felt so alone. I thought maybe . . ." She shook her head and gave him a rueful laugh. "I can hardly say it out loud. But when I went to him and told him that I was ready to run away with him, that we could go to the *Englisch* world and live, he said no. And because he told me no I realized that I didn't want to go. I felt relief. He told me that I just wanted what was in the past. And I did. As sad as it is, I wanted those care-free times. You have nothing to worry about. That was selfish of me. And I'm sorry."

Her heart pounded heavy in her chest. What if he told her no as well? What if Levi couldn't find it in his heart to forgive her? What would she do then?

She would spend the rest of her life trying to make it up to him. And with God's help, she would make him see that she was his one true love.

"Mandy." He rose up on his knees and gently pulled her mouth to his, kissing her as a husband kisses a wife. He kissed her long and sweet, and she was dizzy when he lifted his head.

She bit her lip. "Yes?"

"So you want a baby?"

"Only if you want one."

"The truth, please."

"Oh, Levi, I want a baby so much."

He smiled. "Then let's see what we can do about that."

Mandy returned his smile and kissed her husband once again.

Chapter Fourteen

"Titus?" Abbie peeked into the barn, knowing that Titus was in there somewhere, getting ready to go to church.

They hadn't said much to each other that morning, even as they did the morning milking. They had fallen into a comfortable routine, one that didn't require a great deal of talking. Plus, she had known this morning that there was a lot on his mind. Today was the day he would kneel in front of the church and, after a vote, would be reinstated into the congregation. She could only imagine how nervous he was.

He took a step out of his stall as she came around the corner.

"I thought I heard you out here. What are you doing?"

She held the shirt in her hands and resisted the urge to shove it behind her back as some sort of surprise. Instead, she took a couple of steps toward him and held out the pristine white fabric. "I wanted you to have something special to wear today."

He looked at the shirt and back up to meet her gaze. "I thought you were making a green shirt."

"You can't wear green to church."

"But isn't it for your *dat*?"

She gave him a small smile and shook her head. "It was never for *Dat*."

A grin spread across Titus's face. He looked so handsome when he smiled that Abbie made a note that she needed to make him smile as often as possible.

"For me?"

She nodded. "I hope it fits."

His expression turned wistful as he took the shirt from her and shook it out. He held it up as if testing its size. "I think it'll fit just fine. Perfect, even."

"Will you wear it today?"

"Of course," Titus said and ducked back into his stall to change.

Abbie waited for him, excited to see how it looked on him, but it was more than that. She was reluctant to leave. This day could potentially be the start of a new life for the both of them. Titus had made his decision. He was staying with the Amish, and they were raising cows and camels and she could only hope that maybe one day they could court for real. How wonderful. How joyous! She couldn't think of anything better in the world.

He stepped back out of his stall, still adjusting his shirt and suspenders as he did. The fit was perfect and the crisp white made his blond hair look like golden rays of sunshine.

"It looks good." She resisted the urge to step closer to him and adjust his shirt like she had seen her *mamm* do for her father countless times. But as much as she wanted to touch him, he wasn't exactly hers to touch. Not yet anyway.

"I think it's great, thank you." He stepped closer to

her and took her hands into his. Then he bent close to give her a sweet kiss high on the cheek. He smelled like shaving cream and soap and she wanted to bury her face in the crook of his neck and never let go. Not that she would ever be that forward.

She took a step back, but he held fast her fingers.

Their gazes caught and the moment stilled. "Abbie." Her name was like a prayer on his lips. Soft and sweet. And still their gazes held. He took a step closer, his intentions clear. He was going to kiss her, and she waited with breathless anticipation. Then he seemed to rouse himself out of some kind of stupor. He took a step back.

"I'm sorry," he said. "This isn't the time. It's not the place. But I want you to know, Abbie King, that I would love nothing more than to kiss you right now."

If she had been anybody else, she might've taken a step toward him and lifted her lips in invitation, but she couldn't. She just hadn't been raised that way.

"But after today, after I join the church again, when I have everything back in order, I want us to date. Would you like that?"

She almost cried in anticipation. She would love nothing more than to date Titus Lambert. If someone had asked her two months ago she would've laughed. But Titus had come to mean so much to her in the last few weeks. She would love nothing more than for their business partnership to turn into a marriage partnership. A family partnership.

"I would love that."

He squeezed her fingers and lifted one hand to kiss the back of it. "I just have to get this right first. You understand?"

"I do," she said. It was best for everyone involved for Titus to get his life back in line with God's plan; then they could go forward and do all the things their hearts demanded.

"I'm so glad."

She smiled up at him in sheer anticipation. "Me too."

Titus was way past nervous as he took his place in the front row next to where the bishop would sit. He didn't know why he was nervous. But there was that chance that someone in the congregation would say that they didn't want Titus to come back in. Even in his heart, he knew it wouldn't happen, but he couldn't stop those feelings all the same. If that were the case, he didn't know what he would do. Perhaps he should pray about it. But prayer was something he just hadn't been able to do yet. Nor had he told anyone. One day, one day he would have that ability back, but in the meantime he had surrounded himself with people strong in prayer. But with any luck at all, his inability to talk to God would disappear as quickly as it came.

The elders came in from one side, signifying that church had begun. The minister stopped in the front, while the bishop, the deacon, and the preacher all took seats next to Titus in the front row. It was almost as if he could feel the eyes behind him burning a hole through his back. He tried to tell himself they were just looking at the beautiful shirt Abbie had made for him, no matter that it was mostly covered by his vest. It was better by far than thinking those eyes cutting through him like laser beams belonged to a person who didn't want him back into the fold. He had done nothing untoward since he had come back here. He had walked the line. He had done everything he was supposed to do and was doing his best to start over. He was doing his best to do everything that God wanted of him.

Everyone took up their hymnals and began to sing. Since he was not a member in good standing, he braced his elbows on his knees and placed his head in his hands, covering his face as everyone sang. The last three church services he had sat this way, repentant of the sins he had committed. It was an old custom, and though many of the old ways were being dropped and changed to suit the new modern Amish society, he was glad this one wasn't one of them. He could still hear the sermon, listen to the songs, and enjoy the message, but with his face covered he felt as if he could hide in the words. He could get lost in them without having to come back until he was ready.

The song ended, and the preacher stood. He walked to the front with his Bible in his hands. Titus hadn't known who was going to be speaking the first sermon, but he did know that was his cue.

Titus stood and waited for the minister.

"Titus Lambert."

He took a step forward, then knelt in front of them all.

"Titus, you came before the church and confessed your sins. You have been under the *Bann* for six weeks. Do you believe the punishment was deserved?" Bishop Ebersol asked.

"Yes, I do."

"Do you sincerely ask for patience from God and the church?"

"I do," he replied.

"And finally, do you promise to live more carefully with the Lord's help like you promised at baptism?"

"I do." And he so very badly wanted to.

The bishop reached out a hand and helped Titus to his feet. He gave him the kiss of peace and together they faced the congregation.

"Five years ago, this church was rocked with tragedy. It has taken a long time for us to heal, but with Titus joining once again, that circle is complete. And I believe that we will all be better Christians for it."

Titus only hoped that it was the truth.

"Abbie? Are you listening?"

Abbie turned back to the conversation at hand. "What?"

Emily Riehl nudged Caroline. "I told you she wasn't listening."

"I'm sorry," Abbie said. She hadn't been listening, because she had been too interested in what Titus was doing. She couldn't help but watch him as he finished his meal, threw away the paper plate, and otherwise moved among the members of the congregation as if he truly was part of them once again.

That's all she could ever hope for. Because after today they would be courting, but she couldn't tell Caroline and Emily that.

"It looks to me like you got a certain someone on your mind today." Caroline bounced baby Holly on one hip, and suddenly a baby was all Abbie could think about.

It was a ridiculous thought to have. She had so much to do she could barely take care of it all. Her parents still required quite a bit of attention, though her father's drinking had stopped and her mother seemed to be on the upward climb out of her depression. But a baby . . .

She and Titus would date for at least a year before they would even think about getting married; until then they would have baby cows and baby camels to worry about. The baby humans would have to wait a little bit longer. But the thought of a family of her own filled her with such warmth she was almost beside herself.

"So are you up for it?" Caroline asked.

"Up for what?" Abbie moved her gaze away from Titus and settled it back on her new friend. She really did like Caroline. She had come to Wells Landing as a young widow with a small child and promptly fallen in love with Andrew Fitch. They had gotten married and now had baby Holly, named Hollis after Caroline's father. It seemed that the rest of her family had moved from Tennessee's conservative Swartzentruber community to the slightly more liberal community of Wells Landing.

That was the one regret she had about going to Missouri. It put her life on hold, suspended it to be continued when she returned. But maybe it was a good thing after all. If she hadn't have come back from Missouri when she did, she might not have gotten to know Titus again. She might not have ever fallen in love with him. And they might not ever be planning on courting.

She thought about Alvin. What would he think of her and Titus? But she knew. Titus had been his best friend. And Alvin would love the fact that they were together.

"I asked if you wanted to come over and play games this afternoon. Andrew bought this new game that you play by drawing a picture and then everybody has to guess what it is."

Abbie shook her head. "That sounds like fun, but I can't draw."

Emily laughed. "That's kind of the point. If your pictures are really bad, then it'll be harder for everyone to guess what it is."

"That sounds fine," Abbie said. "Are we doing couples?" It was sort of a dumb question considering that everyone that she had mentioned might be coming over was married. Pretty much the only girl left in their group who wasn't married was Sarah Yoder, Mandy Burkholder's cousin. And Jonah Miller. But Jonah had his heart broken one too many times by Lorie Kauffman, and Abbie wasn't sure if he'd ever settle down.

"Well, *jah*. I mean, we're all married."

Just as she thought.

"I hate to go and leave Titus alone."

She searched him out in the crowd once again, finding him immediately. He looked so handsome in his new shirt. She had enjoyed making that one so much she needed to make him another. Maybe something in that green she had bought the same day . . .

"Abbie?" Emily shook her arm. "Pay attention."

"I'm sorry. I was just thinking about—"

"Titus?" Caroline asked.

"Well, of course. I mean, he is staying with us. I would hate to leave him behind if I came over to play cards."

"And he surely wouldn't want anybody to think that the two of you might have feelings for each other," Emily said with a smile. Her dark blue eyes twinkled with laughter.

"There's nothing going on between me and Titus," Abbie lied. But she looked at her fingernails as she said it.

"It's okay," Caroline said. "Your secret's safe with us."

"I don't have a secret."

Caroline and Emily looked at each other again and gave a knowing nod. "Right," they said together.

"Okay," she said. "There might be a little something. But, you know, it's nothing yet." Except for one fantastic kiss that she had wanted to go on forever and ever and ever, and one beautiful afternoon by a hidden waterfall that not many people knew about. And that wasn't even counting the day in, day out. The boring chores that they performed side by side. Somehow being with Titus made it seem more fun than it had ever been. She felt pretty sure she could be happy her entire life mucking out stalls if only Titus was right there next to her.

"She's got it bad," Emily said.

Caroline nodded. "Real bad."

"You two stop."

"The only reason we know is because we've been there," Emily said.

"It's not a bad place to be," Caroline said. "As long as everything goes okay. Love is a beautiful thing."

Abbie let her gaze stray back over to where Titus was standing with Jonah Miller and some of the other boys in their group. She wondered if he was getting his own invitation to play cards.

As long as everything went okay.

From where she stood, she could see nothing going wrong.

He could hardly believe it. Just this morning he made his vow to court Abbie and now she was sitting in the buggy beside him as they drove to Andrew and Caroline's. It was amazing how things worked out. But after tonight there would be no keeping their relationship a secret. He supposed they could, but only if they went out to Taylor Creek.

There were several buggies already parked in the yard when they got there. The two of them had to go home and milk the cows, then shower and get ready to go back out. It seemed like everyone else had already joined in the fun before they got there.

Titus pulled his buggy to a stop, counting the ones already in a row. There were five total including his.

He set the brake and turned to Abbie. "Are you sure you're up for this?"

She nodded. "I think it will be fun, don't you?"

Fun. He had been asking her about having fun for a long time. And he had tried every day since he had been out of jail to live his life to the fullest each and every day. Time was a very precious thing. It shouldn't be squandered. But somehow this was different. Living life up on the farm was a whole different thing from couples getting together and playing games on Sunday night.

Still, he would have to get used to it. He and Abbie would not have a traditional courting. They were too old to attend the singings, though technically he supposed they could. And their community wasn't large enough to host a whole bunch of friend groups like single couples over the age of twenty-two. They would have to make do. And most times they would get settled in with a bunch of other couples. Then again, why did it matter? If they were to be a couple, there could be no secrets.

"Of course it's going to be fun."

He slid out of the buggy and came around to help her down. He still wasn't able to drive a tractor since he had been back, but he had to admit that there was something special about traveling in a buggy. Nothing beat it.

The sound of laughter met him as they started up the porch steps. Titus had always loved the Fitch place. The big workshop off to one side and the huge barns on the other. It was a beautiful place and sometimes he wondered if he and Abbie would have a house like the rambling white clapboard. He wanted to give her everything, the world, especially since the one thing she wanted the most he could never get her back.

He pushed that thought away and knocked on the door, opening it before anyone responded.

"Did you hear something?" someone asked, though he wasn't sure who it was.

They stepped into the house just as Caroline peeked her head around the corner from the living room. "Come in. Come in." She turned back to the room. "Titus and Abbie are here." He didn't know they'd become a celebrity couple.

"Come on. You're missing the fun. We'll deal you in so you can play."

Caroline hustled back into the living room as Titus and Abbie followed. Just as he suspected, everyone here was married, except for Jonah and Sarah. But he had heard rumors around town that Sarah had set her sights on Jonah ever since Lorie Kauffman had gone *Englisch*. Still, it felt a bit awkward to look around at so many faces and know that it would be another year before they would be among them.

Just another year of living the life, becoming accustomed to being out and all the other things that he needed to do. And maybe even in that year he could learn to pray again.

"Come sit." Caroline patted the spot between her and Emily. "We're playing boys against girls."

The boys all shook their heads. "It wasn't our idea," Andrew called in return. "The girls think they are smarter than us."

Jonah motioned him over. "Come help us prove them wrong."

Reluctantly Titus moved away from Abbie. Some date. He had to spend it across the room from the one he wanted to sit closest to.

* * *

"I'm hungry." Andrew looked pointedly at his wife. Abbie watched the two. They seemed to have something incredibly special, and she could only hope and pray that the Lord had something that great in store for her.

"I'm hungry too." She thought it was Jonah this time. Then a chorus of "let's get something to eat" rose from the male side of the room.

Caroline jumped up from her place on the floor and brushed off her skirt. "Let me see what I can find."

Emily was on her feet in a second. "I know. Let's have a kitchen party."

A series of comments went up all around the room. Finally, Julie said what they were all thinking. "We can't have a kitchen party. We're too old for that."

"Then let's have a retro kitchen party. We can do anything we want. It's our house," Emily said. Then she looked over to Caroline. "I mean it's your house. A kitchen party would be fun."

"Let's do it!" Caroline motioned for everybody to follow her into the kitchen. Abbie laughed and followed behind.

Kitchen parties were always the best. They were especially entertaining when they were teenagers and in *rumspringa*. They would all gather in the kitchen and raid the refrigerator, taking whatever leftovers they could find and turning them into something else entirely. There was something to be said about just hanging out, eating, talking, laughing, and having fun with friends. It was something she hadn't had enough of recently, and she knew Titus hadn't either.

She cast a glance over at him as he stood, leaning up against the counter, drinking a bottle of water and talking with Elam Riehl. Elam was a dairy farmer too. Though she didn't know how he managed to get his milking done and be at the party before her and Titus. Of course he had lots of sisters and sisters-in-law to help if he needed it.

"We've got those leftover hamburgers," Caroline said.

Julie and Sarah had stationed themselves at the pantry. "There's crackers and beans," Sarah said.

"We could make chili," Julie added.

"It's ninety-five degrees outside," Andrew said.

"Better yet," Julie said. "You have all those little bags of corn chips you bought at Sam's."

"Frito pie!" someone called across the room; this time she thought it was Danny, Julie's husband.

"How about tacos?" Emily suggested.

"There's a little bit of chicken in here too," Caroline added.

"Do you have lettuce?" Sarah asked. "There's a jar of salsa."

Ten minutes later they were all eating taco salad out of individual bags of chips. Caroline heated the hamburgers on the stove, tearing the patties into small pieces. Then they crunched up the chips, added the meat, lettuce, and salsa along with a sprinkle of cheese.

"So," Julie said, sidling up beside her. "You and Titus."

Abbie shook her head. "He's a nice guy," she said, scooping up a bite. She couldn't say much more, her mouth was full of food.

"I know that," Julie said. "He always was."

"I'm sorry," Abbie said. "He's a little sensitive about things sometimes; I think it makes me the same way."

"There's no need to be. He's back in the church, he's working, he has a job, now he has you."

Abbie liked the sound of that. She had Titus, and Titus had her. She very much believed that Alvin would approve. She and Titus might've gotten off to a bit of a rocky start. But she was glad she had worked through all those negative feelings. She felt better for it and came out with a man she loved in the end.

She looked over to where Titus was eating his own food. Even though they didn't have to separate when they ate, like they did in church, somehow they found themselves sitting on opposite sides of the room again. Of course it was really easy to see the men when they were across the room. And she loved to watch Titus. He was different from the other guys. It was his time in the *Englisch* world. He had lived a different life than they had in the last few years. And it had turned him into a strange combination of a few things *Englisch* and a few things Amish. More than just the average Amish man.

It was impossible to be Amish in today's world and not gain some influence from the *Englisch* people. The trick was knowing what to keep and what to throw away. Somehow Titus had spent the last five years among the *Englisch*, and the worst *Englisch* out there, and managed to retain his Amish demeanor while adopting so much of the *Englisch* ways as well. She found it intriguing, and it also helped her to remember every day that he had lived so differently from the way she had in the last few years.

"I heard about your camels."

Abbie smiled and took another bite. "They're something else, that's for sure."

"We'll have to come out and see them." She laid a hand on her belly, the action drawing Abbie's attention.

"Julie," she started, "are you going to have a baby?"

Julie beamed. She was the last of their group to have a baby other than Abbie herself and Sarah Yoder. Though between Abbie and Sarah, Abbie supposed she was the closest. At least now that she and Titus were officially courting. And although she wanted a baby and looked forward to that time in her life when that would happen, she knew she was in better shape for making those dreams come true than Sarah. Sarah had just hitched her wagon to the wrong star.

Though Abbie had noticed Jonah was watching Sarah very closely as they sat across the room from each other.

But more than anything, Abbie was so very thankful that the Lord had sent Titus her way. He had done so much for her family, brought her father back from the brink of drinking himself to death, brought her mother back from the pit of depression. He had helped her heal in ways that she didn't herself understand. And she was a better person for it. She was more tolerant, more understanding, and more diligent in making sure that life was lived to the fullest. And that was exactly what she planned to do, with Titus at her side. She was going to live life to the fullest every day.

Chapter Fifteen

"I wish you didn't have to do this." Abbie crossed her arms as she watched Titus lug his meager possessions to the back trailer attached to his buggy.

"I told you it's necessary. I can't court you and live on your farm. It's just not seemly."

Abbie rolled her eyes. "Who uses a word like that these days?"

Titus chuckled. "I thought it fit."

"I didn't say it didn't fit," Abbie said. "I said no one uses words like that these days."

Titus slung his bag into the trailer and turned back to her. "I do."

And that was why she loved him so much. One thing was for certain: Titus Lambert was his own person. And he was definitely a person she didn't want to move out of the barn. It wasn't like they would do anything unseemly. They were just now starting to date each other. They had more than enough to do raising their cows and getting their camel farm started. The last thing he needed was to have to run back and forth between his house and hers in order to get the work done.

But that really wasn't the reason she didn't want him

to move out. She slept better when he was in her barn every night. She felt secure and somehow closer to him knowing that she could get out of bed and go talk to him anytime she wanted.

She never would. It just wasn't proper, and she wouldn't want her parents to think that something sinful was going on under their roof. But she wanted Titus close. And if he was staying at his parents' house, he wasn't nearly close enough, as far as she was concerned.

"It's just what we have to do, Abbie. You know how it is."

She nodded, then gave a tiny shiver as her prayer *kapp* strings tickled her neck. "I still think it's stupid," she said.

"It might be. But that's the way it has to be." They finished the afternoon milking, fed the animals, and made sure no weeds were taking over the garden. Then they started loading his stuff into the trailer.

"Are you sure you don't want to eat supper here?"

He shook his head. "I would love to, but *Mamm* is expecting me tonight." He grinned sheepishly. "I think she's kind of excited to have me back home."

Abbie could understand that for sure. "And you're coming back in the morning?"

"I'll be here as early as I can. Probably around five or five-thirty." It would push their milking back a little bit later than normal, but that was better than not having him there to milk with her at all.

"Okay, I'll be waiting on you. Are you eating breakfast there or here?" When did she start sounding so much like a wife?

"What would you rather I do?"

"I'd rather you be here," Abbie said.

He smiled and gave a small nod. "Okay, I'll wait to

eat breakfast here, and I'll probably go home for dinner. How does that sound?"

"Good."

"Speaking of dinner," Titus said. "How about we go out to eat tomorrow night. I'll call Bruce Brown. Maybe he can take us over to Pryor. I heard they have a new Chinese buffet over there."

Dinner out! And not just anywhere but at a brand-new restaurant in Pryor. If he kept up that she would start feeling like she was Queen of the World.

"I'll bring a change of clothes, and we'll leave from here after the evening milking. Does that sound okay?"

Abbie smiled. "That sounds perfect."

Bruce dropped them off at the door of the restaurant, promising to return to pick them up in an hour and a half.

Abbie couldn't contain her smile as they walked through the door. Her first real date with Titus. This made it official. She was so happy, nothing could dampen her spirits.

"There are a lot of people here," Titus said.

"Well, it is a new place to eat." She glanced up at him, and the look on his face was pensive. "Is something wrong?"

He shook his head. "I just didn't expect so many people to be here."

He was right. The place was packed. Almost every table was full. Members of the waitstaff rushed around clearing off dishes and getting the tables ready for the next people to sit down. Others brought out more food to the buffet. The place was bustling.

It smelled heavenly. The decor was nice golden yellow with bamboo plants on every table. Asian art decorated the walls and the loudspeakers played some type of Asian music, the likes of which Abbie had never heard. Still, it was pleasing, and she smiled even wider as she stood next to Titus.

She glanced up at him and his expression was even more concerned than before. "Do you want to find someplace else to eat?"

He swallowed hard and shook his head. "No, this place is fine."

She had to agree, but she couldn't help feeling that there was something else wrong with Titus. He hadn't changed his mind, had he? He had been with her at the farm all day. He'd come at five-thirty as promised to do the morning milking. Everything seemed to be going just fine. He'd stayed clear through to the evening milking, then showered and changed clothes as they had planned the day before.

Bruce Brown had picked them up and twenty minutes later they were at the restaurant. So why the sudden change in mood?

"Are you sure you're okay?"

"Yeah, I'm fine." Titus took a deep breath and let it out slowly.

"Is the crowd bothering you?" She had to admit that so many people in one closed-in place was a little unnerving. She'd never been in a restaurant this large, and she felt like it was some sort of adventure. But she knew everyone didn't feel that way.

"It's fine. I just want you to be happy and have a good time." He visibly relaxed and sent her a smile.

She couldn't help but notice it didn't quite reach his eyes. She would have to find out what was bothering him another day. "I am happy. I'm with you."

The hostess came and escorted them to a clean table. On her heels was a waitress who explained to them how the buffet worked. She got their drink orders and moved away.

"Let's go get a plate," Titus said.

Abbie followed behind him to the buffet. "I hope they have orange chicken," she said.

He smiled. "I'm sure they do. It looks like they have just about everything."

And that was the truth. They had dishes she had never heard of along with batches of seafood, three different kinds of rice, and two different kinds of noodles.

"Do you want to start with a salad?" Titus asked, giving a nod to the salad bar on the right.

"Are you kidding?" The salad looked green and fresh, but she'd come for Chinese food.

Titus chuckled. "I was just making sure."

They grabbed plates and got in line, starting with the rice and other goodies. But she liked to look at the whole buffet before deciding on her main dish. What if she got to the end and didn't have room for her favorite orange chicken because it was on the other side?

After serving up some rice, she headed down the buffet taking note of different dishes as she went. Chinese green beans, she loved those. Sweet and sour chicken, lemon chicken, lemon shrimp, orange chicken. She reached for the spoon and scooped some onto her plate.

A noise arose somewhere around the start of the buffet line. Even above all the racket of the place, the Asian music coming through the speakers and the chatter of the many diners, she heard the clatter as something hit the floor, then a noise like shuffling feet. Abbie looked up, but couldn't see anything over all the people milling around. Someone screamed. Others gasped. Murmurs arose, accompanied by more sounds of scuffling.

"Somebody call the police!"

The crowd parted and she so very clearly saw Titus—her sweet, loving Titus—grab a man by his arm. He twisted it behind the man's back and shoved him head-long into the salad bar.

"Titus!"

His face was red and blotchy, his breathing heavy. She abandoned her plate and ran to his side.

The man pulled himself off the salad bar, brushing bits of peas and other vegetables from his shirt. "Dude, what is wrong with you? I said I was sorry."

"What's going on here?" A tall, thin man in a plain black suit approached. Abbie supposed he was the manager, but she couldn't ask. She didn't have the words. Had she really just witnessed such a violent display from her Titus?

Beside her, Titus started to shake. She wasn't the only one who noticed. A man at a nearby table stood and took Titus by the arm, helping him to his recently vacated chair. The man was older, gray-headed, and wore a leather vest and a baseball hat that said VIETNAM VETERAN.

"Just rest," he said, patting Titus on the shoulder.

Abbie silently thanked the Lord for the kindness of strangers. She didn't know what had just happened, or even how it could have happened, but something was wrong. Terribly, terribly wrong.

"I was just getting some food," the other man said. "I accidentally bumped into this guy. I didn't see him there. He dropped his plate, and the next thing I know he's got me around the neck, my arm behind my back, and I'm flying into the salad bar. I didn't do anything."

"Are you hurt?" the manager asked.

The man shook his head. "No, I'm fine, just dirty." He brushed at his clothes once again.

"Do you still want the police?" someone nearby asked.

The manager looked to the two men. Titus was sitting in a chair hunched over and still trembling as if he had been in the cold for days.

The other man was young and Abbie was afraid that he would want the police to come just to cause trouble. But he seemed to recognize something in Titus.

"I guess not," he grumbled. "I mean he's Amish, right? I thought they were pacifists."

The manager turned to Titus. "Do you want to tell your part of the story?"

Titus didn't look up, just barely shook his head. Though Abbie was a good five feet from him, she could hear his teeth chattering.

"What's wrong with him?" she asked. Was he having some kind of fit? Did they need to get an ambulance?

The man in the Vietnam veteran hat grimaced. "I'm no doctor, but I'd say it's PTSD."

She shook her head. "What's that?"

"Post-traumatic stress disorder," the manager grimly stated.

Behind him some of the waiters and waitresses started to move the patrons around and focus them back on the buffet.

"I don't understand."

"Is he a veteran? Has he seen combat?" the gray-headed man asked. "We see this all the time over at the VA hospital. A man comes back from war, and he just ain't the same."

"He's a vet?" the young man asked. "Aren't Amish people against the army?" He turned to Titus. "Dude, I'm sorry. I didn't know."

Abbie hated letting them think that Titus had served in the armed forces, but she couldn't tell them that he had been in prison. It wasn't any of their business.

Right now all she wanted to do was get Titus out of there. "Is he okay?" she asked. "Should I take him to the hospital?"

"It might not be a bad idea," the older man said. "Just to be on the safe side."

Titus pushed to his feet, swaying a bit as he stood. "No hospital," he said, sounding so much like her father that it nearly brought tears to her eyes. "I'll be fine. I'm sorry about the mess. About everything."

To her dismay, tears rose into his eyes. "I'm taking him home," she told the manager. "Do we owe you anything?"

He looked at the mess, then shook his head. "No, just get him some help. Too many of our boys are coming back from over there all messed up."

She nodded. "I will. Thank you."

She ignored the looks they received as she walked him to the front. Unfortunately, she had to stop at the counter and use the phone to call Bruce and have him come back to get them.

The hostess offered for them to sit in the lobby waiting area, but Abbie thought it best that they wait outside. They had upset enough people for one night. The quicker they got out of sight, the quicker they would be forgotten.

"I'm sorry, Abbie."

"Shhhh . . ." she crooned. She didn't care who was watching. They sat beside each other on the bench outside. Abbie pulled his head down to lay on her shoulder. "Don't worry about it. Everything's going to be okay." But she didn't know that to be the truth. She didn't know the first thing about this disorder. In fact, she had never even heard of it. She didn't know whether or not it was dangerous or harmful to the person. All she did know was that it could take a normally loving and kind man and turn him into something else entirely.

They didn't have to wait for long before Bruce pulled up to the curb. He left the engine running and hopped out of the car, rushing around the front of it to where they sat. "What happened?" He helped Titus to his feet.

"I don't know, really. I think someone bumped Titus and knocked his food out of his hands. The next thing I know, he shoves the man headfirst into the salad bar."

Bruce frowned. "That doesn't sound right."

Tell me about it.

"I'm sorry," Titus said. It seemed to be the only thing he could manage.

"Should we take him to the hospital?" Bruce asked.

"He doesn't want to go to the hospital," Abbie explained.

"No doctors," Titus mumbled. "I'm so sorry."

Bruce helped Titus into the backseat, then snagged Abbie's gaze. "What do you think?"

She didn't know what to think. She didn't have any experience in such matters. "The man in there said it might be some kind of stress disorder. They thought he had served in the army."

"PTSD. We see it a lot. These days especially." Bruce shook his head sadly.

"Does he need medical care for that?" She didn't know what to do.

"He should definitely talk to someone. A therapist or maybe a doctor. A psychiatrist."

Abbie's heart fell in her chest. "Is it that bad?"

"It can be if not treated." Bruce went around and got behind the wheel.

Abbie climbed into the passenger side, then turned to look at Titus. He was slumped in the backseat looking dejected and embarrassed all at once. She wasn't sure if his sluggish state was due to his actions or the disorder. She only knew that she needed to get him home, back to his parents so they could figure out what to do.

"Don't worry too much, Abbie. I've been around Titus quite a bit since he got back into town. He doesn't appear to have too many triggers. I'm sure this can be easily controlled."

"I hope you're right." She turned back around in her seat. She couldn't imagine what horrors Titus had faced in prison and how he had survived at all.

Lord, please help me find a way to help him. Amen.

He had come to mean too much to her over the past few weeks. She didn't know what she would do without him and she prayed she never had to find out.

Bruce dropped them at Titus's parents' house. Titus seemed to have gotten some of his bearings back. He thanked Bruce for his time and offered him money, though Bruce refused to take it. "Just take care of yourself," he said before he got into his car and drove away.

The last thing Abbie wanted to do was explain the incident to his parents.

But one thing was certain: they needed to come up with a plan before they walked through the door.

"So what are we going to do?" Abbie looked to Titus as he stood there in the driveway not moving.

"There is no we." He looked out over the pasture as he said that, not even meeting her gaze as he spoke.

"What do you mean?" She had an idea, but just the thought of it made her mouth dry and her heart pound painfully in her chest.

"Don't you see?"

"Maybe I do. Maybe I don't. Why don't you tell me what it is you want to say, Titus?"

He turned on her, his eyes hard and cold. "Go home, Abbie. It's over."

She swallowed hard, but refused to let him see her pain. He was hurting too, she understood that. But how could they get through this together if he wouldn't allow her to be by his side?

"There can be no we. It's over. Because I can't have you near me. Not like this."

"Titus, it was one incident. You just need some help."

He shook his head though he had lost some of his earlier anger. "This time, maybe. What about next time? I can't take the chance that I might hurt you."

"Don't you think that should be up to me to decide?"

He folded his arms and expanded his chest as if somehow that would intimidate her into giving up and going home. She was doing neither.

"Do you know why Mandy married Levi?"

She shook her head. "What does that have to do with anything?"

"He told her that even if I did come back, I wouldn't be the same person. And you know what? He was right. He saved Mandy from being married to a monster. The last thing you need is the same trouble."

She ignored the zing at the thought of being his wife and instead concentrated on his stubbornness. "Of course you're not the same person, Titus. Even if you had gone away to a spa in the mountains of Colorado for five years, you would have come back a different person. No one lives anywhere for five years without changing. And you're kidding yourself if you think that you could have. What you have to do is learn how to deal with those changes."

He shook his head. "I can't."

Angry tears welled in her eyes. "After everything you've done for my family, after everything you've done for me, and everything you've done for everyone around you, I never figured you to be a coward."

He opened his mouth and shut it again as if he didn't have words to say. Or maybe none of them were nice.

"Go home, Abbie."

Chapter Sixteen

His heart burned in his chest as he turned away from her and stalked up the porch steps. He slammed into the house without looking back. Knowing it was for the best even if his heart was shattered. He could not risk her life, her well-being, even her happiness, because of what he suffered. He had heard about post-traumatic stress disorder. He'd thought at times that he might have a few problems with it. Here in Wells Landing, the chances of those encounters actually happening were slim. But he couldn't live his entire life holed up in the barn. He would need to learn to survive, but he couldn't jeopardize Abbie's well-being until he learned to work through it. And after that? Could he ever really trust himself after tonight? When that man had knocked his food out of his hands—even though he knew and understood later that it was an accident— something went through him. All at once he was back in jail being threatened by the block bully, who liked to go around slapping food out of other prisoners' hands. He always managed to do it when no one was looking or when conveniently no one saw anything. So the poor

person didn't get anything to eat. The first week Titus
was in prison, he ate three meals. All because of this
bully. The tray clattering to the floor at the buffet line
brought all that back and more. Suddenly he wasn't
standing in Pryor in the new Chinese restaurant; he was
back in jail, fighting for his life, fighting for food. Nothing like starvation could take a man back to an animal
state. He'd spent three days in solitary confinement for
fighting back. But he had learned real quick that he
had to fight or become a victim. He thought then that
if he could only learn to fight back, maybe he would
come out of jail closer to the person he was going in,
but even that had changed him. He had learned to
use physical force to keep himself safe, and every day
he told himself that it was a necessity. But every day he
hated himself more.

"Titus?" June was sitting at the kitchen table, a stack
of greeting cards next to her. "What happened?"

He looked down at himself, only then realizing he
was a mess. He had food splattered up around his legs
where the tray had dropped to the floor at his feet.
Could feel the heat in his face and had a feeling that his
eyes might appear a little wild. It had been a rough day.

"Abbie's outside."

She looked at him blankly.

"Can you take her home?"

"Why can't you take her home?"

"June, can you just take her home for me, please?"

Something in his tone must've conveyed that he was
at the end of his rope.

June stacked the cards neatly and set her pen aside.
"*Jah.* Okay. Sure."

She brushed past him and out of the house, allowing
the screen door to slam behind her as she did.

He'd been too harsh with her. And he owed her an

apology. But he could not go back out there as long as Abbie was around. As soon as June got back home, he would tell her he was sorry.

She would never know how sorry.

Titus plowed his fingers into his hair, feeling as if his head were about to spin off. All the thoughts, all the problems, all the everything. It was too much. His best choice now was to leave. To leave it all behind.

"Titus?" He turned as his *dat* came in from outside. "What's going on? June just stormed by and took the tractor to run Abbie home." He looked Titus up and down. "What happened to you?"

"I tried," Titus said. "You'll never know how hard I tried. But I can't stay here."

His father shifted in place. "Okay, but I don't think it's a good idea for you to sleep in the Kings' barn if you're going to date their daughter."

Titus shook his head. "I can't date Abbie anymore."

His father's expression changed to one of understanding. But how could he truly understand when he had not lived what Titus had. "Let's go into the living room and sit down."

Titus shook his head. He could not allow his *dat* to talk about this. Not while he still had it in him to walk away. He had to leave now while he still could.

"I've got to go." He took the stairs two at a time, then hurried into the room he shared with Gabe Allen. He gathered what clothes he had, some *Englisch*, some Amish, and shoved them into his backpack. He had that one photograph of him with Eli, Alvin, and Blaine. Someone had taken it up at the lake that summer. Those were the days when they'd still been living like they were supposed to live, before they decided that they needed one last party before they settled down into pious Amish life. That photograph meant so much to him. It was the one thing he kept with him always. The Amish didn't allow photographs, but he cherished it. They were all smiling and laughing. That was how he wanted to remember everybody, not the way it ended up.

A knock sounded on the door. He didn't need to look to know who it was. He knew.

"Would you mind explaining this to me a little better?" *Dat* asked.

What good would an explanation do? It wouldn't change anything. "It doesn't matter," Titus said.

"Why don't you let me decide?"

What was it with everybody thinking they could make the decisions for his life? "I can't do it," he said. It was as simple as that. All the explanations and everything else were just words. For whatever reason, the fact still remained. He could not live the life of a pacifist after everything that he had been through in prison. And he wouldn't hurt those he loved just to be there with them. He would rather live alone for the rest of his life than hurt Abbie or June or anyone else in the wonderful community of Wells Landing.

"Can't? Or won't?"

Titus met his gaze. "Can't."

His father thoughtfully scratched his beard. "Does this have anything to do with Mandy?"

"Why would it have anything to do with her?" He hoped Mandy had gone back to her husband like he told her to do. It was one thing for him to walk away, but he would not take another man's wife with him.

"Wells Landing is not a big place, Son. Rumors fly around here like bats. She's been out to the house I don't know how many times since you've been home. Probably more times than she came around the whole time you were gone."

"The rumors are wrong."

"So if it's not Mandy, what about Abbie?"

"I love her, but I can't stay."

"You aren't making any sense."

Titus zipped his backpack. He'd been here for over six weeks and still everything he owned would fit in one small bag. "I can't stay here and live the life that you want me to live."

His father took a step toward him, but Titus held up one hand to stop him. "That's where God comes in," *Dat* said.

"God doesn't listen in prison. I stopped praying a long time ago. And I have no reason to believe He'll start listening to me now." He slung his bag across his shoulder and brushed past his father and down the stairs.

Dat was right on his heels. "You're a grown man now. You can walk out that door and never look back. You can walk away from Abbie even though you claim to love her. But God can't listen to you if you're not talking to Him."

Titus started down the road the same way he had come in—backpack on his shoulder and one foot in front of the other. He had no idea where he was headed. Just away. He had to get away before he did something he regretted. Something he couldn't take back.

He was halfway to nowhere when June pulled up in the tractor. He just kept walking.

"Where are you going?" she asked.

"Away," Titus said.

"Can I have a few more details than that?"

"Tulsa?" He shrugged. "Does it matter?"

"Are you going to walk there?"

He hadn't given it much thought. He would probably have to hitchhike once he got to the highway.

"Get in. I'll take you somewhere."

He wanted to just keep on walking, but he couldn't. This was June. "You can't take me all the way to Tulsa in this old thing."

She shrugged. "Then don't go to Tulsa. Maybe you should go to Abbie's and make up with her."

"You don't know what you're talking about," he said. He climbed up on the tractor next to her.

"Really?" June asked, pulling the tractor into motion once again. "That's how you want to handle this?"

"You don't understand." How could anyone understand? No one had gone through what he had.

"I understand this. I just took home a girl who is heartbroken but still loves you."

"I don't want to talk about it," Titus said. He didn't want to think about how Abbie was feeling right about now. The thought of her crying, heart breaking, was almost more than he could handle. But he was doing this for her. Maybe one day she would understand that. "Where are you taking me?"

"Eli's."

"What if I don't want to go there?"

"Too bad," June said. "You're going anyway. Maybe he can talk some sense into you."

"Just so you know, I'm leaving tomorrow." Titus felt it best to get things straight from the start.

"And why is that?" Eli asked.

June had dropped him off at Eli's house without much fanfare. She simply made him get off the tractor and told Eli to "talk some sense into him," whatever that meant. Of all the people in Wells Landing, Eli had perhaps the best idea of what Titus's ghosts were like. Though Eli had no idea what it was like to be in prison. No one did. How could anyone help him if they didn't understand?

"Get us a drink, Titus," Eli said, with a nod toward the fridge. "We need to talk."

Talking was the last thing that Titus wanted to do. He was talked out. Tired of having to explain himself. He should have told June to take him over to the highway so he could hitchhike into Tulsa. He could have stayed with Luke Lambright. They had been good enough friends once upon a time. Maybe Luke could help him get a job.

He opened the fridge and peered inside.

"I think June made some lemonade yesterday."

Titus pulled the pitcher from the refrigerator and closed the door with his hip. "I take it she spends a lot of time over here."

"She comes over every day. She worries about me being out here by myself all day." Eli's parents ran a resale shop in town. The youngest of five, Eli was the only one of his brothers and sisters who still lived at home.

"She thinks you can't take care of yourself?" Titus poured them both a glass of lemonade then put the pitcher back in the fridge.

Eli shook his head, his mouth turned down at the corners. "No," he said. "She loves me."

Titus stopped, the glass suspended halfway between the counter and his mouth. "What just happened here?"

"I think you just had an epiphany." Eli chuckled.

"An epiphany?"

"June got me a word-a-day calendar for Christmas last year."

Titus would have to figure that one out later. "So what are you saying?"

"I'm saying you have a big chip on your shoulder and somebody's going to knock it off."

"It's not that." Titus shook his head.

"How about you start by telling me why you broke up with Abbie King."

Titus explained the situation, what all happened at the restaurant. He was shaking when he finished his tale. He still couldn't believe that it actually happened. That he had physically laid his hands on someone without it being absolutely necessary.

"But in that moment," Eli said, "it was necessary. That's what you've got to get through."

"How am I supposed to do that? Who am I supposed to talk to? The bishop? He doesn't know how I feel."

"The first thing I realized in the hospital when I woke up and knew that I would never walk again was that nobody would know how I felt. Maybe Johnny Flaud. Then again, he's in much worse shape than I am."

Johnny was a year or two younger than they were, a fun-loving, sweet guy who accidentally fell off the barn and broke his neck. He barely had any use of his arms as well as his legs and had to have constant care.

"And then I realized," Eli continued, "I don't need everybody to know how I feel. I don't want anyone to feel like I do. All I need is somebody to help me deal with it myself."

"Which leads me right back to where I started. Who do I talk to?" Not that it truly mattered. Yes, he would get help. But he still would never be able to trust himself around Abbie. How could he? How could he possibly jeopardize her life for his own selfish wants?

"You have to get help from an *Englisch* doctor. It's the only way. But I can tell you this, there are people out there with varying degrees of what you and I have."

Titus stopped. "You have it too?"

"A form of it. Not exactly like yours but it took me a long time to want to get back on the road in any sort of vehicle. A long time. It still makes me nervous, but I learned how to breathe through it and deal with it. It's something that will always be with me. That's the first thing you have to realize: you'll never be completely over it. You just learn how to cope."

And that was the exact reason why he couldn't go back to Abbie.

"So I'm sunk either way," Titus said.

"What are you talking about? You get help, and you move on with your life. You don't have much choice. And for not having much choice it's a pretty good one, don't you think?"

"I don't know what I'll do without her."

The words fell like a soggy sponge. "Then pray you don't ever have to find out," Eli said.

Titus threw his hands in the air. "How am I supposed to be around her if I always have the potential to hurt her?"

"I think you're missing the point. I think you do need to be around her because you need someone to help you tame this beast inside you now. You've been through a lot. More than most people our age can say. And anybody that you can surround yourself with, anyone supportive and loving, find them and never let them go."

Titus shook his head. He turned around and looked

out the kitchen window. Darkness had truly fallen. He couldn't see three feet in front of his face out there. He shouldn't have come here. He should've gone on to the highway and hitchhiked into Tulsa. He could have stayed in one of those shelters for the night. The thought of all those people in one place together . . . He shuddered.

"You think about this tonight," Eli said. "If you don't have her, what do you have?"

Titus woke up around two o'clock in the morning unable to fall back asleep. Once again the room felt a little too big, but he had decided he was staying in place. He wasn't going to get up and go into Eli's horse barn. He had to learn to live like a man again. Somehow, someway if he and Abbie were to have any chance at all, this was the first step.

He flipped over in the bed and stared at the darkened ceiling. Only the solar-powered security lights outside offered any illumination. And that wasn't saying much.

Titus sighed. He should get up right now, somehow find his way to Abbie's house in the dark, and beg for her forgiveness. She was the one he wanted more than anything. His stomach hurt when he thought of that look on her face yesterday when he told her they were through. She didn't know he had her best interests at heart. All she knew was that he was breaking it in two. After all his vows to stay with the church, to court her, to stay in Wells Landing and be her business partner, he had blown it all. Now he could only pray that when he got to her house later that she would be open to hearing what he had to say.

As much as he hated to admit it, Eli was right. He had a chip on his shoulder. And he couldn't go around expecting everybody in town to know how he felt. And he certainly couldn't go around town making sure everybody knew that they didn't know how it felt. No one would ever know how he felt and that was something that he needed to start dealing with. Immediately, if not sooner.

He could only hope and pray. Pray. That was something he hadn't done in a long time. He had been faking it for the last few weeks, bowing his head when it was expected of him and hoping no one would recognize the insincerity. He didn't mean it that way. But he just couldn't find the words for prayer.

Try now.

The words ran through his mind as clear as day. He could pray now. Right now.

He got up from the bed and knelt beside it. Clasping his hands on the mattress, he lowered his chin until his forehead was touching them. But where were the words? "Dear Lord . . ."

No, that wasn't right.

"Father God," he whispered. That sounded strange. But he didn't know why. He had prayed that way his entire life.

"God in heaven," he tried again, and then he remembered Jesus's Sermon on the Mount and his teaching the multitudes how to pray.

"Our Father who art in heaven, Hallowed be thy name. Thy kingdom come, Thy will be done in earth, as it is in heaven. Give us this day our daily bread. And forgive us our debts as we forgive our debtors. Lead us not into temptation, but deliver us from evil: for thine is the kingdom, the power, and the glory forever. Amen."

He felt as if a burden had been lifted from him. He might not be able to find words of his own, but the words of Jesus would work just fine.

He got up from the floor and crawled back into bed, drifting off to sleep almost as soon as his head touched the pillow.

Chapter Seventeen

Bright sunlight filtered through the windows, accompanied by the sweet chirping birds. Titus lay there for a moment taking time to get his bearings back. He knew he was someplace different. He wasn't in the horse barn, and he wasn't at his folks' house. And he wasn't in jail any longer. The last thing was a definite blessing. But where was he?

He opened his eyes, allowing them to settle on certain hints and clues. He was at Eli's house. And it was morning and—

He jumped from bed. The morning! He had been planning to go to Abbie's first thing. He had hurt her yesterday and abandoned their partnership. The least he could do today, along with his apology and begging her to take him back, would be to help her with the milking. But if the position of the sun was any indication, it was closer to lunch than it was to the morning milking time.

He stood and pulled on his trousers. He slipped his suspenders over his shoulders, then he hustled down the stairs, taking them two at a time as he raced to get to the kitchen.

He came to a skidding halt, realizing that he was alone.

Where was Eli? He heard an unfamiliar squeak and looked out the window just in time to see Eli push his wheelchair up the ramp that led from the back porch. It was then that Titus realized that none of them had been spared injury from that accident. Eli's might've been on the outside, but Titus's were hidden. Yet they were there all the same. And after people were injured they got help. And that was exactly what he would do.

But first he had to go to Abbie.

"Hey! You're up." Eli rolled himself into the house and shut the door behind him.

"Why didn't you wake me up?"

"Good morning to you, too, Titus. It is a lovely day."

"Seriously," he said. "I was going to help Abbie this morning. She has fifty cows to milk, you know."

"So I see you had a change of heart last night." Eli said.

Titus tried to relax. The time had already passed. "Yeah, you could say that. Or you could say I was being really stupid."

Eli laughed. "I like the last one best but whichever you prefer."

He rolled himself to the fridge. "Are you hungry? *Mamm* left a pan of biscuits and bacon on the stove for you." He nodded his head toward a pie plate on the stove.

Titus's stomach twisted into knots. He had to get over and see Abbie. He had to ignore this worry he had. Once he did that, he might eat, but for now . . . "No, thanks. I appreciate it, but I need to get over and see her."

"I thought you would say that." Eli tossed him a set of keys. "These go to the tractor."

He shook his head and handed Eli the keys back. "I don't drive."

Eli studied him a minute then gave a quick nod. "Suit yourself," he said. "Take the buggy if it makes you feel better. Just get over there."

Titus raced from the house and headed for the horse barn. He had to go now, before he lost his nerve, before she wouldn't forgive him at all.

There was a lump in his throat, his stomach was in knots, and his hands were shaking. He had never felt more alive. Now he could only pray that she would accept his apology. He'd been harsh with her yesterday, but surely if she loved him then, she loved him still.

Titus got out of the carriage and looked across the yard, but nothing stirred except for a few birds and some ducks. She needed a dog. That would be fun. Maybe he would get her a puppy. Maybe one of Obie Brennaman's golden retriever puppies.

No one came out of any of the outbuildings so he loped up the porch steps and knocked on the door. No sounds came from the house. They were gone. That made sense. This time was for them. There weren't any chores this time of day. The morning milking was complete and by now all the animals had been fed. Of all the days. He needed to talk to her more than he needed air to breathe, and she was nowhere to be found.

He stopped. Was that something on the other side of the door? Some kind of muffled sound. He reached for the handle and let himself in the house, his breath stolen away as he saw Emmanuel King lying at the foot of the stairs, one leg bent at an awkward angle. He had a bruise on the side of his face and blood trickled from the corner of his mouth.

"Emmanuel!" Titus cried, and rushed to the man's side. The minute he got close enough he could smell the liquor. "What happened?" He needed to get him to a doctor and fast.

"Fell down the stairs," Emmanuel groaned.

"I'm going to call someone now. Just lie still, and I'll be right back. Promise me you won't try to get up."

"Promise," he whispered. His eyes were closed, and Titus felt certain that he would do as he had been asked.

Titus raced from the house and into the shed where the Kings kept their phone. His fingers trembled as he dialed Bruce's number. There was no answer.

He ran a finger down the list of numbers next to the phone and started to dial the first one on the list. He had to find someone to take them into town. Anyone.

A truck horn sounded from the road.

Titus dropped the phone and raced outside. The camels! His two new camels were scheduled to arrive today. How could he have forgotten about that?

And they came in a truck.

"Hey!" Titus ran across the yard, waving his hat at the driver. "Hey! We need your help."

The driver got down from the rig, clipboard in hand. He sneezed and wiped his nose on a paper towel. "Abbie King?" He looked Titus up and down, then sniffed.

"I'm Titus Lambert."

The driver checked the clipboard.

He drove a dually with a magnetic sign on the door. The trailer was separate from the truck and looked like it had been rented.

"I need your help," he cried again.

The driver frowned. "What's wrong?"

"The owner, Emmanuel King. He fell and is in pretty bad shape. I need you to take us to the hospital."

The driver sucked in a deep breath and sneezed. "Why don't you call nine-one-one?"

Why didn't he call 9-1-1? "They'll take too long to get here. They have to come all the way from Pryor. I don't know how badly he's hurt. He might not have that kind of time."

The man started patting himself as if he had misplaced his keys. "Can't . . . breathe . . . ," he wheezed.

"What's wrong?" Titus stared at the man.

"Asthma." He gasped. He pulled out an inhaler and took a puff. That seemed to help, but he still appeared to be struggling for breath. "Too much dust."

"I need you to be okay," Titus said. He needed this man more now than he had ever needed anyone.

The man nodded. "I will be."

"Can you help me get him into the truck?"

"Can he walk?"

Titus shook his head.

"Let's go."

Titus nearly cried when they lifted Emmanuel off the floor. He was in terrible pain, and Titus hoped that the alcohol in his system had kept some of it at bay. The man was really going to be hurting tomorrow. But for now, they had to get him to the hospital and fast.

They managed to load him into the backseat of the truck. He passed out somewhere along the way and for that Titus was grateful. He could only pray that the man didn't have any internal injuries and they hadn't made it worse by moving him.

"I'll get the camels. You unhook the trailer," Titus said. He wanted to have time to visit with his new creatures, but that would have to wait until later. Maybe tonight after he and Abbie talked, he could come out and get to know the beasts a bit better. He unhooked the latch and got down to work.

What seemed like an eternity but could have only been a few minutes, the camels were in the pasture.

"Here." The driver handed Titus his keys.

"What's this?"

"You drive."

Titus shook his head. "I can't drive."

"Can you drive one of those tractors?"

"Yeah, but I don't."

"You have to," the man insisted. "I can't do it. I need to catch my breath and we don't have time for that." He shook the keys at Titus and rubbed his eyes.

Titus stared at the keys. He hadn't driven anything with a motor since that fateful night. But it took only a second for him to decide.

Heart in his throat, he grabbed the keys and slipped behind the wheel.

Lord, please help me get them there safe.

His palms were sweating and his fingers trembling but somehow he managed to get the truck out onto the road.

Beside him, the driver took another puff from the inhaler.

"Are you going to be okay?" Titus asked.

The man nodded and tugged on the ribbed collar of his shirt. "Yeah, I'm just allergic to some animals and dust."

"You have asthma and agreed to bring two camels to a dairy farm in Oklahoma all the way from Kansas?" It didn't sound like the smartest move.

The man leaned his head back, still sucking in air like a fish on a river bank. "My youngest has been real sick. I needed the money."

He wasn't sure how to respond to that, so he just kept his eyes on the road.

"I mean, it's not cancer or anything," the driver continued. "But she's had to go to a lot of testing. Brain doctors and all sorts of clinics."

"Oh, yeah?" He felt he had to say something, though he wasn't entirely sure that "oh, yeah" qualified.

"They think she's autistic." He shook his head. "I thought only boys got that. The worst part is no one knows how to treat her."

Titus didn't know much about autism, only what he had read in the article about camel's milk. He turned to look at the man. "I may have something you might be interested in."

Titus pulled the truck up to the entrance of the emergency clinic and ran inside to get help. He didn't want to move Emmanuel himself again, worried he might have more damage than they could immediately see. They admitted him immediately, then whisked him away for treatment.

Two members of the hospital staff took one look at the truck driver and began his treatment as well. Titus was left calling loved ones and telling them what had happened. He tried to remember if there was any blood on the floor of the house. That would surely upset Priscilla and Abbie if there was. He called the family of Stan the driver and told them that he was being checked out and would surely be okay. He hated the sadness he heard in his wife's voice and vowed to do everything he could to help the man. Stan had quite possibly saved Emmanuel's life. Titus would do everything he could to help the man and his daughter.

There was no answer at the Kings' residence so Titus

called the bishop and explained. Bishop Ebersol promised to help him get the word to Abbie and Priscilla.

Titus leaned back on the hard plastic seat and wished for somewhere more comfortable to sit. He only wanted a few minutes to gather himself. It had been a long couple of days. Had it just been twenty-four hours since he had been in Pryor, on top of the world and about to eat Chinese food with his girl?

"Titus."

He turned at the sound of his name to see the bishop striding down the hallway toward him, Abbie close behind.

"How is he?" Bishop Ebersol asked.

"He's in surgery now. He broke his leg pretty bad. Nothing he can't recover from." Now was not the time to talk to the bishop about Emmanuel's drinking, but soon.

The bishop settled down into the seat next to him with Abbie on the other side. Titus would have loved to have her close to him. But he knew that wasn't the best idea. She needed time to worry about her father before Titus started begging for her forgiveness.

They didn't have long to wait. The doctor came out twenty minutes later.

"The surgery went well," the tall, dark-skinned doctor reported. "He's in recovery now. Hopefully, we'll have him in a room in a little bit. And you'll be able to see him then."

Titus stood to shake the man's hand, but Abbie was there before him. She shot him a triumphant look. "Thank you, Doctor."

She plopped back into her seat and stared straight ahead. "Bishop, can you find out from certain people why they were at my house today?"

The bishop swiveled his head from her to Titus, then

back again. "Titus? You want me to ask Titus why he was at your house?"

"*Jah,* please."

The bishop shook his head and turned back to Titus. "Abbie would like to know why you were at her house today."

"You can tell her that I was there because I wanted to talk to her."

The bishop turned to Abbie. "He says he was there to talk to you."

"Would you please tell him that he said all he needed to say last night?"

Bishop Ebersol stood and turned to address them directly. "I'm not sure what's going on, but the two of you need to be talking, and I need to be out of it."

"But—" Abbie started.

He shook his head. "I'm going to get a cup of coffee, and then I'll be back." With that he sauntered away.

Titus took a deep breath. "I came over to tell you that I was wrong."

She opened her mouth to say something, but he cut in before she could speak.

"I know I was wrong, and I admit that I was wrong. But if I hadn't been there then your father would still be lying at the bottom of the stairs."

Tears filled her eyes. "Did you really drive him here?"

Titus nodded. "I sort of commandeered a delivery truck."

Abbie dabbed her eyes. "I can't believe you did that. You drove a truck to save my *dat.*"

He shrugged. He only did what anyone would have done. "Where's your *mamm?*"

"They are having her fill out paperwork. She's making *Dat* go into some sort of rehab. I don't know.

Do you think he'll be okay? Do you think that he'll be able to stop drinking?"

"I do," Titus said truthfully. "He drinks because he's sad. We just need to make sure that he's not sad any longer."

"And you think that will work?"

"I guess it's a simplistic view of things, but he didn't drink before Alvin died, only after. And we got him to stop drinking and then I threw you that party."

"You think he started drinking again then?"

"I do. I don't think he could handle the party and not having Alvin there."

"So how do we get him past that?" Abbie asked.

Titus sighed. "I don't know. I guess we have to leave that up to the professionals."

They sat in silence for a moment.

"What about you?" she quietly asked. "How are you going to deal with your PTSD?"

"I think I need to go talk to somebody. Because I can't live without you and I can't live with you if I think there's a problem with me."

"Oh, Titus." Abbie stood and pulled him to his feet. "There's nothing wrong with you. You've just been through a lot. Now all we have to do is get you past all that."

"We?" he asked.

"We." She smiled. "I let you go once, but it ain't happening again."

Sweeter words he had never heard. "Please don't." He pulled her close and regardless of the few stares they received he held her in his arms.

"I love you, Titus Lambert."

He was wrong. *Those* were the sweetest words. "I love you, too, Abbie King."

Someone cleared his throat nearby. Titus looked up

to see the bishop smiling over a steaming cup of coffee. "The doctor wanted me to tell you that your father's awake."

"Oh, good," Abbie said. She stepped back, and Titus reluctantly released her.

"Maybe we should talk to him soon about a having a wedding this fall," the bishop suggested.

Abbie and Titus shared a look. That would be a mighty quick courting time, but Titus couldn't think of anything he wanted more.

"Really?" Abbie breathed.

"You think that will be okay?" Titus asked.

The bishop smiled. "I can't think of a better healing balm than love."

He was right. Love was the best medicine of all, and he was going to make sure that Abbie King felt loved for the rest of her life.

Connect with

Books by Bestselling Author
Fern Michaels

___The Jury	0-8217-7878-1	$6.99US/$9.99CAN
___Sweet Revenge	0-8217-7879-X	$6.99US/$9.99CAN
___Lethal Justice	0-8217-7880-3	$6.99US/$9.99CAN
___Free Fall	0-8217-7881-1	$6.99US/$9.99CAN
___Fool Me Once	0-8217-8071-9	$7.99US/$10.99CAN
___Vegas Rich	0-8217-8112-X	$7.99US/$10.99CAN
___Hide and Seek	1-4201-0184-6	$6.99US/$9.99CAN
___Hokus Pokus	1-4201-0185-4	$6.99US/$9.99CAN
___Fast Track	1-4201-0186-2	$6.99US/$9.99CAN
___Collateral Damage	1-4201-0187-0	$6.99US/$9.99CAN
___Final Justice	1-4201-0188-9	$6.99US/$9.99CAN
___Up Close and Personal	0-8217-7956-7	$7.99US/$9.99CAN
___Under the Radar	1-4201-0683-X	$6.99US/$9.99CAN
___Razor Sharp	1-4201-0684-8	$7.99US/$10.99CAN
___Yesterday	1-4201-1494-8	$5.99US/$6.99CAN
___Vanishing Act	1-4201-0685-6	$7.99US/$10.99CAN
___Sara's Song	1-4201-1493-X	$5.99US/$6.99CAN
___Deadly Deals	1-4201-0686-4	$7.99US/$10.99CAN
___Game Over	1-4201-0687-2	$7.99US/$10.99CAN
___Sins of Omission	1-4201-1153-1	$7.99US/$10.99CAN
___Sins of the Flesh	1-4201-1154-X	$7.99US/$10.99CAN
___Cross Roads	1-4201-1192-2	$7.99US/$10.99CAN

Available Wherever Books Are Sold!
Check out our website at **www.kensingtonbooks.com**

More by Bestselling Author
Hannah Howell